There had always been whispers and warnings among the peasants and the townsmen about the one who lived in the wooded hills, an ageless being who supped on the blood of her people, which nourishment linked her unbreakably to this ancient soil. They had always spoken of her with fear and with warding-off signs given them by their priests; but they spoke of her with a kind of pride, also.

Ah, he thought, she is real.

"And I know you, Karl Ivo Maria von Cragga," she said, in tones richly thoughtful and insinuating. His nape prickled, but he listened, breathless and spellbound.

"I can smell your blood," she murmured, "so rich with the courage and pride of your line. Warrior of many battles, you must know that you are wounded to death."

"Then drink from me," he said, dragging himself up on his elbows in a surge of desperate energy.

the **Ruby Tear**

◆

Rebecca Brand

TOR ®

A Tom Doherty Associates Book
New York

This is a work of fiction. All the characters and events portrayed in this book are either products of the author's imagination or are used fictitiously.

THE RUBY TEAR

Copyright © 1997 by Suzy McKee Charnas

All rights reserved, including the right to reproduce this book, or portions thereof, in any form.

A Tor Book
Published by Tom Doherty Associates, Inc.
175 Fifth Avenue
New York, NY 10010

Tor books on the World Wide Web:
http://www.tor.com

Tor® is a registered trademark of Tom Doherty Associates, Inc.

ISBN 0-812-57132-0
Library of Congress Card Catalog Number: 96-29342

First edition: April 1997
First mass market edition: April 1998

Printed in the United States of America

0 9 8 7 6 5 4 3 2 1

CONTENTS

Casting

◆

I don't believe it," Jessamyn said. Her voice rose, threatening to break out of her control. "Walter, what are you telling me? I don't believe it!"

Walter Steinhart, looking not just rumpled (as always) and harried (likewise) but downright uncomfortable, held up both hands, palms out, placating.

"Jessamyn, I just need to have you very clear on this, all right? You've got to realize that if things turn out badly—"

"If you decide to give the part to Anita MacNeil, you mean," Jess said bitterly. "Even though I'm twice as good, and you know I'm twice as good, and—and I need this job, Walter. You know that too."

Never, never in her life in theater had she stooped to begging. Her throat closed and she bit her lips to prevent the escape of any more self-demeaning words.

Walter Steinhart sat folded into the beat-up swivel chair

behind his paper-drowned desk, his scarred leather flight jacket gapping open over his belly. A balding, stocky man with some resemblance to a slightly mangy monkey, he rubbed his palm repeatedly over the bald top of his head as if trying to coax some new and better thoughts out of the brain beneath.

Jessamyn automatically noted his dress, his mannerisms, everything about him that expressed his discomfort with this whole situation: it was her job to notice such things in people so that she could reproduce versions of them to express the same interior conditions on stage.

It was her job now, again; after more than two years of recovery from the accident (*My god, was it really that long?*)—or it would be, if only she were allowed to do work!

"You know how I feel about it," Walter said. "I agree, you're the best we've found to play Eva. Anita is a competent second choice. She might even grow into the part and become better than competent, but she'll never bring to it what you have to bring. I don't mind telling you, Jess, part of that is something to do with your climb back up out of—well, recovering from the accident, I mean."

Though he lived on words, a playwright's words and then his own as director, sometimes words failed him. This was one of his more endearing qualities, and he knew it. But Jess was not susceptible to endearing qualities today, which clearly showed in her face, for he hurried on earnestly.

"It shows, Jess. The trauma, the despair, the resolution, and the struggle to rebuild your life, they've all marked you in ways that make you stronger and better for this part."

Rebellion prompted Jess to make some snide reply to the effect that maybe all theater people should get bashed up in car wrecks as part of their training, then. But this was not something to say to Walter Steinhart.

Walter was one of the best directors in New York, and if anyone could steady her and help her over the last long hill of her recovery and back into performance, he was that person. The things he said to actors were carefully chosen to strengthen them and improve their work, and his instincts in this were of legendary rightness. From him, she could accept this kind of talk, which normally she despised.

So she said nothing, only folded her arms tightly across her chest and paced the narrow room in angry silence.

"If it were solely up to me," he added, "there would be no contest. You know that. And it may still work out."

"How?" she demanded. "If Nic doesn't want me—" Her voice broke. "Walter, I can't believe he's doing this to me. Honest to flipping God, am I crazy or what? If anything, he *owes* me this part! He was driving the damn *car*."

Tears stung in her eyes. She stopped at the big, dirty-paned window and leaned her forehead against the cold glass. Down in the alley below, a couple of prop-shop workers hustled in through the stage door, back from lunch break.

"I can't believe I said that," she added miserably.

"Why not?" Walter said with a sigh. "It's true."

"Okay, then: he was driving the car; and he was going to marry me, Walter. That can't be news to you; I'm sure everybody knew our little secret."

"Well, not everybody," Steinhart said. "People close to you both did expect to see you become Mrs. Griffin, though. But everything's different now. Like it or not, you were changed by the accident. So was he. And for whatever reason, he doesn't want you in this play."

"In the play?" she cried. "My God, not even as—as what's-her-name, the old woman—not playing any part at all? Jesus, Walter, what has he got against me? He's ignored me ever since the damned accident, he's as good as refused to see me, and now he says I'm not good enough to be in his play?"

"That's not what he said," Steinhart corrected gently. "And I've already told him I think you're the best Eva we've seen. Maybe—maybe it's some feeling that people might think he was trying to repay you by giving you the starring part in this show. You know, the part as contrition instead of as recognition of your talent for the work. Maybe he's trying to protect you, in a stupid, high-handed way.''

She stared at him, trying to penetrate beyond his words into his mind because what he said was too incredible to be understood. ''Is that what *he* says? Because if it is, it's the lamest, most pathetic—''

''He doesn't give a reason, that's the weird part,'' Steinhart said uncomfortably. ''You know, Jessie, I knew Nic when he was a rich kid, a playboy type in school; and I knew him when he started getting serious about the world and the stage; but I barely know him now. I don't think it's any use to try to understand his present behavior according to what he used to be, let alone judge it.''

''I don't,'' Jess said. ''Anybody would know he's matured tremendously, just by reading that script. It's a good play, a much better play than it was in the old version. For all I know, he may have turned it into a great play.

''And without any explanation he refuses to let me in on it. Just like that, go away and drop dead! It's horrible.''

''It's also not settled yet,'' Steinhart said crisply. ''I've been talking to the theater board and to a couple of the big contributors. You're forgetting, the final word on the casting isn't left with the playwright. I want you as Eva, and I'm doing everything I can to get you.''

Simmer down, she thought; *simmer down*. That was what it felt like, too: jamming the lid down on a pot that was boiling over. *The man is a talented professional, he's your friend, and he's trying to help. Don't kick him in the chops for that because you're furious with—somebody else*. Helplessly furious, without a chance in hell of fixing the situation.

Better to bow as graciously as possible to the inevitable. *But I will never forgive Nic; never!*

''Thank you, Walter,'' she said. ''But if that's how things are, maybe you should leave it alone. How can I take the role against Nic's will? It would just make problems for the show, if the author is dead set against me.''

Steinhart scowled, fished out his pipe and began packing it with sweet-smelling tobacco. "Don't go all noble and silly on me, Jess. At least wait for the final word to come in."

"Walter, I've *been* waiting," she said. She sat down on the broad sill of the window, clasping her hands to keep from waving them around in frustrated gestures. "I waited to get out of the damned hospital, I waited through a ton of physical therapy on my hands, I waited for my eye socket to heal so I don't look like the bride of Frankenstein's uglier sister, and I waited to get my nerve back, which was the hardest part of all. I'm through waiting. I'm ready, Walter. I'm ready *now*."

"I know you are. You look great," he said, glancing up from his pipe with an appreciative glint in his eyes. She could have kissed him for that lecherous look. "The doctors did a wonderful job. *You* did a wonderful job."

"Don't say I look better than before, Walter, or I'll start throwing things."

He grunted and concentrated on sucking flame down into the packed bowl of the pipe.

"There's nothing else in production in New York that's worth spitting at this season, and you know it," Jessamyn added. "And I'm righter than right for this part. But Nic Griffin says he doesn't want me in his play. Seriously, Walter, maybe I need to get out of this now, before everything I've been working on in myself since that damned crash unravels over this."

Walter sat back emitting a stream of aromatic smoke from his nostrils. "Jess, you do what you have to, and I'll do what I can, and we'll see where we come out, okay? But if you turn your back on us now, all my effort goes down the drain with yours."

She got up and grabbed her coat off the back of a scarred oak armchair from some long-dead high school office. Ah, the glamour of the theater! "Low blow, Walter."

"I hit wherever I can," the director said with a grin, "when winning is important." He pointed at her with the stem of the pipe. "Go home, cool down, rest, and don't toss the script, all right? Work on those lines, Jess. You may be needing them in spite of what Nic says."

On the way out she stopped in the rest room to splash cold water on her aching eyes. In the mirror her face was pale, her eyelids puffy, and her short dark hair clung in sweaty curls to her forehead and the sides of her cheeks. The only visible scar left over from the accident cut slantingly across her right eyebrow, giving her a faintly quizzical expression. The silver streak in the dark hair sweeping back from her temple seemed deliberate, like a romantic inspiration from a makeup artist.

No one could tell by looking at her what a narrow escape she had had, or how much it had taken to overcome her injuries. No one could see now the pain and despair the recovery had cost her.

To the world she was the lucky one, having been thrown clear of the wreck. She had come out of the crash with her beauty not lost but changed, marked with a distinctive shadowing of melancholy that people seemed to find attractive. She knew this and sometimes managed to take some pleasure in it.

But not today. She turned abruptly away from the mirror, pulled on her outdoor boots, stowed her shoes in her tote bag, and went downstairs with her coat over her arm, too tired and depressed to think. Anita MacNeil was in the second stairwell, talking intensely to one of the contenders for leading man, a ginger-haired kid with a classical profile.

"—with lots of projection," she was saying. "Marko has to give out a sense of authority and stability so that when he breaks up in Act Two it *means* something."

"Hello, Anita," Jess said as she approached.

"Hey," Anita said. She gave Jessamyn a quick up-and-down study, and offered a rueful smile. "Shit, you look great. I hope I have a chance in there."

Jess smiled back, hoping the effort didn't show. "There's always a chance."

It was a cold, gray afternoon in the city, another freezing

day in a freezing winter of blustery gray days and paralyzing snowstorms. She wrapped her scarf around her head, tugged on her fur-lined gloves, and walked uptown, shoulders hunched against the wind.

How could Nic do this to her? Her eyes blurred with tears that she fiercely refused to shed.

But memory washed over her like a sweet, warm tide, only curdled now with her bottled-up rage at him. On a day like this, with just this damp edge to the wind (and she had been wearing these same gloves then, too), the two of them had walked from their favorite bookstore in Greenwich Village all the way downtown and taken the Staten Island Ferry, just for the hell of it.

She had leaned at the rail, drinking in the wind as fast as she could because if she paused to think about it, the air would be too painfully cold to breathe. Behind her, Nic pressed close and enfolded her in his arms, heating her like a furnace, whispering his warm breath into her hair and hugging her tighter when she burst into helpless groans and giggles at the things he was saying. He had specialized in collecting and memorizing really terrible lines from failed stage comedies.

"—Because the dog ate the banana!" he had cried in a lunatic European accent, and when she laughed, he stooped over her and kissed her till she melted, until she had barely felt the headwind off the Hudson razoring the exposed skin of her neck and cheek.

Home again in her apartment that night, with the playful silliness and half-drunken hysteria of nearness to each other worked off, they had fallen into a ferocious embrace with the apartment door still open. She had managed to kick it shut behind her before sinking with fierce joy into what seemed like an endless age of ravenous feeding on each other's hot-breathed mouths and slick, shuddering skins.

And then they had lain in the tumbled bed all night, drowsing but too happy to sink out of joy into mere sleep. They had kept each other up by whispering tag lines about love from Shakespeare, until their bodies fell to feasting again. She remembered lying against his back in the morning with her face pressed to the flat of his shoulder blade, and inhaling the scent of his skin until she felt intoxicated.

Jess veered aside on unsteady legs and stood at the showcase window of a boutique. She leaned her forehead against the icy glass and breathed great gulps of knifelike air, while her eyes prickled and stung with tears.

They had had everything, been everything to each other that anyone could ever ask, never even bothering to discuss their future together; it was a foregone conclusion from the start, and they both knew it.

But that was then. Now he refused her everything: his bouyant vitality, his shameless sensuality, his company, and now even a part in his miserable play!

He couldn't. She wouldn't let him.

Inside the store a salesgirl was refolding a sweater and furtively watching her, no doubt dreading the necessity of calling an ambulance for the lady collapsed outside on the sidewalk. Jess checked her wallet, fumbled out some bills, and on impulse turned her course toward Grand Central Station.

She hadn't been to Nic's family home outside Rhinebeck since the accident. It was time she went.

Rhinebeck

◆

The cab from the station cruised through the pretty town as if the driver was used to taking visitors on a leisurely sightseeing tour. Today, though, everything looked cold and wet and draped in pocked and dirty snow.

"You should see this place in the summer," the driver said. "Though it's getting boutiqued and gift-shopped to death these days."

"I have seen it," Jess said. "Things are lively, then, at least. Winter always looks so grim in the country."

She cringed to hear herself chattering away like this out of simple nervousness. She wore black woolen pants and a rust-colored turtleneck under her hooded loden coat, and she looked like a grown-up, she knew, a capable adult; but she must have sounded like a silly schoolgirl.

The driver said, "I don't get a lot of fares out this way, but I do a lot of fetching and carrying back and forth to the Griffin place. It's a shame, what happened to Mr. Griffin. I'd sure hate to be stuck in a small town like this without being able to drive.''

"Oh, I heard that Nic Griffin has gotten around a lot already in his life," Jess said cautiously. "Maybe he's happier staying put for a while. That old house has been in his family for generations, too. He probably enjoys being home."

"Yeah, I heard he used to be quite a traveler," the cabbie said. "War zones, places most people stay away from."

Jessamyn did not rise to the invitation. She felt a bit embarrassed at having said as much as she had. It was one thing to prattle about herself, another to talk about Nic with a stranger.

About a stranger with a stranger, in a way. She wasn't sure she knew Nicolas at all anymore. What kind of man would she confront today at the Griffin house?

When she had first met Nic, in a summer-stock production of *Barefoot in the Park*, in which he had tried his hand at acting (not very well, as it happened), she had gone out of her way afterward to pump friends and acquaintances about him. She had been attracted right from the beginning and had sensed a reciprocal interest.

What she had learned was not very reassuring. Nicolas Griffin had grown up rich, a reckless and destructive young man who had been tossed out of several prestigious private schools. His love of theater was a taste he had only allowed himself to indulge after the death of his tycoon father, and a modest talent had immediately shown itself. Right after college he had dashed off a couple of light comedies which his own money had paid to mount in small theaters, to no outstanding success.

He had inherited even more money, and the Rhinebeck house as well, on his mother's death not long thereafter, and had shut the house down and gone off to write travel columns for a magazine catering to wealthy travelers who had worn out the ordinary cruise circuit and were looking for more exotic adventures. Here, too, Nic had, people said, a small but pleasing gift.

At length his wanderings had taken him to Sarajevo. The ethnic upheavals in Eastern Europe had fascinated him, and he had stayed much longer than expected; longer, in fact, than *Time and Tide* were willing to pay for.

But he had continued slogging through the destroyed and dangerous Eastern European countryside to talk to local people and record their stories, paying his own expenses and writing in his journals for his own eyes only. The experience had changed him. He had come home to write his first serious play, originally titled *Blood Kin*. As part of connecting with serious American theater he had taken a role in the stock company, where Jess was spending her summer that year as well.

A flighty man, a bit of a dilettante and somewhat spoiled, but with an awakening passion for justice, some people had said. But it really hadn't mattered what they said or thought: Jessamyn was hooked.

What a spark had lit between them, what a time of overheated senses and pounding hearts had ensued! They had met privately whenever and wherever they could, spent all their working time together, and had become the stock company's Major Item that summer, provoking sympathy, pleasure, and envy all around—none of which impinged on them at all until rumors surfaced long afterward. They had been too wrapped up in each other to notice other people's reactions.

A magical summer; it was painful to think about now. So much had been promised—so much to be wrecked, later on.

Since the accident, he was drastically changed. He had no more relatives living in the East, but people who had known him before—people Jess had once been jealous of because they had known him longer and better than she did—were no longer welcome company. Word was that only visitors on professional business came to the Griffin house these days—like Walter, conferring with Nic about details of the proposed production of his rewritten play.

Well, she was changed now too, and it was time they

had it out, whatever "it" was—the barrier that had slammed down between them when the car crashed, destroying their future together.

Until now she had not had the energy or the courage to force the issue. All initial approaches had been stonewalled. She knew that he wouldn't take calls from her anymore. Walter said Nic screened all his calls now, and lived as a virtual recluse in the old house outside the town. But since he no longer traveled and did not drive because of his stiff leg and a stubborn refusal to have hand controls fitted to his car, she would pretty surely catch him at home if she showed up without warning.

Assuming he didn't simply slam the door in her face.

The cab was approaching the turn that still made her shiver when she saw it, off the roadway onto a shortcut, unpaved, that ran down a woodsy slope to link one winding country road with another. The dirt track dead-ended at the lower road, the one to Pie Corners, with sharp turns left and right.

Jess had flinched from even thinking of the place since the accident. Now, it seemed like a sort of good-luck gesture, a healthy spit in the eye of Fate, to deliberately go and look at the scene of her old life's end.

"Stop here a minute, will you?"

The cabbie turned onto the dirt and pulled up facing downslope toward the Pie Corners road, which here widened slightly into a meeting of ways beneath a single, thick-bodied oak tree. The sky was dark today and the paving of the Pie Corners road gleamed dully wet with melted snow. It looked no different than it did in the dreams she still had about the accident.

The worst dream always began with sound: the purr of the engine, and the spill of Nicolas's laughter, and the rush of wind. They had been celebrating that afternoon: word had just come; *Blood Kin* had been accepted for production, and Nic was to meet the following weekend with the staff at a Chicago theater for contract talks.

Jessamyn knew—had known for days—that once the

deal was signed, once the play was slated for production, Nic would turn to her with the question, with his life. He would ask, and she would answer, and they would begin a new, formally joined course together.

Instead, the blond man with the finely chiseled face of a poet, the cool gray eyes that always warmed for her, and the mouth from which she had drunk so many drowning kisses, drove her in his car for the last time.

Sunlight had glowed on the golden hairs along his fore-arm as the gleaming green BMW, a car as dark and sleek as a German forest, skimmed down the hillside between the two paved roads. He'd had the sleeves of his blue chambray shirt rolled back to make the most of the glorious sunlight after a week of unseasonable rain, and she had watched the play of light on his skin with exhilaration: this was going to be forever, she was as sure of it as she had ever been of anything in her life.

He talked excitedly as he drove, his eyes flashing again and again from the road to her face. One of his long-fingered hands kept leaping from the leather-clad steering wheel to shape the air, caressing the idea of the coming success he planned for, down to a share of the proceeds being earmarked for a fund to build a theater in Sarajevo.

God, how his passion for that battered city and his ve-hement generosity had thrilled her then! She remembered her eyes actually tearing up with joy in her own good luck: this man was special, and he loved her as consumingly as she loved him.

"Watch the road, silly," she had said, laughing and nudging his shoulder with hers. She was not really afraid. He had a pure, clear sense of the strength and reflexes of his body that she had come to trust totally.

Then she had looked ahead and seen—nothing out of the ordinary; nothing but the paved Pie Corners road crossing the dirt one they were on, a turn they had taken a hundred times before on the way into Rhinebeck. It had all been perfectly normal: the stop sign, the double-headed arrow in black on yellow indicating that the dirt road dead-ended here, the oak twisting crookedly toward the sky from the earthen bank above the paved roadway.

Just what she was looking at now, and just as empty: there had been no oncoming traffic, no tractor trudging noisily along, no van or truck or bus—just an empty junction alongside a farmer's field.

But Nicolas had exclaimed in surprise and stamped hard on the brakes. The tires had slid on the dirt surface, and the BMW had fishtailed and careened downhill, out of control.

"Nic, what—?" She had grabbed his arm; she had stared in helpless horror as he dragged the juddering steering wheel hard right, heading the car straight for the double-arrow sign and the thick old oak leaning above it.

Jess remembered being plunged into a jolting rush of light and dark as the car hit the rootbound bank and bucked, leaping upward into the tree trunk with a punishing impact. The sunny afternoon had exploded instantly into silence.

Like the silence now, on another day in another season, another year. (So much time, healing took so much time!) Only gradually did she register today's faint noises of dripping snow and trickling meltwater finding its way along the seams of the countryside.

Jess took a deep breath and walked briskly down to the oak, her hands stuffed deep in her coat pockets. The tree was boldly scarred from the crash, but appeared to be still alive. Amazing, that no living thing had had the life crushed out of it by that stunning impact—except, somehow, her relationship with Nic.

Afterward, everyone had agreed that it was extraordinary that both she and Nicolas had survived. There had been some question at first about Nic's mental state: He'd regained consciousness raving about seeing a woman riding across the road ahead of them, whom he had braked and swerved the car to avoid. But as soon as he'd gotten his bearings he had stopped talking about this, and then he had refused to discuss the crash at all.

He had turned instead to rewriting his playscript, which

he had pulled from the theater in Chicago. He had gone
into virtual seclusion with the work, and the script had
emerged now, over three years later, ten times better than
it had been. *The Jewel* was no longer the good, solid war
melodrama with a peace message that *Blood Kin* had been.
The play had become a tense, tightly focused family tragedy with somber metaphorical resonances. This version had
quickly found a berth at the small but prestigious Edwardian Theater in New York.

But Nicolas, too, was changed: he had become a withdrawn, reticent, watchful man, his conversation brusque, his
patience short, his former easy athleticism spoiled by a
heavy limp. Jess remembered one brief conversation with
him, running into him outside the physical therapist's office, and encountering the new Nic had thrown her so badly
that she could never recall later what they had talked
about—only that her own joyful words had been withered
in her throat by the Arctic chill emanating from him, and
the flat, cold stare of his eyes.

Well, maybe she *was* lucky, not to be married after all
to a moody, darkened version of the exuberant man she had
loved so much. He was gone, replaced by a taciturn
stranger. But Jess did not feel lucky.

At the moment, kicking angrily at the edge of the tarmac
by the oak tree, she felt bitter and betrayed. She had no
illusions about her interrupted career. She had been a theatrical lightweight before the accident, with no serious ambitions to reach higher. If she had died in Nic's car, her
talents would not have been greatly missed.

Now she had a chance at something more: the role of
"Eva," part human, part Spirit of Time and Place. By turns
a supernatural being and a battered street urchin, this character appeared to different members of the trapped family,
meaning something different to each of them. All this took
place in the pressure-cooker environment of the castle basement where the family had taken refuge from bombardment
by their unseen and relentless enemies.

The Jewel was a powerful piece, full of passion and discord as the little group quarreled over old grudges and over the treasure left by their dead patriarch to whichever of them could make the best use of it: the jewel of the title. Greed, pride, ambition, idealism—the family members fought and schemed their way through alliances and betrayals, triumphs and reversals, as the castle was bashed to bits about them. The allusions to the post-communist fighting in Eastern Europe were clear and wrenching.

Only a man of deep feeling could have written *The Jewel*, and although Jess no longer had access to the author, she was determined to do his work justice—if only he would let her!

Now, looking up at the twisted branches of the oak, she acknowledged to herself that there was more to it than getting her career back in stride. She still harbored hopes about Nic. After all this time and bitterness, there were other reasons she had postponed a return to the stage than simple terror of failure. She hadn't had the nerve to even try, until she heard that Nic's rewritten play was to be done at the Edwardian.

She still hoped that he would come around, once she got the part, once she gave it everything, using the extra depth that Steinhart was not the first to see in her since the accident.

If only she could still face an audience, if only her study, performance, and memorization skills hadn't been hurt or withered by the crash and the long recovery, if only Nic himself could be persuaded to let it happen!

She was freezing out here, trying to warm herself with *ifs*. She turned back toward the cab, trudging moodily up the dirt road. The driver got rolling again without a word. Soon they were driving alongside a fieldstone wall with tall trees reaching up behind it. Then the trees gave way to a sweep of winter grass mounting to a white, gabled house on a rise set back from the road. The cab turned in at a passage between two stone pillars and ran up the driveway under arching, leafless branches.

Jessamyn sat a moment, gathering her nerve and staring

at the front steps where a few wet leaves clung. She took
a deep breath and got out of the cab.

The house was tall, broad-winged and silent. Its roof
slates glimmered with the moisture of melting snow, and
its curtained windows were elegantly set off by the glossy
black shutters pinned back against the white walls. Aloof,
sure of itself, the Griffin house crowned the low hilltop with
a pristine perfection of form. She had forgotten how beautiful it was.

"Call when you need to get back to the station; ask for
Bart." The driver handed her a card printed with the name
of the local taxi company and drove away.

Alone now and feeling her skin dampen with anxiety,
Jess mounted the front steps. The paint on the railing was
new. Nic had obviously had the house refurbished, as if he
had finally decided to settle in for good. Fixing up the
house was something they had discussed doing together.
Maybe he had found some other woman to share the project
with, someone Walter Steinhart had avoided mentioning?
Biting her lip, Jess stabbed at the bell.

From inside the house came the ring of door chimes and
the deep, fierce barking of dogs. The dogs were something
new, a part of Nic's peculiar, almost paranoid withdrawal.
Walter had warned her about them.

"Dobermans," he'd said, shuddering. "I can't help it, I
hate the damned things!"

The paneled door opened and Nic stood looking down
at her, unsmiling. She swallowed, wordless at the sight of
him. It was as if she had seen him just yesterday, it was as
if the explosion of the accident in both their pasts knit them
together more tightly than ever now, obliterating the inter-
vening months. They had so much to tell each other, so
much to say about that experience that no one else could
begin to share or understand, and in that telling they would
surely move toward each other again.

I should have come before, she thought.

If only she could find the right words to begin with.

What words? Her mind was blank. She flushed with anger. *For God's sake, why was it up to her? Why didn't he say something?* He was using a cane, but he stood solid as a wall and as unmoving.

She had an urge to rush forward and overcome the distance between them with the sheer energy, the need of contact. Here he was at last, her golden, beautiful lover—surely a hug couldn't hurt? She imagined the warm, enveloping strength of his body so sharply that tears sprang into her eyes.

But if he pushed her away, or even stood cold and unresponsive in her arms, she knew she would break down. She would hate herself, she might even hate him, and that was not a thought she could bear.

"Hello, Nic," she said finally, in a voice that sounded subdued and hopeless in her own ears. "How are you?"

He looked at her with a tense expression that she read as badly disguised dismay. He moistened his lips, but did not speak.

She plowed doggedly on. "I'm sorry if this is a bad time, but it seems to me that we have some things to talk over."

Abruptly he stepped back to make way for her. Behind him two large dogs stood, powerful forelegs braced. They began barking again as she stepped inside.

"Quiet, there!" Nic commanded. "Mac! Beth! Settle down. Better let them have a sniff of your hands, let them know you're not a visiting ax-murderer."

"Are you sure of that yourself?" Jess said. "For a second there, I thought you were considering leaving me outside to freeze."

She was uncomfortably aware of Nic watching in dour silence as she sank onto her heels and reached out, crooning, to fool with the dogs. Now that the ice was broken, they provided a warmer welcome than Nic seemed willing to extend.

The larger Doberman stretched forward and gave her an approving lick on the cheek, daintily using just the tip of its tongue. The smaller, a glossy male with crazy-looking greenish eyes glowing avidly from the dark mask of his face, flopped on his back and waved his paws, begging for a belly-scratch.

"You've got a way with them, haven't you," Nic said, sounding rather put-out that they were so easily tamed.

Jess smiled, slowly rubbing the male under its armpits. The dog stretched ecstatically, mouth open and eyes glassy with pleasure.

"My mom raised Dobies when I was a kid," she explained. "They're pussycats, until some moron gets hold of them and brutalizes them into becoming the dangerous lunatics he wants them to be. My parents quit breeding because they couldn't stand the people, not because of the dogs."

"Well, you'd better stop scratching him," Nic said irritably, "or you'll be down there all day, keeping Mac happy. Come inside and get warm."

He limped on ahead of her, leaning hard on his cane, into the airy room to the left of the entrance hall. Painfully she remembered sitting back-against-warm-back in the window seat there, sharing the Sunday *Times* and drinking coffee as strong as paint thinner. He had always taken great pride in grinding the coffee, his own secret blend of beans, fresh in the little electric machine she had bought him for their first Christmas together.

Pair of yuppie fools, she thought now, achingly jealous of the easy, playful confidence of those dead days.

Now, as then, a fire leaped under the mantelpiece and deep, golden tapestry drapes held in the heat. Where rather stiff family photographs had hung, small landscapes in oils glowed richly, jewellike with deep layers of varnish and color. Nic's uncle Robert had been a well-regarded local artist. A cache of his work had been stored in the basement the last time Jess had been in this house.

"You've changed some things," she said, pausing in the doorway to kick off her muddy boots. "It looks good. When did you get the dogs?"

"A year ago," he said. "They're trained as guard dogs,

though you'd never know it to look at them now, would you?''

"That's the way you want them," Jess said, walking forward on the pale Chinese rug in her wool-socked feet. She draped her coat over a brocade chair. "Fierce with strangers, relaxed with your friends. They're a handsome pair, and you were very smart to get them professionally trained. That way they know what's expected of them."

Silly chitchat, but being with Nic again made her feel shaky and foolish. Already she sensed failure: he would not be moved by this awkward visit from her.

The house, which she had always loved, today felt peculiarly cold and unfriendly. It wasn't just the winter light slanting in thinly through the French doors to the snow-scarved terrace in back. It was the dogs (Mac was pressed against the side of her leg, madly licking her fingers), and the lighter, colder color of the walls and the new pictures; it was Nic himself, changed like everything else important here.

Jessamyn took a seat on the massive plush sofa and untied her white cashmere muffler. Nic sent the dogs out into the garden so that they wouldn't make affectionate nuisances of themselves. He moved with the slow deliberation of a much older man, and she felt a physical ache, noting this.

His natural beauty, a kind of radiantly confident good looks, was subdued now, masked by lines of habitual tension around his eyes and mouth. A frown cramped his golden brows into an expression of watchful apprehension. He wore his fair hair cut closer than was the fashion in theatrical circles. It was almost a military cut, minimal and severe.

His clothes were good but casual, as always—tan slacks, a camel sweater over a pale linen shirt, and low-topped brown boots with a mirror shine. The cane in his left hand was a straight blackthorn with a brass handle. On his other hand—a lean, graceful hand—he wore a heavy golden ring.

It had, she knew, the figure of a rampant gryphon

stamped into the bezel, and was an heirloom piece. He always said that he wore it for that reason, but she suspected that he was vain of his beautiful hands and wore the ring to draw attention to them. She had loved that little weakness in him. She could still imagine the grip of that warm, shapely hand on hers, and the bite of the ring's inner curve into her own fingers. The memory was far more painful now than the pressure of the ring had ever been.

She saw now that she should never have come. But then she would not have seen him, and that was worth everything.

Jessamyn was used to being around attractive men—theatrical men—but Nicolas had always been different: attractive without that instinctive, manipulative charm all actors owned. From the beginning Nic had been completely straightforward and direct, not busily trying to impress. She had always felt that she was seeing the man himself, candidly offered for her inspection without deception or apology.

Now he seemed clenched and guarded, even from her. Especially from her.

"How about a glass of wine?" he said abruptly, and she became aware of the long silence she had allowed to build between them. "I'm about to set out on a trip to the cellar to get something and open it for later."

She jumped up from the couch, relieved to have something physical to do. "Tell me what to bring, I'll get it. I do know my way around down there, Nic. Still."

After a moment of awkward silence he suggested a California chardonnay. She ran down the stairs and paused at the bottom to inhale the deep, acrid scent of earth and stone.

The light of the single naked ceiling bulb showed no changes here. She and Nic had spent one weekend cataloging all the wine stored in the rows of cobwebby bins, and Nic had shown her the secret safe in the wall and joked about "family jewels."

"A piratical pack, my ancestors," he'd said wryly. "There are all kinds of ill-gotten gains stashed away in there. They never let anything valuable out of their own keeping. That was back in the days before every third American was a burglar!''

He must have trouble negotiating the cellar stairs with his cane. Maybe a glass of wine with a meal was a rare treat for him these days. People with unreliable legs couldn't afford to get tipsy.

How the hell did he *live* out here now, all by himself? She waited, scrubbing dust from the bottle with the tail of her shirt, until she got control of a racking surge of mixed pity and outrage. She could not help but think, *If only he had let me stay with him, he would never have been brought so low. Guard dogs!*

Back in the living room, he wielded the corkscrew efficiently and set the open bottle on the heavy antique sideboard to breathe.

"I've got to take the dogs walking soon; they need the exercise, as I do myself." His expression indicated that this duty was not something he looked forward to. "What did you want to talk to me about?"

"The play, of course," she said, suddenly desperate to get this over with. What did she want with this painfully eclipsed sun of a man, once her lover? It hurt to look at him.

"I hear you've really impressed Walter with your reading for Eva," he said, carefully seating himself across from her. His eyes were downcast as if he were ashamed to look at her; a bad sign.

"And I'm ready to impress you, Nic," she said. "I've got my whole first scene down. I can do an audition for you right here, right now, without the script."

"No," he said forcefully. "I told Walter, and I'm telling you—I don't want you in the part. I don't want you in the play. I don't want you in the theater, Jess—not while *The Jewel* is playing there."

It was like being punched in the throat. How could her friend, her joy, her heart's delight, have become such an enemy? With tears in her eyes, she struggled to frame a coherent question.

He leaned toward her over the inlaid coffee table between them. "There's no point arguing. I've made up my mind. So have a glass of wine with me, Jess, for old time's sake—and go home. A better play will come along. You look—you look wonderful. You'll do fine, but not in my play."

"Just tell me *why*," Jess cried.

Nicolas sighed and sat heavily forward, wrapping both hands over the head of his cane like an old, old man. Jess forced herself not to look away. "It wouldn't make any sense to you."

"Try me," she begged. "Nic, please!"

After a moment he said, "Remember what I said after the accident, about the woman on the horse, the person that I saw and you didn't? My explanation would be like that, Jess; more of the same. You don't want to hear it. You'll say I'm crazy, and frankly I'm just not up to fighting about it."

"I won't fight you, I promise," she begged. "Just tell me, Nic; *please*."

He struggled to his feet and limped over to the sideboard where he poured two glasses of wine with a steady hand. "I'm sorry you've had this long trip for nothing. Better go call that cab back. I don't drive these days, and town is too far to walk."

A Man at Bay

 **N**icolas Griffin walked his dogs along the back wall of the long garden behind his house. Although the trees that lined the stone boundary fence were leafless now, their branches would at least partially shield him from the view of anyone who might be snooping around in the woods behind the place.

Anyone: the enemy, faceless and nameless and unknown, and all the more dangerous for that! It was a strange thing to have an enemy, a peculiarly personal terror. He'd had rivals before, and angry men opposing him over some issue or some prize. But this was someone moved by a malevolent will to destroy him because of who he was, and who his father had been, and his grandfather and on back, no one was sure how long. This was something far beyond mere social or professional friction, the bristling of hackles, a flurry of threats and insults or even punches.

Among other things, it was invigorating. Nicolas walked

without his cane, not easily and not fast, but with determination: today he would do the whole fenceline with hardly a trace of the limp he had exaggerated for Jessamyn, and
he would do it on fierce self-discipline fueled by adrenaline.
Tomorrow he would do it without limping at all.

Small, hot needles of pain darted through the muscles
above his knee with each step. He accepted the pain as a
sort of penance for deliberately deceiving Jessamyn, and
hurting her; he had seen the hurt in her face. It had nearly
been too much for him. He had come close to killing her
in his car, and had made her miserable recently over the
play: there could be no penance too great.

Level with his knee, the two dogs paced together, alert
but quiet, heads high, watchful eyes gleaming yellow in
their dark-masked faces. He had named them Mac and Beth
in defiance of the old theatrical superstition that Shakespeare's *Macbeth* carried bad luck. The gesture, originally
a flash of rebellion in the face of Fate, seemed puerile to
him now.

He had had dogs as pets, before, because he loved their
beauty and their cheerfulness. These were trained guard
dogs, and he had them because he needed them.

Nicolas walked, his gloved hands swinging tensely at
his sides to give him balance and momentum—and to
break his fall, if he did fall. At least these days if he fell
it wasn't because he had no strength to keep himself up-
right, but because the lame leg weakened when he was
tired, and his foot sometimes dragged and caught on a
root or a rock.

The sun wallowed in cloud-wrack low behind the trees.
He shrugged his duffle-coat collar higher around his ears,
his breath misting the air in front of him. Early or late, cold
or warm, he walked every day, without his cane.

He did not want to have to count on the dogs. He needed
to be able to trust his own strength. He needed to be able
to run, to pivot, to plant his feet firmly so he could back a
punch fully with his weight, or a kick.

Because his enemy was near. The play would bring him nearer. That was its purpose.

This was the enemy Nic had never believed in, the enemy his uncle Rob had hesitantly told him about just that one time, after the funeral of Nic's father. He remembered pressing Uncle Rob for more details of that incredible story, but his uncle had retreated into anxious silence. Later Nic had threatened, mockingly, to write a comedy about just such a "family curse."

Rob's story was ridiculous on the face of it. Nic could admit now to himself that he had been made uneasy by it all the same, even on that first hearing. He had wanted to mock Rob into retracting it. There had always been a bit of a rivalry between Rob, the artistic one, and Nic's tycoon father. He hadn't been willing to let his uncle rattle him.

It was true that many male heads of the family had died young and violently, a few even by their own hands. But surely that had more to do with their reckless pursuit of wealth than with some sort of crazed supernatural enemy stalking them relentlessly down the centuries!

If you were going to seek your fortune shipping slaves from Africa, you might expect someday to fall victim to a revolt on board. A man who went eagerly West burning with gold fever might find himself outgunned over the sluice-chute on a rich claim. And one who ran down rumors of a lost emerald mine in South America could fall afoul of people down there and not be seen again, which was what was thought to have happened to Nic's father.

Even if there was some kind of darkness over the Griffins, all you would do by worrying about it was to make a fool of yourself; worse yet, a miserable, frightened fool.

At first Nic had ignored the package in the safe, which Uncle Rob said held the evidence. Let it sit there and fester, whatever it was; let it sit in the dark and rot, deprived of the nourishing fears of the latest head of the Griffin family. Nic was not going to play into the hands of any so-called curse.

But then he had wandered into the battlefields of central

Europe, and the dark history of that bleak but beautiful part of the world had drawn him into a strange, grim mood that left a flavor of melancholy even when it lifted. In a fever of haste he had written the first version of the play, at that time called *Blood Kin*; and when it was accepted for production, he had gone out to celebrate, driving down toward the city with Jessamyn, the woman he loved.

No one believed him, but he knew what he had seen that day: a woman in dark, floating garments sitting astride a milk-white horse of enormous proportions, like a medieval warhorse. Horse and rider had simply appeared in the middle of the junction with the Pie Corners road, halted there, dead ahead. They had waited, composed in emblematic profile, except that both heads were turned as if with mild curiosity toward the skidding car.

First the Woman on the White Horse comes, Uncle Rob had said, and shows herself to the victim. Not long afterward, he dies.

Nic had almost died right there on the dirt cutoff, first from a surge of fear so huge it had felt like the bursting of his heart, and then from the impact of the crash. Later he had for a time considered suicide.

He had not welcomed the realization that in his arrogance, his foolishness, his partisan distrust of Uncle Rob, he had nearly cost Jessamyn her life. She was the one person in all the world whom he had loved with his whole being from the moment she had come staggering, swearing, and laughing onto the stage that day in summer years before (having tripped becomingly over a lighting cable). And he had come close to destroying her.

In the hospital he had dragged himself from his room to hers, watching over her in a relentless turmoil of pain, fear, and remorse. For days she had lain in drugged sleep, her head and hands swathed in bandages and her broken arm set with pins. He sat there for hours on end, beyond tears, deprived by the bandages of even a decent look at her. That had hurt, because he had known in his gut that this would be the last intimate time he would spend with her.

He could never forget the sight of her in the hospital bed, so swollen and bruised and feverish with pain. His dreams were haunted by the bloody vision of her crushed eye socket, which had hit the cornerpost of the windshield, before the doctors reconstructed it. He remembered watching, feeling sick and full of self-hating grief, as a nurse unwrapped the raw chunk that had been her left hand; he had fled the room that day, hobbling down the hall scarcely aware of the agony of his unhealed leg.

It had been a mercy (and an unbearable deprivation) to be allowed to go home, away from her. Luckily, he had something to do there, to give him a new focus in his life. First came the lady on the white horse, and then came— what, exactly? What was he to expect?

The package in the safe was waiting, and with it the end, he knew, of the rich and happy life he had always assumed was his by right. The first thing he had done upon his return home was to make his painful way down into cellar and open the old-fashioned wall safe.

There was the spidery writing on parchment, so old that it was surely a museum piece, and unreadable to him; and the typed, modern version that his grandfather had provided. And other papers, bound in a black silk ribbon, pertaining to the incredible situation the letter had described.

And there was the ruby.

It was a dusky, bloodred stone the size of a small bird's-egg, simply set and hung like a medallion on a chain of broad gold links. No maker's mark, no karat stamp could be detected on the gold—this was something old, he'd been sure. Something rich, with a crude, brooding beauty quite different from that of modern gems, which were cut to sparkle.

The documents hinted at an unbelievable story of how because of this jewel his forebears had died cruel, early deaths, pursued by an implacable enemy who claimed ownership of the ruby; as he must die before long too, in his turn.

Unless (maybe) he could regain his physical confidence

and his sharp reflexes, enough to put up a fight. He could not allow himself to drift in the direction of despair. So he had made a plan and set it in motion, instead of waiting passively for the other to come to him. He had turned to his one true talent and had begun revising the play, shaping it into the weapon of his response.

Sequestered from everyone while he worked, he had still phoned Jess's physical therapist every week for a report on her progress. Much later still, he had made it his business to know even about her paralyzing attacks of stage fright. The problem had struck, embarrassing her horribly, when she was called on to deliver lines in Ernie Wilkes's class for professional actors—just to say lines, in a class!

Actors went to school all their lives to keep their skills sharp. But Jess had been turned into a beginner again; worse than a beginner because she was older than most beginners, and because, Nic was sure, she was afraid that her looks—not a matter of vanity but the foundation of every actor's toolkit—had been ruined.

She was never to have been involved in his struggle with the Griffin nemesis. He had already taken too much from her to risk costing her anything more. He was bitterly resolved to stay away from her, to drag his heart from its moorings in his love for her and die of the rupture before he would endanger her again.

Not, above all, with a part in *The Jewel*.

The rewritten play was a flag to signal his enemy, a coded message that could not be mistaken: *Here I am; I know about you; come and face me.*

Jess must not be anywhere near when an answer came.

Nic had never imagined that she would venture to try out for the part of Eva, not in the face of his cold disconnection of his life from hers. He was still furious with himself for not foreseeing this and forestalling it somehow, anyhow. And he was filled with aching admiration for her spirit, the spirit he could no longer think of linking with his own.

This visit today had been hard on him, very hard. She

looked different, she carried herself differently, her voice soft with hesitancy, her eyes so anxious. He had felt himself falling in love with her all over again, longing to comfort, explain, draw her close instead of driving her away.

He should have refused to see her, keeping to his decision to armor her in distance from himself. Letting her into the house and spending even that brief time with her had been a mistake. He was still raw with it, and could not calm his breathing or the thunder of his pulse.

Jessamyn had steeled herself to come here to him in spite of everything, and he had denied himself even a handshake, a touch on the shoulder, enough closeness to feel the warmth of life radiating from her body. One touch, the ghost of a touch, would have broken him and leached all his resolve out of him, and that he could not risk.

But loss gnawed at him, and he felt the weight of the red gem like a boulder on his heart.

So he walked, his breath showing pale in the evening chill, with the two dogs pacing at his side; and it was not for the pain in his leg that the tears shone on his cheeks. It was not for the bite of the cold air, or from the pressure of fear for his own life. It was for the loss of someone he could not live without, but must live without.

That was why his eyes brimmed bitter tears as he limped the last hundred feet of the stone fence back to the house, his left leg beginning to drag.

Blood Angel

Lying on his bed in his clothes, the pale young man slept his light sleep and dreamed the only dream he had dreamed for centuries. It never changed.

In the dream, he could see the castle walls reddened by flames, and glints of firelight gleaming from the armor of figures fallen around him. Someone groaned nearby, and he turned his head to see. Pain lanced from the joint of his neck and shoulder down into his chest and took the breath he needed to scream with, and his sight went dark.

Then he heard a horse nickering in the night, but no men's voices called. In despair he realized that this was no helpful rider searching for survivors, for the sound was moving away as the animal wandered, trailing one rein from its bit.

Alone and gnawed by relentless pain, he craned his neck to see about him. The moon had risen, and its light silvered the curved surface of a breastplate on a still form a yard from his right hand. He knew the design engraved on that armor as well as he knew the crest on his own shield, but the name of that old friend and comrade, survivor—till now—of a hundred skirmishes and pursuits, eluded him.

He could not recall the names of his uncle, his two nephews, and his younger brother, all of whose hacked-off heads he could make out jammed on the spikes on the wall beside the open gateway into the forecourt. Or the names of his mother, the sister who had never married and who ran the estate better than any man, or the names of many others who lay dead or dying all around him because he had come home too late.

There was one name: Magda, who was to have been his wife, missing from among the dead. She was ravished away, a prize not of war but of treachery. Her name was seared into his heart with a great hot iron, where it stung and burned like the spit of the Devil bubbling on the flesh of the damned.

They were all dead, and his home tumbled stone from stone and consumed in flames, and all the treasures of his lineage robbed away by strangers. He should have been praying for the salvation of his immortal soul (he had seen enough of death in battle to know that his own wound was fatal) but instead he cursed and swore in a wild whisper, picturing the enemy: mercenaries in foreign gear, ruthless men who had lain in ambush for him in his own home and cut him down and thrown his bleeding body out here with the rest.

He who had spent years fighting for his church against unbelievers and heretics of all sorts now called not upon his God, but upon the legions of Hell, and begged them to give him the strength to strike down his family's murderers.

Someone came: a sturdy white warhorse, stripped of its trappings, walked placidly among the tumbled bodies. On it rode a woman, seated sideways on the horse's broad back. She was a stranger to him, a white-faced woman in dark garments with long, black hair swirling from her head as she turned to look this way and that, studying the dead.

Perhaps she was some surviving wife or daughter or leman of a man of the castle, seeking her butchered lover or father to pray over. She passed nearby, black against the moonlight. He tried to call out to her, but could only groan.

God, how it hurt simply to breathe!

Yet she must have heard, for she turned to ride closer, and she slid down from the horse, which stood motionless where she left it. Her skirts whispering, she knelt beside his good companion in battle, poor Pero (that was the name of that wretched hulk), handling him somehow, but without sobs, without tears or prayers. Handling him—raising him up a little—to rob the corpse? Was it some peasant woman, come here on a strayed or stolen war mount to seek bloody enrichment among the corpses of her betters?

He uttered a croak of outraged protest and managed to lift his head.

She turned, and her face shone pale and still with a stillness like the calm of the moon's own face. Ebony hair floated about that pallor like a lowering cloud, and the white column of her throat drove down in a gleaming arrow amid the sable stuff of her gown.

"Woman," he whispered, "who are you?"

He could feel a chill in her gaze, from eyes invisible in their shadowed sockets. Her lips were black, because the redness of blood shows black in the moonlight.

"I am the Blood Angel of this land, Baron," she answered in a voice that seemed to glimmer and glow like watered silk in torchlight. "You have glimpsed me sometimes in the past, while you hunted in the forests of your father's domain. Where blood is spilled, there I drink; and with the blood I take up memory, I take up oaths and curses and destinies. I take up the crimes of the past and the promises of the future, Baron. You know me."

Why yes, he thought with muzzy astonishment, *I do.*

There had always been whispers and warnings among the peasants and the townsmen about one who lived in the wooded hills, an ageless being who supped on the blood of her people, which nourishment linked her unbreakably to this ancient soil. They had always spoken of her with fear and with warding-off signs given them by their priests; but they spoke of her with a kind of pride also.

And yes, he had thought he had seen her sometimes when he was out hunting his father's woods; but those sightings he had never spoken of, for could a Godly man be prey to such visions?

Ah, he thought, *she is real. And Pero must be not quite dead, for she would not drink blood from a corpse.*

"And I know you, Karl Ivo Maria von Cragga," she went on in tones richly thoughtful and insinuating. His nape prickled, but he listened, breathless and spellbound.

"I can smell your blood," she murmured, "so rich with the courage and the pride of your line. Warrior of many battles, you must know that you are wounded to death."

"Then drink from me," he said, dragging himself up on his elbows in a surge of desperate energy. "Leave poor Pero; he is a good soldier and has been devout all his life. Let Heaven have him, for he has earned a sweet rest from this misery of iron and death. But I have failed in all that I sought to do."

"Be sure of what you offer," she answered from those dark and shining lips from which he could not avert his eyes. "Perhaps it is only your fear of death that speaks these reckless words, Baron von Cragga."

His mind, slowed by suffering and the onset of darkness, caught up with events: she addressed him by title, for the second time now, because his father the Baron was dead. Egon, the true Baron and respected (if not precisely beloved) father of Ivo, had been butchered by the raiders, egged on by the taunts and laughter of their leader, the blond foreigner with the white gryphon on his shield whom the family had hired as head of their castle forces in Ivo's absence. So Ivo was Baron now; the dying heir to an old line.

"Take my blood, I tell you," he said, trembling with a rage he could ill afford. "And give me your kind of life in return. My family is destroyed, my line is ended, my wife-to-be is the booty of a treacherous thief, and the treasure of the Craggas is stolen away as well. We had it from the hand of Charlemagne himself and we have kept it safe until now! So as the last of my name I have work to do, the work of revenge. But I cannot do it like this—help me, I beg you!''

I am dreaming, he thought, floating in a sea of pain, *for hurt as I am, how could I speak aloud to her? My lungs are lanced through, I am surely already in Death's hand myself, and this is a dream of the torments of Hell.*

The woman with the bloody lips inclined slightly toward him, attentive and unhurried. ''It is a wonderful treasure that you have lost,'' she agreed, ''a gem beyond price. And these have been terrible deaths that the betrayer has thrust upon your family. But haven't you had enough punishment, Baron? What you ask of me is no favor, believe me. What you beg from me now, you will curse me for in ages to come.''

''Listen to me curse, then, and laugh at me!'' he cried. ''I would willingly be the butt of your sport in that cloudy future, if I can only live long enough to avenge my family! Lady of the Night, come and drink from me before all my blood runs out of me. Give me whatever kind of life you can in place of this warm, lost life of mine. I will do whatever you bid me do, at whatever cost.''

She came nearer and touched his forehead with her cool, pale wrist. ''Do you think I am lonely, Baron? Do you think I long for your companionship?''

''No more than the moon longs for another moon in the night sky,'' he said, and paused, coughing blood. ''The longing is all mine, Lady. The pain I feel is nothing to this longing. I will never trouble you, for if I live with the life you offer, I will go hunting on the trail of my enemy. No matter how long it takes, no matter how far I must range, I swear to return to him and his the slaughter he has given me, until the last of his line is dead and the Cragga treasure is again safe in my hand.''

"Well," she murmured, "that sounds a good purpose for a brave young man of noble blood."

She drew down the hood of his mail shirt, exposing his neck to the chill night air. Her fingers rested lightly against the throbbing artery of his throat. Her touch was the touch of ice.

"You will leave this place, then, on your travels but come again if I call you; and you will be unable to create others like yourself, for with that power I do not part; and I will speak to you from time to time, through the link the land's blood creates between my mind and yours."

She leaned close, and her cool breath glided on his skin. "I will agree to all this, if you give me your oath and it satisfies me. The men of Craggenheim have not pursued me or set priests and Inquisitors after me. By the orders of your family, I have been let go my own quiet way for generations, and I am appreciative of that. The women of Craggenheim have bought favors and powers from me and paid the fair price. Something is owing for that, too, and your own lady mother was one of those women.

"So: what you must do is give your word to obey my rules. On what will you swear, Baron?"

"On my blood," he choked, darkness dancing in his wavering sight. With agonized effort he reached up to touch her temple with his bloody fingertips, and he guided her pale face down. Her stained lips pressed cool against his throat, and he felt points of ice sink into his taut skin. The cold of the blackest spaces of hell flowed into him and took the place of the warm blood pulsing out of his body. He floated away on a freezing, inky tide toward the night-black shore of a sleep from which he knew he would awaken changed forever.

Ivo started up with a low groan from the shallow well of sleep. The dream, sharp and bright as a stained-glass rendering of some saint's agony, faded at once. It didn't matter. He knew it by heart, and felt a sad fondness for it sometimes—his one true relic of the old life, still faithfully his.

He stood up and stretched, and went to the window of the bedroom. He hugged his chilliness to him, rocking gently on his heels and thinking of what his sworn oath had brought him, and the culmination that soon would come. Not *too* soon, though; nothing spoiled revenge like haste. He had had time to learn that lesson well.

On the whole, he thought he had made a good bargain.

Victory

◆

Jessamyn walked into the upstairs work-room of the Edwardian Theatre for the first rehearsal. The board had given Walter Stein-hart the go-ahead: If he wanted to sign Jes-samyn Croft on as Eva, he could do so; and he did.

Jessamyn, filled with a mixture of triumph and misery, had refused to commit herself until Nell Clausen, the theater's business manager, took her into the business office and showed her a copy of Nic's contract for the production. The playwright had, according to the words on paper, a right to participate in the casting process and to contribute his input as he saw fit. He did not have veto power over the director's choices.

Moreover, since Nic had not come to the city for any of the auditions for Eva (or for any other part, for that matter), the board members held that he could make no case for interfering in Walter Steinhart's decisions.

The cast gathered around a scarred oak table in a musty

room with a cracked mirror on one wall. The stage itself would not be available for rehearsals until the building and fitting of the sets was finished, three weeks at least. They were all used to doing preparatory work in settings like this. Jessamyn herself found the casual shabbiness downright comforting; it was so familiar.

The first thing Walter said to them, once he got them to stop chattering and doing somersaults and other physical warm-ups on the carpeted floor, was that Nicolas Griffin was not going to attend the rehearsals.

"You all know," Walter said, "that Nic and I have had some disagreements about casting." Everybody pointedly avoided looking at Jessamyn. "Disagreements in which I have, luckily for our show, I think, prevailed. In the interests of harmony, Nic says he'd rather stay out of it entirely. If there are questions we can't resolve among ourselves here, I'll go up to Rhinebeck if I have to and get his input. On no account will he come barreling down here, demanding changes."

At Jessamyn's side, Anthony Sinclair cast his eyes heavenward and intoned with feeling, "Thank you, Jesus!"

Jess felt impelled to defend Nicolas. "Nic Griffin has never had the reputation of second-guessing the director. Ask people who've worked with him."

"Which Nic Griffin?" Anita MacNeil said with a quizzical grin that took some of the sting out of her words. "The guy who wrote *Olympic Apes and Blood Kin*, or this new Nic that nobody knows, the author of *The Jewel*? Anyway, I'm glad—I'd just as soon not have the writer breathing down my neck and judging me with looks of stifled pain during rehearsals."

Bella Mason, who played the matriarch of the fictional family in the play, twiddled with the knitting she had brought with her and inquired, "What about changes asked for by us? I have a couple of lines that certainly could benefit by a little judicious redesign. I'm thinking about little things like finding someplace to breathe."

Walter, his hands clasped on his potbelly, nodded solemnly. "I'll take any such requests to him, of course. He says his text isn't set in stone but let's remember, too, this isn't a workshop production. Try to keep changes minimal, and get them in early, folks.

"Now, can we try a read-through of the first act?"

And so, in their sweats and jeans and sweaters, sipping sodas from the machine in the hall to keep their mouths moist, they began working through the play. They stopped after each scene to discuss the shape and pace and emphasis of it, like a chamber-music group running through a score for the first time.

This was the part of theater work that Jessamyn loved the most: the early moments, when everybody was equally ignorant and hesitant. They began the process of feeling their way along together, under the guidance of the director, toward a coherent intepretation. Nobody expected anything of anybody yet, so everyone felt as if anything was possible: any insight, any revelation, any achievement.

In reality Walter already had a firm idea in his mind of how the play should look and move and sound, toward which he would more or less subtly move them all. They depended on him for that vision. It was the backbone of his work, and he had the reputation of being very good at it, which meant they could trust him not to let them make fools of themselves onstage.

So there was a good atmosphere in the rehearsal room, tingly with apprehension and anticipation but basically confident. Jessamyn basked secretly at this warm fire that she had missed so much since the accident.

She threw herself into the first round of the reading, and the round after that, trying to find the melancholy center of the doomed and prescient Eva and establish it as a touchstone for each line, each word as she spoke it. It was too soon for this, of course; but you could only get there by starting somewhere, and after so long she felt starved for some sense of competence and craft in herself.

As for the others, she hoped for the best. Bella Mason was a known, dependable quantity and a comfort to have on board. Jess knew Anita MacNeil, who had gotten the lesser part of Hildegarde, and she had heard of Anthony Sinclair for years but had never worked with him before. The other four were strangers.

Before long they would become tighter than the family they would portray onstage.

After the rehearsal, feeling jazzed and exhausted and dizzy with potential ways to go with her part, she wandered down to the dressing rooms and stuck her head in the one that the stage manager said would be hers.

It was a small space, crammed full with an illuminated makeup mirror, a bare table with scarred legs, and a single chair. A battered wicker wastebasket occupied one corner. There were several clumsily patched places on the grimy walls, but at least she saw no roaches.

A vase of flowers, some pictures, and a colorful calendar would help. You had to make your working space into home for a while. She thought of a pretty little music box that she had used in her last dressing room, that horrible hole in the Holtby Theater—but no, the box had been given to her by Nicolas, and Nicolas did not want her here at all.

But she wanted him. She would have given a lot to see him pop in here and make some wise-ass joke that meant, "Good luck, I love you, I hope you do well!"

Instead she had her victory over him, and its taste was as bitter as it was sweet.

So, she thought, sitting down before the makeup mirror, *I win this round, and that is important*. Not, she admitted ruefully to herself, just for her own self-respect, but because even this initial triumph carried in it seeds of the hope she could not give up.

If the play was a success, maybe he would come after all and see her part in the making of that success, and fall in love with her again.

Meanwhile, damn him to hell if he did anything to try to ruin it for her!

Someone was out in the hall, a short, stout woman with

a belligerent jaw, walking up and down peering at the dressing-room doors.

"Marie," Jess exclaimed. "Are you working in this show?"

"I'm your dresser, Miss Croft," the short woman said. "As long as they can afford me."

Jess smiled. She had worked with Marie before, and she recognized Walter's hand in this—hiring extra help they could probably ill afford. But by doing so he had done his best to give Jessamyn a stalwart and completely partisan ally in the production.

"Come on in and have a look," Jess said, giving Marie as much of a hug as that small and sturdy person would accept. "It's no palace, but it's not as bad as a cell in a Turkish prison, either."

By the third day of rehearsals, the dressing room had been transformed. Marie knew how to "dress" spaces as well as people, and to Jess's rather limited ideas she had added some touches of her own: a porcelain figure of a seventeenth-century gallant bowing on the windowsill, a beautiful batik-print cloth from Indonesia hung to mask the worst wall, and a colorful rag rug, a peaceful oval shape, hiding the worn center of the painted concrete floor.

"Oh," she said, "and there's something else, I almost forgot."

She paused in her work to search among the tubes and jars on the makeup table. There was to be a party celebrating the launching of the production at the home of the head of the Edwardian's board, and Marie was halfway through making Jess up for it in an initial stab at Eva's spectral looks.

"Ah!" she exclaimed, pouncing. She held up her prize. "I found this on the dressing table this morning: a gift from an admirer, I guess."

Jess's eyes widened as she took the object. "An admirer of what, for goodness's sake? I haven't done anything yet!"

"Well, neither has anyone else," the dresser said tartly,

selecting a blusher shade and trying a feather-touch of it on Jess's cheek. Marie's lifelong sentimentality over the theater and its folk was well disguised in briskness colored with cynicism.

Unaccountably reluctant to unveil the mystery, Jess turned the gift-wrapped little parcel speculatively in her hands. "You don't suppose it's something inappropriate from Anthony Sinclair. I've heard he's famous for wooing his leading ladies.

"Or it could be just an encouraging gesture," she added doubtfully. She was afraid to say what she really thought and hoped: that this might be a peace offering from Nic.

"Anthony Sinclair is way too old for you," Marie said severely.

"I don't care about age, Marie, but he's a married man."

"You still have a lot to learn about the theater if you think that makes a difference," the dresser said.

Jessamyn hid a smile. Marie had always had a huge crush on Sinclair herself, though she would die rather than show it.

In the box inside the wrapping was a teardrop-shaped pendant in dark metal with brilliant silvery ornaments, tiny rosettes and stars, set on the fine black filigree work. The pendant was strung on a delicate chain of the same black, wiry swirls and turns, like exquisite, miniature wrought-iron work.

Jess's heart thumped. The pendant wasn't flashing with diamonds or dripping pearls, but she knew fine workmanship when she saw it.

Marie blinked at the gift nested on its cotton bed, and stood back with her hands on her hips. "Well, that certainly doesn't come from Mr. Sinclair. That's an antique piece. The dark part is Berlin iron, cast and lacquered, and the bright bits are cut and polished steel. Turn it over, you'll see that it's put together with tiny rivets—see there?"

"Looks like a lot of work. Is it valuable?"

"As an antique only," Marie said, a little flame of greed gleaming in her eyes. "Of course at the time it was made, somewhere in the early nineteenth century I expect, it was the kind of thing that was valued among comfortable bourgeois who couldn't afford the rubies and emeralds of the rich. Any collector would drool all over it, but it's no museum piece.''

"Good," Jess said, although she was disappointed. Nic was a wealthy man, thanks to the Griffin fortune; in a present from him, rubies and emeralds—small ones, maybe, but gems nonetheless—would be more likely. He was not the source of this gift, she was sure now. She sighed and made the best of it. "Something really expensive would make me nervous."

Marie, who collected fine costume jewelry, added shrewdly, "I didn't say it wasn't expensive. These days that kind of thing is collected for its beauty and rarity. Look at the delicacy of the work."

"Then it had better not be from Anthony!" Jess said with a laugh. "His wife would come down here and shoot me, and she'd be right, too."

"Sally Sinclair would more likely shoot *him*. The only way he could afford a fine piece of Victorian jewelry is by having a sideline in bank robbery."

"Then who left this, Marie? It must be a mistake. It can't be fake, can it? A reproduction, maybe?"

"No. That's old work." The dresser peered sternly at Jess. "You'd better be careful, Miss Croft. I don't know who left it any more than you do, but you can bet he's got something more in mind than watching you from the audience."

"Well, so what?" Jess said with more boldness than she felt. Marie's knowing manner provoked her into outrageousness. "He could be tall, dark, handsome, and rich enough to hand out antique jewelry as trinkets, and what would be wrong with that?"

"In my experience," Marie remarked, "the kind of man who sends jewelry looks like a toad and treats women like flies."

"Erk," Jess said, giggling. She reluctantly put the lid

back on the box. "You're probably right. Well, I don't have to accept it, do I?"

"Not if you can figure out who it came from and give it right back."

"Look, can you take it to the office safe later, Marie? Just until I find out more about it. I'd hate to have something happen to this beautiful thing and then not be able to replace the value of it to whoever sent it."

The dresser nodded, took the little package, and secreted it somewhere on her person so quickly that Jess couldn't tell where it was. Marie had done a stint as a magician's assistant, among many odd theatrical and circus jobs. She knew a few tricks herself, and occasionally amused herself by showing them off.

Anthony Sinclair came sweeping in and collected Jess for the party.

"Time to get going!" he announced in ringing tones. "Mustn't keep the backers waiting! Actually, this is exactly my idea of a celebration—*before* you open, when everybody's still full of hope and cheer!" He smiled his famous, fetching, crooked smile. His whole hawklike face seemed softened, radiating warmth and affection.

Could he have sent the pendant? No, of course not—Marie was right, the man was a talented performer and he seemed fond of Jess in a collegial way; but if he could lay hands on such a lovely object he would probably use it to try to woo back his wife.

The Sinclairs were famous for their long-lasting but wildly stormy marriage. At the moment they were in the fourth month of their latest separation. Anthony had always taken back his beautiful Sally before, when she could be persuaded to return to him. He would undoubtedly do so again.

Jess wondered if she would ever find such a devoted life partner for herself (not Nicolas; she must give up the idea of Nicolas).

Suddenly she couldn't wait to leave the cramped dressing room and all the uncertainties it symbolized. She quickly finished dressing—there were no costumes yet, so she wore a simple dress of her own that she thought fit the play's visual quality—and rode uptown with Sinclair to dazzle the subscribers and maybe help squeeze a little more out of them in contributions to the theater's expenses.

The party was on the penthouse floor of a huge old apartment building on Central Park West. All the way there Sinclair talked cheerfully, telling theatrical stories of disasters and saves, ruins and triumphs, and complimenting Jess on what she had done so far with the character of Eva.

"Thanks for the encouragement," she said. "I know I'm not really back up to speed yet. I'm blowing lines that are right there on paper in front of me, for God's sake—"

"Being nervous is perfectly understandable," Sinclair said. His voice, a deep baritone that could reach the back of the largest theater with no evident effort at all on his part, lowered even more with disapproval. "Though I don't think Walter's constant carping helps."

"No, he *is* being helpful," Jess said. "Everybody is."

"Not our reclusive playwright," Sinclair said. "My bet is that he won't even show up on opening night."

Jess sighed. "Don't blame Nic Griffin. That damned accident hurt him a lot more than it hurt me."

"Well, he doesn't deserve to have you sticking up for him," the actor said stubbornly. "I know you and Griffin were an item, Jessamyn, but I have to say it anyway and hope you'll forgive me: maybe he's just got no guts."

"Anthony, don't be unfair," she responded. "Don't you think Nicolas was brave to go to Europe and help carry medical supplies through the lines at Sarajevo? It wasn't his fight, and goodness knows almost everybody else just sat around wringing their hands, not actually *doing* anything! And then to come back and write about it all so compellingly—not just to endure the bombardments and the sniper fire and the deaths of people around him, but to relive it all for the stage—"

"It may have been courage," Sinclair said. His mobile eyebrows gathered in a severe expression. "Or it may have been self-dramatization. And who's out there taking the risks now, may I ask? Who's actually preparing to go on-stage in front of everyone, armed with nothing but someone else's words and her own native wit and talent, to be cheered or jeered when the curtain comes down? You, my dear; you, and me.''

''And Billy Calthorpe, and Anita MacNeil, among others,'' Jess reminded him, amused at how Sinclair's egotism obliterated the lesser members of the cast.

''Jessamyn Croft,'' he said with a sigh, ''I really do wonder sometimes how you have come this far in the theater— and believe me, you have come far—without losing all that extraordinary sweetness and generosity.''

She blushed and began to deny any special virtue, but Sinclair touched her lips with his forefinger to stop her protestations. ''As one who long ago lost his own best qualities, I know whereof I speak; and I know how important it is to be reminded that one can be both a fine performer and a decent human being.''

He caught her hand and lifted it lightly to brush her fingers with his lips; very Old World, and very sexy, too, as he undoubtedly knew very well. She was suddenly very aware of the solid presence of the actor, the broad chest from which that deep and supple voice flowed so richly, the warm pressure of his thigh against her own. Her cheeks grew hotter; good grief, this was all she needed: an attractive man, an accomplished man—a married man, no matter how rockily.

She had to work with the man, and closely, for an unspecified length of time. Besides that, she liked him. What could she say to preserve the distance between them without hurting his feelings?

There was a considerable gap in their ages, and if she felt it, he certainly must. Actors are sensitive about age, and with good reason. Then there was the production to think of. Backstage romances had a way of causing more trouble than they were worth (just look at her and Nic, starting out besotted with each other in *Barefoot in the Park* that summer).

The limousine halted and a uniformed doorman opened the door. At the penthouse floor of the building, Walter Steinhart met them in the foyer of the thronged apartment, drink in hand, his beard bristling and his dark eyes glittering with energy.

"Jess!" he cried, turning away to call out to the crowd. "Here she is, everyone—the perfect Eva-in-the-making, the benchmark performance!"

He left Sinclair with Jess's coat in his hands and drew her quickly after him into the thick of the mob, introducing her to bright-eyed strangers. Some were the bohemian friends of members of the company, dramatic-looking women with stark makeup and outrageous clothes. They looked more like actresses than Jess did, she noted with inward amusement but some shyness too.

People close to her (like Aunt Rachel, back in Virginia, whose presence she suddenly wished for very strongly) insisted that her slight scars had simply made her more intriguing to look at. But Jess could no longer think of herself as beautiful in any conventional sense. In her green silk dress, without her stage makeup or a costume cut just for her, she knew she wasn't nearly as striking as some of these people.

And not just the women, the men too. She glanced covertly at a handsome poet with a silver ring in one nostril and his hair shaven to a fine fuzz all over his scalp. He was too deep in discussion to notice, talking to someone with an impressive, ramlike nose down which he gazed with bored, heavy-lidded eyes like a Byronic laudanum addict of the last century.

The room was large and high-ceilinged, paneled and plastered with old-fashioned opulence. It was already crowded to bursting, hot and noisy. The hired waitstaff had to eel their way through the crowd, performing unnoticed prodigies of balance to avoid tipping drinks and finger food down the guests' collars.

Jess had done more than one stint working for a caterer, before her first theatrical successes had relieved her of that necessity. She felt for these hired servants, at the same time that she hoped fervently that she would never be reduced to that kind of work again.

Walter, who had been taken aside by their host Joshua Whitely—a heavy, round-faced man wearing a rather endearing expression of dazed delight—caught her eye and beckoned to her.

Jess foresaw entrapment in one of those painful situations where she would be introduced to someone she should flatter and charm so that he (it was usually a he) would write a check for a new office computer for the theater, or some new lights, or a replacement for the worn stage curtain, or whatever was at the top of the current wish list.

She was an actress, not a saleswoman. She let some people step in front of her so Walter wouldn't see her slip out through the French doors that opened onto a spacious outdoor terrace.

Cold air flavored with smoke refreshed her. Several people stood by the wrought-iron railing at one end of the terrace, arguing about plays and performers, unions, critics, and producers. They were mere silhouettes against the brilliantly lit buildings of the mid-Manhattan skyline, which glowed under stars that the illumination of the buildings far outshone.

Glad to stop smiling for a moment, Jess walked to the other end of the terrace and relaxed against the rail with a sigh of relief, although it was too cold to stay out long without her coat. The conversation inside sounded like insane babble.

So much hope, so much excitement—and so much of it riding on her and her abilities. She should get herself home, fix some hot cocoa, and curl up in front of the television to numb herself to sleep. If she stayed around here, somebody might offer her something stronger, and she might be tempted to accept.

Jess never sneered at performers who used liquor and

dope, though she herself did not indulge. The stresses of
the work were so great, the roller coaster of emotion was
so magnified and so inescapable, more than any outsider
could ever imagine. Those emotional extremes were part of
the performer's talent, after all, and part of her work; naturally there was a price to pay for taking the ride.

Right now she found something very seductive in the
idea of slipping away for a nightcap with Anthony Sinclair,
who for the moment had no loving wife to go home to.
Any more than Jess had someone of her own.

Dangerous thoughts! Jessamyn had once fallen for a married man, and it was not an experience she ever wanted to
repeat.

Better get out of here, she told herself; but how to get
through the crush inside without being endlessly diverted
and detained? If only that airplane droning overhead were
a flying saucer that would drop a transport beam down for
her, she could slip away from all this uproar without having
to first plunge back into it.

"Excuse me, but you are about to spill your drink," said
a male voice, one she didn't know, quite close by. Startled,
she did spill the drink, and jumped back from the cold
splash of vodka and tonic across her instep.

"God, you scared me!" she exclaimed.

"May I take the glass?" said the stranger from the
shadow of a tall shrub planted in a redwood box. Lightly
as a breeze he lifted the glass from her fingers and set it
down under the evergreen. "Someone will retrieve it later,
I am sure."

The shadow of the plant beside him seemed to stretch to
cloak the man in a deeper darkness than that of the city-lit
night around them. Jess could barely make out the line of
his cheek and the shine of his eye. His English was clearly
not native, but accented in an unfamiliar way. Curious, she
cast around for some comment that would draw an answer
from him. Accents were part of her professional interest.

"Thank you," she said. "I barely knew I had that drink

in my hand at all. I might have forgotten completely and dropped it on some poor passerby's head.''

''Ah, well,'' replied the other, his quiet voice shaded with humor, ''an accident of life in the great modern city. It is part of the excitement people seek when they come here.''

''Only a newcomer to New York could say that,'' she said. ''Mostly what people crave is peace, quiet, and not to get mugged in the street.''

He leaned one elbow on the terrace railing behind him, his face still shadowed, and chuckled softly. ''All milieus have their dangers, Miss Croft.''

His voice was a rich, youthful tenor, velvet with a curious, uninflected intimacy. It was as if she knew him so well that he did not need to stress his feelings in order for her to interpret them instantly and unerringly. It threw her back to the early days of her relationship with Nicolas, who had simply opened his heart to her without histrionics, as if even before she knew him she could never mistake his meaning.

''Believe me,'' she said, more tartly than she meant to, ''if there's one thing New York has too much of, it's dangers. And you are . . . ?''

''Someone with a taste for theater but only a limited tolerance for large, noisy parties,'' he answered. ''From your tone, perhaps I have somehow offended?'' He made a sharp little bow with his head, a very European gesture. ''I beg your pardon if I said anything to anger you.''

Who was this man? What did he look like, out of the protection of the shadows? Jess felt a little thrill of interest beyond the merely professional.

''Are you a friend of the Whitelys?'' she asked.

''Mr. Whitely occasionally asks me to consult with him about his collection.''

Jess thought of the various items she had seen exhibited in impressive numbers in Whitely's apartment—Japanese kimonos spread like animal hides to show their designs, South American pottery that ran to goofy-looking little clay people doing uninterpretable things, exquisitely framed historic photographs of old New York . . . "Which one?" she said.

"Most of them," he answered with amusement in his tone. "My experience, and my expertise, are broad."

"Are you a collector yourself?"

"Ah, no," he murmured. "A traveler must keep his possessions light, isn't that what you say?"

At that moment Sinclair hailed Jess commandingly from the open doorway; she spotted his hawkish head silhouetted against the lights within. "Jessamyn, what are you doing hiding out here? Come and laugh at my stories; none of these stuffy kids will!"

As she turned to answer, Jess felt the hidden stranger slip past her with a murmured apology—his breath stirred the hair of her temple, he passed so close—and she saw a man hardly taller than herself, but powerfully built and elegantly tailored, quickly cross the terrace and pass in front of Anthony Sinclair. In a few buoyant strides the man had vanished into the crowd.

Her blood seemed to buzz in her veins as if she'd had something very odd indeed to drink; and she had never even seen the stranger's face. Who was he, anyway, to depart so abruptly and leave her with her skin tingling and her breath half caught?

Warnings from the Past

Nic woke with a gasp and lay staring at the ceiling: Bad dreams again, melted away now, leaving him—where?

The elaborate plasterwork around the base of the lighting fixture was alien, the feel of the mattress unwelcoming, the smell of the room unfamiliar—everything was strange and disorienting. His leg ached and his heart was heavy with a clinging anxiety left over from his dreams.

No sign of dawn yet; he could only have been asleep for a couple of hours, after returning to the hotel from shadowing Jessamyn and her distinguished escort to Joshua Whitely's party. Ridiculous, like some fifth-rate Bogart imitation in a private-eye novel! He was no investigator, and no actor either; he ought to leave such shenanigans to puffed-up characters like Sinclair (who, to be fair, was a puffed-up character with talent; Nic had seen him perform several times, and had been impressed).

Besides, Sinclair *had* been her escort (and maybe aspired to be something more than that, damn him!). It wasn't as if Jess had been wandering around all by herself in the middle of the night; nor, Nic suspected, would his own presence have been warmly welcomed if he had been discovered, by Sinclair or by Jess herself.

After all, he had taken some pains to alienate her and open a gulf between them, hadn't he? And *that* much of an actor he was.

But he couldn't stay away. He couldn't leave Jessamyn to the protection of others, people who with the best will in the world still didn't have any idea of the danger she might be in; any more than she did, herself.

He groaned and threw his forearm across his eyes. It had seemed quite simple, when he had first conceived of his plans for his enemy. What he was doing was a poor exchange for the life he had anticipated with such blithe confidence when Jessamyn had been at his side; but he had accepted another fate now, as the newest head of his family. What was unavoidable had to be accepted, didn't it? With good grace, if possible, and with ceaseless efforts to recast it into something of his own, not just something forced upon him by outrageous fortune.

But the whole thing made him feel old; a thousand heavy years older than his true age. Old in strength—he was never sure that he had enough of that—and old in understanding, too. Much older than he had been before the accident, that was certain.

Here he was waking in the middle of the night like some frail elder, to lie brooding in the darkness while sleep eluded him. There was so much to think about (although thinking didn't change things). His mind ran in its accustomed track, and came, as always, to his father, Eric Griffin.

A hearty man, heartily loving to his only child, but always abstracted somehow, his eyes narrowed in contemplation of his next business triumph; a good dad, when he was there, but a man who had lived the robust and aggressive center of his life outside, in the world, not at home.

As a boy, Nic had adored him.

No wonder there had been such a sudden, sharp change in the man upon Grandfather Geoffrey's death! Eric Griffin's bluff, acquisitive, sometimes callous nature had closed down into hollow silences and brooding stares as he watched his own son study, play, and plan for a sunny, adventurous future.

That had been a hurtful time for Nic, full of desperate anxiety that somehow he himself had failed his father, that he was the cause of the change. God, the incredible self-centeredness of youth!

In self-defense he had begun calling Eric "Old Sourpuss," behind his back of course, which had made him feel worse—cowardly and treacherous, but also more adult, as if he had somehow seen through his father's facade to the "real" man. He supposed some sort of estrangement like this had to happen in all families, one way or another, for a boy to separate from his parents enough to become a man himself. But those last years had been so ugly and full of wounds given and taken, and he deeply regretted his behavior now.

His mother, too, had been hurt, as much by her own bafflement and increased distance from Eric as by Nic's disparagement. He was sure now that his father had never spoken of the curse to Serena Griffin, either. Eric had hugged it fiercely to himself in silence, trying—who knew exactly by what harsh means—to wrestle it out of existence.

What showed outwardly was this: he had gone on increasingly long and obviously wearing "business trips," ending in the disastrous one to Colombia from which he had not returned.

Serena Griffin had recovered some frail cheer afterward and had filled her days by traveling, in company with her widowed older sister. Nic remembered so clearly the times he had rendezvoused with her in Europe or Costa Rica, and how he had sensed the slow dissolution of her anguished conviction that somehow Nic's scorn had contributed to his father's death. They had been drawing shyly closer to each other when a quick series of strokes had killed her.

It was amazing, looking back, how long and in how varied a way the Griffin curse had blighted Nic's life along with the lives of his parents. His one comfort was that his mother had never known about the strange fate that had destroyed Nic's father, as Jessamyn must never know. A strong man protected the people he loved, or how could he respect himself? How could he be worthy of their love in return?

Besides, in some way that he could not quite explain to himself, this mysterious affliction was strictly a matter for the Griffin men. Perhaps it had something to do with the sense of shame that came with it, although shame for what, precisely, he was never sure.

Jess, and what he had done to her, was already cause enough for shame and regret in his life. She mustn't be drawn any farther into the terrible chain of events than she already had been by the crash of that damned car. He was determined on it.

But he was deeply afraid now, whenever he went to sleep and each time he awoke. Haunted by a relentless sense of being dragged toward darkness by an inexorable, hidden current, he moved through his days with his teeth clenched in a ceaseless effort to retain control.

But he was not a helpless victim; he had faced his situation and made a plan, and that had helped against the fear. Until now.

Now his strategy for dealing with the enemy was launched—and had veered wildly out of control: through her participation in the play, Jessamyn had involved herself even more deeply, with an innocent courage that broke his heart. He had done all he could, at painful cost, to insulate her from his struggle, and all for nothing, it seemed. Sometimes he was furious with her, in the seething tumult of his own mind, for what she had done.

If only he could find a way to reverse what he had set in motion, expelling her again from his family's terrible story! He was trying, as hard as he had ever tried to do anything in his life; and meanwhile he could not help but do his best to protect her, no matter how vain his efforts. He watched over her. God help him, despite himself he haunted the theater, he observed the building she lived in from a doorway across the street. He fed his weary eyes with the sight of her, hugging his love for her to him like a magical source of warmth that the coldest day could not chill.

He was her tender, futile, desperate guardian angel. What a joke! He was an idiot, and for all he knew, his silent attendance on her only increased her danger.

God, how had he come here, anyway? What an incredible, whole world's-length away from the careless confidence of his younger days, when he had danced and drunk and partied his way through a seemingly endless crowd of admiring male friends and willing girls!

Before he had met Jess. Jess, his life, his soul, his terror, and his despair. What to do about Jess? She was no fainting violet to be moved here and there like a piece on a chessboard, not even for her own good, assuming he could really foresee how that good might be served.

Sleep was out of the question. He rose with a sigh and went to turn on the desk light on the other side of the hotel room. He got a glass of water and pulled on the short white terrycloth robe from the hook in the bathroom door.

Feeling lonelier than he had ever felt in his life, he sat down at the desk, massaged his bad leg a moment, and drew out of the drawer the packet he had brought with him from the safe in the Rhinebeck house.

The ruby, removed from its nest of soft black cloth inside a velvet pouch, he studied for some time, turning it this way and that to capture the light. He hefted its weight thoughtfully in his palm.

How many of the old stories were true? Family folklore had it that the ruby had been used as gambling stakes, and small fortunes had been won by Griffins betting on it. Shares in it had been secretly sold, the money invested, the rich returns used to buy back full ownership with profit to spare. It had never left their possession; but someone else, it seemed, had repeatedly asserted a deadly claim on it all along.

He turned to the documents that accompanied the gemstone. The older papers he had sealed in plasticine envelopes to protect the fragile, yellowed pages. He drew them out with care: a small series of pathetic communications from Griffin men who had come and gone before him.

Maybe there was a solution hidden somewhere here, if he could only recognize it.

From Abel Griffin, slaver:

Let him come, I care nothing. I shall set stout fellows upon him and take him in chains, with his devil-face blackened by bruises and soot, and sell him off in Charleston, and walk away laughing with my profit. A man who has dealt in heathen souls from the darkest Continent of the world has no fear of silly spirits come a-chasing from the Old World after lost plunder. And besides, the stone is mine.

From Turner Griffin before his death in a shipyard accident while seeing to the refitting of his whaling ship *Reaver*. (The captain had been famous for killing even baby whales and their mothers in his relentless pursuit of profit.)

I, Turner Griffin of Wellfleet, master of *Reaver*, have received my patrimony upon the death of my father. It is a deadly gift; but by God's grace and the Griffin Luck, I have made my fortune and I shall take my family away with me to San Francisco, as soon as I have made *Reaver* ready for sale to some captain who will do well by her. The stone I will have made into a brooch for my Lisbeth, for surely the virtue of such a woman can overcome even a hellish curse.

And in another hand at the bottom ran several neat, small lines:

I would have thrown the ruby into the sea after they buried Turner, but my son would not permit it. He has been told a tale of the stone as the anchor of the Griffin luck. Such luck! But he will not listen. Heaven help us all. Elizabeth Devlin Griffin.

There were more: notes and letters and pompous declarations, most mentioning the ruby with pride and possessiveness. The page from Nic's own father was brief and to the point:

To my son:
    The enemy is real, and he demands our treasure, but it's my death that he really wants. The ruby is just an excuse.
    I have tried extreme measures to defend us against him; no use. He can't be killed by any means I know (and if you think I've overdone it, hiring people to kill him, because I failed, you will someday be forced to understand the desperation that drove me to it). I'm sorry.
    I will try to draw him off, away from your mother and from you, Nicolas. Maybe with help from some of my foreign associates (who live in a part of the world more primitive and haunted than mine—they may know some tricks that I don't and that he doesn't either). I can deal with him once and for all.
    If I don't come back and he does, your turn will come—and I have no wise advice to give you. Except that if you are young enough at my death to prevent it, you might consider having no children of your own. Let the line and its curse end, if you can't do anything else.
    I am sorry I haven't been a better father, and a better man. To tell the truth, though, if I had it all to

do over again, I would probably act just the same—
and feel just as empty, sorry, and depressed at the
end. We are what we are. Look after your mother as
best you can, and never let her know any of this.

Good-bye, Nic. You are too good a young man to
be a Griffin anyway, from what I have seen; maybe
our damned demon will see that too, and let you be.
I wish I could count on it. I wish I had believed
before, then I might have figured out a better way to
end all this. But no such luck. May yours be better.

It was signed Eric Turner Griffin, with a p.s. appended
in a shakier, less bold hand: "I tried just throwing the
damned thing away, but could not bring myself to do it."

Nic had sneered over these pages in the past, sure that
his father had been mad, as maybe other Griffin men had
been before him, too. He saw now that he had lived some
of his young manhood in a white heat of impatient hunger
for life's experiences, sure that the real curse was a heri-
table insanity that would claim him too, in due course. His
wild younger days had not been entirely careless and joyful.

He had done impetuous, angry things that he wished he
could undo—later, when he realized that the mad tales were
true. Often, after the accident, he had sat in the cellar at
the house in Rhinebeck to pray, clumsily and without conviction, over these papers, to brood over them in black anger, and sometimes to weep over them.

It must end sometime; to tell the truth, he was downright
eager for the final confrontation with whoever, whatever,
the demon was. But because of Jessamyn all that was tem-
pered now with sickly dread that she would be caught up
in the finish despite his best efforts to keep her out of it.

Driven to some kind of action, no matter how futile, he
called up David Schoen, and after a dozen rings the phone
was answered.

"Yes?"

"Griffin here. Listen, I want you to call the Burch people
again tomorrow, press them for an earlier appointment."

Schoen cleared his throat. "I had to work to get us signed up for next week, Mr. Griffin. We won't get in any sooner."

"Then we'll go up tomorrow and just drive around the neighborhood, check out the library and historical archives, the local newspaper morgue—"

"It's done. That's how I found out as much as I did."

"It won't do me any harm to have a look for myself." *In case you missed something*, Nic thought, but he didn't say it. Schoen wouldn't have missed anything. He was one of the best investigators in the business—he had found out about the document in the Burch Collection, hadn't he?

"All right, of course," Schoen said. He didn't say, *It's your money, pal; if you want to pay me to do a search for you, and then pay me to take you over the same ground that I've already been over, that's fine with me.* He didn't complain about being yanked out of his sleep in the middle of the night, either, or permit himself to sound even the least bit hazy.

Good money bought good help. Nic remembered his father used to say that. He grimaced, not comfortable at seeing aspects of his father's values and behavior in his own now; he had despised the old man at times, and now he despised himself—for rousting the hired help out of bed in the pit of morning because he couldn't sleep himself, and because owning the Griffin money meant he could do that if he wanted to.

But need drove him. He gripped the phone tighter and said, "Tell me again. What exactly is this 'Burch Collection'? I've never heard of it before."

Without even an exasperated sigh, Schoen told him again. (Nic wondered if there was a Mrs. Schoen, sunken in sleep in another room.) "Burch was an eccentric, a sort of mysticism maven—a spiritual seeker, I guess you'd say now—anyway, he was into all kinds of spirit-chasing. He was a devotee of Madame Blavatsky, he corresponded with Conan Doyle on spiritualism, and he traveled all over America attending seances and watching dowsers at work—

that was a secondary speciality of his, actually; there's a whole subcollection on it.

"But his main subject of interest was New England stories, accounts of hauntings, superstitions, that kind of thing. He even visited H. P. Lovecraft at one point, presumably to make sure the old horror-spinner wasn't actually practicing journalism instead of fiction.

"Over the years, Burch built up a sizable file of documents on his obsessions, everything from newspaper accounts to locks of hair and other souvenirs. When his niece found the stuff, she realized that even though most of these objects had been tossed by her mother, she could still save the papers, which she had the sense to see might be valuable someday. She's the one who actually set up the archive and got some funding to modify the Burch place itself to house it.

"Apparently there are dozens of old diaries, ships' logs, office account books, letters, and legal papers—deeds, wills, sworn statements, that kind of thing—as well as a considerable file of oral accounts that Burch either took down himself or had collected by a couple of his students he got to do some of his fieldwork for him. Did I tell you he was a professor of medieval English?"

"You told me," Nic said.

"Well, when I was checking on your ancestors in Wellfleet I stumbled on a retired librarian who remembered hearing that one of Burch's assistants had made a local sweep of old documents back sometime between the two world wars. That was the explanation she'd been given for why there were gaps in the town archives and records.

"The present Burch curator, Mr. Pease, affirmed by phone that they acquired at that time some kind of handwritten document with a Griffin signature, and there's no problem with letting us see it. I got the feeling the old boy was kind of flattered by the interest. He plainly had to juggle his personal schedule to set up an appointment for us. He's only very, very part-time; ditto access to the collection itself. They don't get a lot of inquiries up there these days—bad investments, I hear, have left them with no spare cash for publicity, and rumor has it that they've had to sell off some prime pieces to keep going.''

Nic said sharply, ''You didn't tell me that before. There's no chance the Griffin papers are gone, is there? Sold with other things, and the curator's forgotten?''

There was a pause. ''I don't think we need to worry about that, Mr. Griffin. Not unless they've had hired help selling things out from under them in secret, that is, and I haven't caught wind of anything like that. I've asked around about the Burch Collection itself, you understand. I think we're on firm ground here.''

Nic thought of the unknown enemy, the ''demon'' of the stories on the desk, and shivered with apprehension. But he said calmly, ''Very good, Mr. Schoen. Sorry to have gotten you up. I'll expect you here first thing after breakfast with a written report.''

''Certainly, Mr. Griffin,'' Schoen said. ''Good-bye.''

Tired and chilled, Nic climbed back into bed. He dreaded the idea of leaving Jessamyn here in the city to go up to New Paltz next week; but the Burch Collection find sounded too important to be left to anyone else to examine.

Assuming it was anything at all. Maybe it was just some tale of a poltergeist in the carriage house taken from a doddering groom, or a bit of gossip about ghosts in an old Indian burial ground.

Temptation

◆

Jessamyn had a drink at Anthony Sinclair's apartment after rehearsal. His obvious loneliness had touched her, and tonight she thought she saw the nervous vulnerability he usually hid so well.

While Walter talked with the cast about the improvements he saw he could sweep them all into his own enthusiasm, but afterward—as Jess and Anthony agreed over a light meal when the session finished—seen in a colder light, all it meant was more work, harder work, for the actors—and more exacting expectations of them from Walter.

The play hinged, naturally, on the interaction between the two leads, Marko and Eva. He was the elder son of the powerful family on whom leadership fell with the death of his father. Eva, though essentially a sort of spirit, was also his flesh-and-blood niece, returned home from a life of mystical seeking in the world. She brought with her word of what that family's interests had wrought against poor and helpless people elsewhere; and what price must be paid in return.

Others in the cast encouraged Jess and Sinclair (subtly or openly) to spend extra time together, on the theory that this would help to create a strong undercurrent of feeling between them on the stage. They both recognized this themselves, and went along with it, only partly in jest.

Jessamyn found herself strongly attracted to Sinclair's air of world-weary vulnerability and his surprising playfulness. And why not? There had been no man in her life since Nic. Maybe it was time there was.

It's like being a widow, she thought; here she was, slow-dancing to some mellow jazz in Anthony Sinclair's living room at two o'clock in the morning, mourning the loss of Nic and noting that Anthony was subtly coming on to her, as men often do with newly bereaved women. The actor's cheek, moving lightly against hers as he hummed a counterpoint to the horn tune, was beginning to roughen with whiskers, and the warm pressure of his body was making her bones feel soft and melted.

He was a well-built, graceful man, experienced, demonstrative, probably a dream as a lover—the first few times, anyway. Real-life but short-lived romantic liaisons were not uncommon in productions of plays about intense emotions and family bonds. And she was needy tonight, she realized, in a way she could not recall having been for a long, long while.

Working with a handful of excitable, dedicated professionals on a passionate play, day after day for hours at a time, had roused her sleeping senses and her bruised and timid flesh.

On the other hand, she told herself ruefully, even as her arm tightened around Anthony's shoulders, she was not some dewy-eyed beginner fresh out of drama school. She would never allow herself to believe that she, among all women, would be the one to permanently win Anthony away from his wife's side—assuming that she wanted him on that basis, which was by no means a foregone conclusion. Most theatrical men—like their female counterparts—were fickle, nervous, egotistical people; they had to be, to be able to do their work.

Jessamyn had sown some wild oats (so to speak) of her own as a beginner. She was not inclined to hold a certain amount of sexual adventurism against her fellow professionals. Forever at risk of public failure, rejection, and ridicule in their work, they sought approval and acceptance wherever they might find it.

Sally Sinclair was currently featured in a musical on Broadway. It was said among the crew at the Edwardian that if an opening that suited him appeared in that show's cast, Anthony would find a way to get out of his obligations in *The Jewel* and go join his wife.

Jess didn't need to get any nearer to someone who might be that unpredictable.

"Anthony," she said, leaning lightly against him in apology for what she was about to say, "Anthony, I don't think—"

"Hush," he murmured, turning her in a swift circle with expert pressure where their bodies touched. "Of course you don't, but let an old man dream on a little, won't you?"

"If you're an old man," she responded with fond exasperation, "that makes me what, an ingenue? Not for a long time, Anthony. Not since I did summer stock."

He didn't answer, but his arm gathered her more tightly to him in a hug that was more comforting than suggestive. Everyone knew that Jess had met Nicolas Griffin in a summer-stock company, and theater folk tried to take care of their own.

She felt her eyes tear up. Anthony, bless him, kept her dancing until the cut on the album ended.

"Just as well," he said, stepping away to reclaim his half-finished drink from a side table by the sofa. "Anything more than a friendly dance and Sally knows about it somehow. Then there's more hell than ever to pay. I do not know how the woman does it. She's some kind of genius—the evil kind.''

"Come on, Anthony, you love her to pieces, and it's mutual; who are you trying to kid?''

He looked at her with mournful eyes. ''That's how it looks to you, my dear, but remember—Sal and I are *actors*.''

She laughed and began gathering up her coat and scarf. ''That's a hell of a better line than 'My wife doesn't understand me.' Listen, I'm going to get out of here before we both end up in trouble, okay? Have you seen my shoes?''

Sinclair raked his fingers back through his thick, graying hair and yawned. ''Look under the sofa, I thought I kicked something in that direction a few minutes ago. I'll take you downstairs.''

"Oh, Anthony, don't be silly—what's going to happen to a sleepy little actress dragging her weary behind home from work?''

"Exactly,'' he said emphatically. ''On her way home at an hour when only a certain type of woman is supposed to be out on the streets all by herself!''

She sputtered with laughter at his old-fashioned attitude and turn of phrase.

He frowned. ''Seriously, Jessamyn, I can't help worrying. Anita told me about the marbles someone dumped on the floor of your dressing room. You could have taken one hell of a fall! That's more than a prank.''

"Yes,'' she admitted reluctantly, ''I don't like it either, but I've put up with nastiness backstage before; we all have. If I don't make a fuss it'll probably go away, or at least dwindle down to your odd, mean gesture.''

In fact, she had been considerably shaken up by the incident. But the last thing in the world she wanted to do was to give the unknown prankster the satisfaction of a big public reaction. Besides, she had too much riding on this comeback to allow someone's malice to upset it all.

So she and Marie had cleaned up and said nothing (or

maybe not quite nothing, since Anthony and Anita and presumably, by now, the entire company already knew about it).

"Lunatic business," he muttered, scowling at himself in the hall mirror and setting his tie straight. "You know, I wish Nic hadn't named those damned dogs of his after the Scottish play. It's never wise for theater folk to tempt the Fates; we're so much at their mercy as it is."

Jess noted with humor that even in complaint, Sinclair avoided saying the actual name of "the Scottish play" out loud. It was really too bad that Walter had let slip that Nic's dogs were named Mac and Beth.

"I'll be all right, Anthony. Whoever it was has probably worked off their hostility with those marbles. Trust me, he or she is sitting around tonight feeling all shocked and horrified at the thought of what might have happened because of their spite."

"Well, I think you should take precautions," he said. "You locked up that pretty pendant you wore to rehearsal tonight, didn't you? It fits your Eva so well—you don't want to tempt this sneaky swine to walk off with it."

"I'm taking care of it," she said, grinning at the thought of a tiptoeing pig. "After all, it's not really mine. I expect whoever sent it to show up any minute and ask for it back." Or for something else instead; but that was best left unsaid.

She pulled her coat on and held the apartment door open while Sinclair checked his appearance one more time in the hall mirror.

"So you have a mystery admirer," he grunted, showing himself first one profile and then the other, "and now a mystery attacker, too. It's too damned much mystery for my taste, Jessamyn, on top of a play that's about a mystery as well!"

He meant the mystery of how the great family treasure, a gorgeous emerald, had come into the possession of Marko and Eva's forebears. This was a subject of intense argument in the play, and the beleaguered situation and fate of the family members hinged upon the truth of the matter.

The central question was whether they were now reaping the vengeance sowed by their ancestors' evil actions, in which case they had best bow their heads and accept their punishment; or whether they were being persecuted by greedy villains upon whom they could justifiably wreak a treacherous revenge of their own.

And then, of course, came the question of what to do with the emerald, regardless of its origins. These questions worked themselves out amid bombardment and deprivation, becoming an allegory of virtue and violence with much wider application than post–Cold War European politics.

It was satisfying to work in a play that had real resonance to major issues. If not for the marbles in the dressing room and the inexplicable opposition of Nic Griffin, Jess would have been completely happy to be back at work again— this part of the work, anyway: the crucible of preparation.

On the way downstairs her foot hit a child's rubber ball that had been left on the steps. It bounded down ahead of them. Startled, she laughed and clutched the banister.

"Life imitates art," she said. "Anthony—what if the marbles were a code version of the old stage expression 'Break a leg'? Maybe somebody was just wishing me luck in a bizarre sort of way!"

"Somebody crazy, maybe," he muttered, peering down the remaining flight of steps as if he expected to see a hit man lurking in the foyer.

He waited outside in the cold with her until she was able to flag a cab. It occurred to her to wonder, briefly, whether he would have been so gallant if she were heading home from his bed, instead. An ungenerous thought, but appropriate to dozens of actors of both sexes whose beauty sleep was far more important to them than any courtesy.

Putting it firmly away from her, she thanked him for his company and said good night. He gave her a chaste, bourbon-scented kiss and waved her off.

When she looked back through the cab's rear window, he was still standing there, hunched up against the cold. She felt a stab of sympathy. There was nothing to stop a man from being truly lonely, even if he would fly back home to his one true love if she so much as crooked her little finger at him.

A far cry from my one true love, she thought tartly. It would serve Nic right if she had stayed with Sinclair tonight. *Oh hell, oh hell.* She dug a Kleenex out of her purse and blew her nose.

Oh, hell.

Her own apartment, across town, was warm and dark and blessedly quiet. She locked herself in with a sigh of relief— *Should have come home hours ago*! Wrapped in the fleecy robe her aunt had brought to her in the hospital, she wandered into the small front room, stirring hot milk and cinnamon with a dash of vanilla. It was her favorite bedtime drink, and she had even converted Nic to it.

Oh, Nic.

She sat on her bed, sipping milk and pawing through a pile of photos from the bedside table drawer.

Here was Nic, tanned and grinning and hugging his arms across his chest in boyish pride after a sailing race. Only he wasn't a boy, he was a willowy man with the long, sliding musculature of a runner or a swimmer; an experienced and well-traveled man who would still gladly crew for someone else in a boat race to Bermuda. (Couldn't keep his own boat, he always said; too much trouble and expense, and he was never home long enough to get the value out of it.)

And here he was again, fixing a loose board in the porch of his house; he swung a hammer like a skilled workman. And here he was sitting in the gazebo out back with a book in his long-fingered hands, grinning at her around the pipe-stem trapped between his teeth.

And here he wasn't, at Jessamyn's side in her apartment—not anymore. So much for the romantic notion, staple of a hundred films good and bad, that if two people came through a disaster together they were bonded for life.

Crawling into bed, she thought of his youthful beauty, a kind of sunny good looks radiating the confidence that had carried him through a hundred dangerous situations in far-off places. Jessamyn could still feel—or imagined that she felt—the pressure of his warm, solid hand on hers.

She was used to the interest of attractive men, but Nicolas had always been different: completely straightforward and direct, not busily trying to express himself in the most effective way possible so as to charm his current audience. He had allowed her to see him clear and plain, candidly offering his true self for her inspection, without wiles.

But not anymore.

She thought, *I should have stayed at Anthony's. Next time, maybe I will.*

And she slept.

A Vampire at Prayer

◆

 **O** Dark One, are you watching me? Do you spare a quiet thought for my affairs, here in this brash new world where my search has brought me?

Cragga stood on the small balcony of his apartment, looking down on the night-shrouded trees enclosed within the block's outer rampart of condo towers and brownstone row houses. His night-sharp eyes could pick out each leaf, each sleeping bird, each soft-footed cat shinning up the fences between the patchwork of smaller backyards and gardens. Most residential blocks in this city contained such hidden jungles, and they fascinated him.

He sipped wine from a stemmed glass—watered wine, just enough to warm him and rest his thoughts a little after the turmoil of Whitely's party. How they churned his feelings, these hot, living folk, when he spent any time among them! Fortunately, over the generations he had learned to consume a little of what sustained those still human, and that sun-grown nourishment enabled him to endure their company (and also the daylight of their working lives, if the sky was not too bright).

Still, northern cities pleased him most, especially in winter, with their lowering clouds and short, dim days.

And their teeming human life, from which a vampire might take his slender supper without notice so long as he was discreet and not greedy. The people of such cities were normally too busy with their own affairs to pay much heed to one denizen's modest, though singular, appetites.

That thin old woman hunched into her quilted housecoat down below, now, opening her back door on a sweep of yellow light to call her pug dog in from the yard where it digs nightly with mad, ineffectual paws. She might notice a young man standing at his window with his drink, addressing the night on the dark of the moon and emitting no cloud of vapor when his breath hit the cold air (he breathed, but not the heated breath of living humans).

Would she think anything of it if she did see him but saw no plume of hot exhalation from his lips? Probably not. Would she speak to anyone about it? In what terms, without making herself sound naive or crazy? In a city like this one, the naive and the mad were taken deep advantage of; they did not survive long, once the common run of urban predators had identified them. No. She would mind her own business.

He raised his eyes to the sky again. Not a star to be seen, thanks to the brilliance of the city's own artificial lights. What a crowded, noisy, dazzling world it was these days! He was proud of himself for being still in it, not driven out by change and change again, not even deflected from his sworn purpose.

Dark One, watch over me as my elder; help me keep my promise, help me take what belongs to me by right.

And, came a voice as light and as sable-black as a raven's feather, what will you do then, Baron?

Whatever I will.

The voice whispered, You do not know what you will.

Your mind is already blurred with interest in a living woman, a performer of fictions onstage—a professional liar. Beware, Baron. Your youth betrays you. I fear you venture out of your depth.

Nonsense! He scowled into his wineglass. My "youth" is only apparent, as you well know; as for the woman, she is an actress, a person of some talent, but it is transient, like everything else of the daylight world. To me, she is simply a person close to the person I pursue. In her own right, she can be no one special. A pawn, Lady, no more.

You have been thinking of her.

I have been thinking of how best to make use of her. Don't you think I have had enough, in my long life, of pretty ladies—the best and the worst of them? And this one is something less than beautiful, with the scar on her face and the scars of fear and loss in her eyes. Such a sad person; depressing.

Then why do you picture her so closely in your thoughts, Baron?

To know her better, the vampire said in the sparkling darkness of his mind under the flat, washed-out darkness of the city's night. To help me make no error here, and risk no loss.

Then you are a fool, came the answer, light and careless and almost fond. For you are already lost.

Cragga smiled at the pallid sky and lifted his glass in a toast to the unseen speaker. Dear Dark One, I was lost the night you drank away my human life and gave me this shadow life instead.

I gave what you asked for.

True. I do not complain, I merely observe.

Really, Baron? What, then, are you doing at your window on this cold night, winging your thoughts away over the midnight seas to me in our blood-soaked homeland?

He sighed. Pursuing my purpose, Lady, pursuing my purpose; without that, what could I be doing, still in this world that no longer has a place or a need or a use for me?

You are moody tonight, came the reply. I think it would

be best for you to find yourself a meal. Moodiness is dangerous for our kind. We can die of moods, we can throw our lives away at a gloomy whim.

Cragga laughed softly. Never fear, Lady; I am hot on the trail of my true prey, and I won't stop short of my triumph.

For a moment there was nothing but the distant honking of horns at some knot in late-night traffic and the roar of a plane overhead. Then the answer came, See that it is so; for I do not appreciate the casual use of my gifts, Baron.

Which is as it should be, he responded calmly, and drained his glass. Farewell for now, Lady, and do not worry on my account. I will go take my food as you suggest; and in time I will take also the prey that belongs to me, and take back my property too. This woman with the sadness in her eyes will help me without knowing it, and touch me not at all. For although we touch, your kind and mine, we are not touched in turn; or not for long, nor deeply.

To this there was no answer; and after a moment Cragga went in, to shrug on his dark wool coat. He covered his russet hair with a soft black hat, and drew onto his muscular hands soft, snug-fitting gloves. Then he went down into the pale night of the city, to assuage his hunger.

And he felt no fear at all, for he believed what he had told his dark ally.

The Bailiff's Tale

Nic could scarcely believe what he was reading. How had his father missed this?

By being a man of action, probably; by rushing off into action instead of researching. And Grandfather Geoffrey, before him? The Burch Collection had been strictly a private hobby of an obscure professor in his time. He had doubtless never heard of it.

But here it was, the answer—maybe—some answers at last. The room smelled of clutter, dust, and furniture polish, and the bulb in the brass reading lamp was rather dim. Alone and still wearing his coat and scarf (the heat had been turned on and the building opened for his visit), he read eagerly.

The original account, faded ink on stained paper sealed now in plasticine, had been transcribed onto white typing paper as crisp and clean as if no one had ever handled it since.

Testimony of Stephen Leigh Griffin, of the village of Hale's Hay in Herefordshire:

I, Stephen Griffin, wish to put forward here my account of what has been told to me by my father, George Turner Griffin, in the days before his strange and lamented death. We are farmers well rooted in this colonial soil, but it seems that a devilish history linked itself with us ages ago in the land of our origin, and has been passed from father to son and with it sad and early death, despite prosperity in our family's outward undertakings.

My father said to me that the fortune of the Griffins began in the ninth century, when Griffin was the name of hereditary bailiffs for a nobleman, the Earl of Banford near the village of Lesser Banside in the county of Wessex. By thrift and good service to their lords and by the grace of God, their fortunes waxed. Yet the bailiff Stephen Griffin incurred much rancor on the part of villagers and serfs whose interests he crossed in the furthering of his duty to his lord.

So much so that he received many curses and revilements, including a public cursing by one Alice Riggs, thought to be a witch, to the effect that one of his sons would bring to the Griffin family a bloodred bane that would follow the Griffin men down the generations; until such time as there would come a son of this house who would loose his grip and lay bare his breast, that his treasures be open to plucking from him as the petty treasures of the Earl's people had been taken from them by the bailiff in the performance of his duty.

Now, it was said even then that the Griffin men were hard men, but in those days hardness flourished. Yet with life and livelihood ever uncertain, the third bailiff forebore to share his worldly goods between his two sons in his will, reserving nearly all of it to the elder son, Simon. A small portion only he bequeathed to the younger, Adam, to outfit him for soldiering where he might win riches of his own.

Thus at his father's death Adam Griffin went abroad, fighting where he was hired in foreign wars, and often no word of him was heard for years together. Meanwhile his brother Simon prospered and became himself a wealthy small-holder as well as the new Earl's fourth bailiff of that name, and thus he established his family.

And then Adam Griffin came home from the lands of the Germans and the pagans, bringing with him the scars of many battles, and a great red ruby as big as a walnut that was a wonder to see, and a fair-haired woman that he married; but she never said one word in any language that anyone could puzzle out in all the days she lived in Griffin Hall.

Of the gem, Adam said to his brother that he had it in payment from a nobleman who had promised him gold and a fine warhorse for his brave services, but had tried instead to kill him when payment came due. And so Adam Griffin took what payment he deemed owing for the many battles and skirmishes he had fought in this lordling's service, and brought away also the young woman named Magdalene, who had been a ward in the foreign lord's household. For Adam Griffin said he had thought that otherwise she would have been spoiled and killed in the upheavals of that country due to the ruinous wars and lack of law of either man or God, and she with no protector left to her at home in her own sad country.

Before very long, word of the ruby reached the Earl himself, some say because Simon was jealous of this treasure and could not bear his brother having it if he could not have it himself, for they were in great anger with each other over it almost as soon as Adam Griffin set foot back in his own land. So the Earl demanded to see the famous carbuncle, and when Adam would not show it, the Earl of Banford had him thrown into a dungeon and put to torture, and so he died.

Simon Griffin was himself taken before the Earl in the same matter, but he said that the foreign woman, Magdalene, had taken the great ruby and run away with it, and though much search was made, the Earl and his men never saw her nor the stone again. But the Earl never forgave Simon Griffin for the loss of the stone, and years later falsely accused him of embezzling tax moneys, and had him executed.

It is not known what became of the foreign woman, Adam Griffin's widow Magdalene; but the stone itself returned somehow to the hands of the Griffins (if indeed it had ever truly left, for no Griffin after was ever able to put it surely away from him and his, once for all).

Their possession of the stone was kept secret afterward from all the outside world because of the evil fate the gem had brought upon the brothers. Yet the curse of the witch fell upon the eldest Griffin sons ever after, one sorry doom after another, as the red stone passed down the generations hidden and guarded, a source of fascination to each son in the line direct from Adam in his turn.

And my father says that in the reign of Charles the First of England, William Griffin claimed to have seen a strange dark-haired woman in a vision, and he went away to London to lose himself among its citizens, for he had been told by his father that this vision of a woman on horseback was the first sign of the approach of the Griffin doom.

The second sign was his meeting with a stranger from abroad, a young, smooth foreign man whose name no one but William ever knew. This foreigner accosted William by night in a street in London outside a tavern and gave him a token: a brooch in the shape of the claw of a dragon, empty where a stone should be set.

And this stranger said to him, "This brooch is

mine, but that which should be set in the grasp of the claw is in your possession, although it belongs by right to me. I have come to claim my property, such of it as survives, and with it I will take your life. For which purpose I have prolonged my own mortal days by a hellish bargain, the terms of which protect me from any threat or wrath of yours."

And then he disappeared, and was not to be found anywhere.

William straightway returned to Griffin Hall and had all his retainers keep sharp watch for the foreign man in league with the Devil, or the strange pale woman. But no one spoke of seeing either of them. Yet within a fortnight William died, knocked from the bridge over the River Ban in what men said was a drunken brawl with persons unknown. And the stone passed to his son, who was grandfather to my father.

My father says that this same demonic stranger has appeared to other heads of the Griffin house, after first they have seen the woman on the white horse; and soon or late thereafter, the foreign man has caused them to come into possession of some small token, and each time death has followed shortly.

And frightfullest of all, he says that the stranger is always the same, not just to look at, but the same man entire, his back unbowed by age and his face no more lined than when it first was seen. His devilish bargain has conferred upon him an endless life in which to pursue the prize the Griffins hold as the very foundation of our family wealth and progress; for since the great ruby came into our possession, the Griffin fortunes have waxed large and generous, so that none would part with the stone despite tales of curses and evil proceeding from the stone itself, for fear of falling into poverty and ruin.

I must write of the cursed stone, red as the heart of Hell itself, and founder of our family's wealth. It was brought by my father, Jeremy Griffin, across the ocean, and wrought its magic to establish his family in prosperity almost from the first year they were here.

I myself wish the object had been left behind, or thrown into the ocean on the journey from Bristol Harbor; but although I have even tried myself to be done with it, at the last moment all my other goods were lost in a fire, and I had to borrow against the stone to begin again, which loan I successfully repaid, redeeming the red gem, after a hard, long time; for without the stone the Griffin luck deserted me.

So I could not bring myself to part with the carbuncle even though I have seen the woman, and a fine ring was left for me in the pocket of my coat while I was foolishly taking my ease in Andrew Mull's tavern; and now the foreign man himself, the Griffin demon, has struck me down, and my own time is very short.

For those of the Griffin blood who come after, know this: the grip of his hand is stronger than iron, and he casts but a very slight shadow, and he will meet you at dusk or in darkness rather than in the brightness of day; but though he may wrest your life from you in the end, meanwhiles use your sharp Griffin mind to preserve the great ruby from his grasp and thus ensure the continuing fortune of our house and our blood. Life need not be long, if you are full of decision and the courage of your heritage, to make your mark on the world and to gather riches for your posterity.

If we persevere long enough, perhaps one day a Griffin heir will live in times which are more than a mere demon can command, and our enemy's hold on our future generations will be broken forever and he himself cast down into the flames his Master lives in; and in that time, the stone of our fortune will be worn openly by the Griffin women to follow, under the protection of the triumphant Griffin men.

There was no signature on the transcript.

But maybe there was hope in it. Maybe.

Certainly there was terror. Here it all was. Nic had seen the harbinger, a woman pale as white marble with hair and garments like flowing black ink, on a white horse like a spectral being, and from that day he had launched his plan.

And a token had been delivered.

To Jess. Not to him, but to Jess: the delicate brooch of Berlin iron, metal blackened to the hue of an iron fence around a graveyard. Walter had described the piece to him.

He was angry and afraid, but most of all he was filled with renewed dread for Jessamyn. But it was still too soon to take action, especially now that he had all this new information to consider and to study for any help it might offer. He had little enough such hope as it was, and if there were any way of increasing it, he could not in conscience ignore the opportunity. He must meet the monster armed to the teeth with all the weapons he could find.

He thought of offering to buy the original document and the transcription both, but he hesitated. Let the story remain here, safely out of the way, for someone else to find—in case something happened to him and to what belonged to him

Because he was the last, there was no Griffin heir after him: and if the demon came and got him, all other evidence of the Griffin curse might vanish with the stone itself.

Heart pounding, Nic got up and called for the curator, who would have to accompany him to someplace where the bailiff's story could be copied. The Burch Collection was too poor to own a copying machine.

"I want to copy this, Mr. Pease," he said. "And I think you can expect a hefty donation from me in the near future."

Closed Rehearsal

◆

Then there is no past?'' Eva said passionately, turning from the mirror to confront her tormentor. ''What you say means that the past is as good as dead, from the moment time moves onward.''

''Would that be such a bad thing?'' Marko demanded. Jess knew that from the audience the pleading gesture of Anthony Sinclair's right hand (that was blocked from her own sight) would be visible, signaling the underlying longing of Marko for understanding, and more than understanding. . . .

''Then past crimes never have to be paid for,'' Eva said bitterly. ''What a comforting thought, to criminals and thieves!''''

''Are you so spotless yourself, then?'' Marko demanded. ''You love any pack of ragged foreigners better than your own flesh and blood. Your virtues are our shame, Eva!''

''And what about *my* shame?'' she cried, and dried on the rest of the line. She called to Walter, without looking away from Sinclair, "I'm sorry, what is it?"

From his place at the back of the theater Walter fed her the rest of the line. She repeated it, and then they backed up and did the scene all over again.

They went through the entire first act again. Jess was jumpy. All afternoon she had had a feeling of being watched, not in the professional way she expected and in fact needed from people like Walter, but with an intense and covert emotion that she felt like an electrical current stirring her hair. Nic might well bring just such attention to watching his own play in rehearsal, and of course she, of all people, was sure to sense that attention.

Maybe he was out there in the house somewhere, stopping by secretly for just a glimpse of his play.

No, that was foolish. He hadn't come before, and he wouldn't come now. No matter how uneasy she felt, it was only the director's judgment that she had to worry about—and to depend on.

"Marko," Walter said from out in the empty hall, "what would happen if you turned a little when you said that line, so that you're looking both at Eva and at her reflection in the mirror when you deliver the kicker? Does that feel right to you?"

Anthony grimaced in mock despair, which only Jess could see, but for Walter's benefit he drawled pleasantly, "There's an easy way to find out."

They ran through the confrontation scene one more time, ignoring the sounds of hammering from backstage. The set crew was reconstructing the "stone" steps that had collapsed under Jessamyn in the first hour of the rehearsal period today. Her shoulder had taken all her weight for a moment. It throbbed now, and Jess was still shaken by that shock when she let herself think about the fall.

Better to throw herself into this last go-round of the scene; but she was tired, and she felt her concentration draining away.

She saw Anthony noticing—his light blue eyes, hooded and watchful in his eagle-face, caught every signal she sent and some she didn't, which was what made working with him so amazing. He visibly cranked down his own energy to match hers. He was a wonderful colleague, to take such care not to show her up.

Walter knew better than to beat a dead horse. He stopped the scene, thanked them, and ended the session. "Jess, go home and take a hot bath," he told her in a mock scolding tone. "If that arm stiffens up on you, give me a call. My masseuse is a wizard with muscle soreness."

She insisted that she was fine, and he seemed satisfied.

"It's not so simple," Anthony muttered. "It can really rattle you, having an accident like that. I know."

He vaulted off the front of the stage and began gathering his cold-weather gear from the front row. He might call himself an old man, but he was never averse to showing off how fit he was.

"Honestly, are we sailing under a curse?" he added in a tone of concern. "I'd consider skipping out myself, if I didn't need the paycheck. This production seems to have a malicious spirit haunting it."

"Oh, baloney," Jess said sharply. "Quit trying to scare me, Anthony. Life is tough enough."

Sinclair grinned and shrugged. "You're right, accidents happen. Did I ever tell you about the time I split my scalp doing a warm-up exercise right before the opening of *Ghosts* in Sacramento? Blood all over the place, you wouldn't believe it; nothing bleeds like a head wound."

She had heard the story twice since they had started rehearsals for *The Jewel*, complete with the dash to the emergency room, the sympathetic nurse who loved theater and so rushed Sinclair through to the doctor ahead of several other waiting patients, and the opening night performed with a six-inch gash stapled shut along the crown of the actor's head.

Sinclair always swore that he would never have had a bald spot at all if not for that blasted scar. He regularly and roundly vilified whatever fool had moved the prop table on the stage from its accustomed place so that it had ended up

right behind where he was sitting when he had tipped backward for a nice, spine-loosening flop onto the stage.

"Of course I've heard it, but you tell the story so well—"

"Old windbag that I am," he sighed, looking mournful
as a hound. "Why doesn't anybody ever shut me up in
time to save my reputation, such as it is?"

"Because we love you, you balding beast," Anita Mac-
Neil chimed in, reaching out to ruffle his hair as she hurried
past. Tall and as beautiful as a model (which in fact she
had been for a time), Anita had a flirtatious streak that
Anthony always responded to.

Now he clapped both hands to his head and loped away
up the side aisle of the small theater, bellowing that she
was trying to sabotage his career by pulling out even more
of his thinning hair. She pursued him, protesting her innocence, laughing, and struggling into her down coat.

"Actors!" Walter said, rolling his eyes with affectionate
exasperation; and he went off to talk to the publicity people
in the theater office.

Jess stayed behind, hunting for a glove that had gone astray.
She felt wrung-out. As a newcomer to serious drama, she got
a lot of support from her fellow players. Yet she sometimes
felt left out of their easy camaraderie. They entertained each
other by endlessly telling stories of theatrical disasters, feuds,
and last-minute saves, which they did extremely well. Being
out of circulation had withered her ready humor, she thought
unhappily; she didn't often contribute.

And tonight she could have used a little extra attention.

The fall through the loosened board had shaken her more
than she wanted to admit; this was a step beyond the marbles on the dressing-room floor, and might have caused
worse than bumps and bruises.

On the other hand, nothing terrible had actually happened. She felt that moaning about small problems was
childish and self-indulgent at the best of times, and downright puerile in professionals merely portraying the actual,

frightful sufferings of people in Eastern Europe.

Nicolas's play used the siege of Sarajevo as a generalized backdrop, although in his hands the situation of the beleaguered city had become symbolic of ethnic and religious conflict all over the world. *The Jewel* was a serious piece; which was why Anthony and Anita fell so easily to cutting capers, in order to bleed off some of the accumulated tension of rehearsal.

Jess wished she could join in, but she felt depressed and depleted, exiled in some chilly country of denial, as if she had no right to a good time. Surviving a potentially lethal car crash seemed to demand an extra degree of seriousness in her approach to the life she had miraculously retained.

Or maybe, though the physical wounds of the accident were healed at last, her bruised spirit still mourned the loss of her heart's desire.

The lighting people began flicking the spots off, sinking more and more of the stage and the rows of seating into velvety gloom. Time to go out into the winter cold. Her apartment would be warm, at least. She could have some well-earned rest and solitude, and try to soak her shoulder's stiffness away in a steaming bath. She winced, working her sore arm into the sleeve of her coat.

But the sleeve drew easily on, as if moving on its own over her awkwardly extended arm. Startled, she turned to find a stranger standing right behind her, smoothing her sleeve with the lightest touch of his hand.

"Who—?"

"Forgive me, please," he said in a soft, clear voice edged with an accent. "I did not mean to startle you, but I saw that you had some difficulty."

She recognized that voice. It was the man from the terrace, that night at Whitely's party.

The backstage hammering continued, lights came on again as the lighting staff worked through some cue sequences—nothing could have been more comfortable and familiar than business as usual in the Edwardian Theater late on a rehearsal afternoon.

But Jess could scarcely breathe. What was affecting her, she realized, was the nearness, and the stillness, of this stunning young man whose thick and beautifully cut hair shone like polished bronze and whose skin was as pale and smooth as fresh, rich cream.

He had a strong face with a touch of the exotic about the high cheekbones and broad forehead. Lines already framed his sculpted lips, signs of a deeply lived life. His eyes, long and with a tilt at the outer corners that suggested the East, were very steady of gaze, smokily dark, and thickly lashed.

He was only an inch or two over her own height, but he stood solidly planted as if nothing could move him that he did not allow to move him, and he carried his head and shoulders with an innate pride that was the next thing to an unstated challenge. She could not judge his age; he looked as though he might well be several years younger than she was, but though his skin was clear and smooth and his bearing was vibrant with youthful energy, he exuded an easy authority that made him seem older.

With a start, she realized that she was staring like a bird fascinated by a snake. She said lightly, "Thanks, it was kind of you to help. Have you been in the theater long today? I didn't know anyone was watching the rehearsal."

"I came a little time ago," he said. He seemed oblivious to the fact that he was standing nearer than people ordinarily stand for casual conversation. Jess was damned if she would give ground like a timid girl.

"Then you didn't see me almost break my neck on those stairs earlier," she said. "I took all my weight on my left arm. It's time I went home and tended to it; I'm just starting to feel the soreness now."

"If you are hurt, surely your cohorts should not have left you behind," the stranger said disapprovingly. "May I escort you?"

"Oh, it's not that bad," she said; yet she felt reluctant to simply walk away. For one thing, he was devastatingly attractive. He had that faint swagger to his well-tailored frame that she had come to think of as typical of Continental men, but hardly ever seen in Americans. This was a man who would look perfectly natural with his overcoat slung dashingly from his shoulders, like the hero of an old war movie.

"Are you an actor, mister . . . ah . . . ?"

He smiled, and she could scarcely believe the transformation. So much lively humor shone in his face that he might have been a different person. He looked like some carefree kid, someone attuned to matters outside himself rather than internal musings, someone—happy.

"I have performed various roles in my life," he said. "But am I an actor like your colleagues here . . ." A graceful turn of his square-palmed, muscular hand indicated the empty aisle up which Sinclair and Anita had laughingly left only moments before. "No, I cannot claim so much."

Like hell, Jess thought, drawing back a little now with a sense of regaining balance, solidity, and common sense. *If you're no actor, mister, you're missing the best bet of your life!* There were performers who would kill for this man's bearing, his striking face, his rich, expressive voice. Actors went to classes all their lives trying to acquire such presence.

And of course he must know it. He was using it all on her right now. People who had this quality of magnetism did that; it was inevitable, unavoidable, and one reason (among many others) that Jessamyn did not look for a life partner among professional performers. They were always "on"; and you could never be sure you had reached the true inner man.

And, she noticed, the stranger hadn't supplied his name, either.

She turned away from him and started up the aisle, speaking rather crisply over her shoulder. "These are closed rehearsals. How did you get in?"

"I came at the request of Miss Lily Anderson," he replied. Lily Anderson was the production designer, a very private little gnome of a woman; it was odd to think of her in connection with this stunning man.

He answered her unspoken question. "At Mr. Whitely's party, Ms. Anderson saw in a catalog some fine old pieces of jewelry that have passed through my hands. She contacted me and asked me to help with some details of this production's design that do not satisfy her. We have conferred several times, but when I came here today, as arranged, she did not meet me. I looked, but could not find her. So I wandered in here, to see what I could discover about your play for myself."

Funny to feel a little stab of jealousy; but face it, she told herself with an inward grin, how often do you run into a man whose good looks are unusual enough not to remind you of shirt-ad photos, as the common run of young actors invariably did? If Lily Anderson could latch on to a gorgeous man, more power to her!

"Lily's little girl is sick, I think," she said. "She went to pick her up from school and take her to the doctor. Look, the lights are going out for real now; the place is shutting down for the night, Mr.—is there some reason you won't give me your name?"

"My name is Ivo Cragga," he said. "Now that you know it, do you know anything more about me than you did before?" He lifted his chin and regarded her with a haughty stare.

Who did this guy think he was, anyway? And why should she stand here talking with him? But there was something, apart from his startling good looks, something alluring about him; and discomfiting, too. Part of it was that though he was probably her junior, she simply could not think of him in terms of being a fresh kid—but why not? She felt a little stir of anxiety, a nagging unease from a source she couldn't pinpoint.

Get going, she told herself, *don't hang around here with some guy you've never seen before; well, never seen clearly, and he is an unknown quantity, and with the things that have been happening around here—*

But the words that came out of her mouth were, "There's a little place nearby where I stop sometimes on the way home from rehearsal. I'll need a little pick-me-up if I don't want to fall asleep in the bathtub and wake up wallowing in cold water at three in the morning. Join me for some coffee?"

She was rewarded not by that blinding smile—which, she realized with chagrin, she had been hoping for—but with a steady, assessing stare followed by a short nod, almost a bow.

She turned away and hurried on ahead of him, propelled by something overwhelming in his advance, a pressure born from the athletic vigor of his frame, his compact muscularity moving toward her with the smoothness and speed of a tiger.

I must be exhausted, she thought distractedly, *to be reacting like this! Good thing he's not a mind reader, or I'd sink through the floor with embarrassment at some of the things I've been thinking!*

"'Night, Miss Croft," Johnny Wagner called from the box office, where he was manning the phones. His round, friendly face fell as he registered the presence of her companion.

"See you, Johnny," she replied, giving him a big smile. Poor kid, he couldn't hide his crush on her. Her newfound escort could hardly fail to interpret Johnny's fiery blush correctly. Jess had a feeling that Ivo Cragga's smoky eyes didn't miss much in any case.

The evening air was like an icy knifeblade against her face. She shivered at the first intake of freezing breath. The man at her elbow said quietly, "You did not dress warmly enough, Miss Croft, and winters have turned cold again. You must pay attention to such things. After all, it would do the production no good if you were to come down with some flu bug from a chill."

She had to smile at the way he said "flu bug," like a man picking up an interestingly novel but basically unappealing insect with the tips of his fingers.

''Don't even suggest such a thing around here,'' she cautioned. ''Actors are insanely superstitious.''

''Are you?''

Hurrying along toward the Two White Cats, her favorite coffeehouse, she shook her head. ''Can't afford to be. Theater is scarey enough without jumping at every little mishap.''

''Like your fall on the stairs? This sounds like perhaps more than a mishap.''

She shrugged. ''I can worry about the stairs, or I can worry about remembering my blocking and my lines. Which would you choose?''

His hand closed lightly on her elbow and he steered her deftly around a patch of glistening ice that had spread under a leaking standpipe.

''Your choice sounds good to me,'' he said. ''But then I know very little about your professional world.''

True, or part of his line? She hoped there was more to him than a very slick pickup technique.

''So what do you do, Mr. Cragga?'' she said. ''Apart from consultations with people like Joshua Whitely?''

''I import rare objects,'' he said. ''I search out and gather for sale old pictures, objets d'art, antique jewelry.''

She blinked. The pendant. It must have come from this man. So now he was putting the moves on her! But he was far from Marie's horrible ''toad,'' and besides, she was curious.

Nic *had* cut her loose, hadn't he? Painfully and definitely. And foreign men were always interesting, as long as you made sure to keep control of the situation and of yourself. At least this one wasn't an actor! Well, maybe he wasn't; she was still not convinced.

She decided not to ask outright about the pendant. If Cragga had initiated some odd, secretive game about it, better to wait and see what the next move was to be, instead of rushing into behaving like a foolish, shallow American, all surface and no patience or depth.

Somewhere along the line she would find out the answer.

Meanwhile, she would certainly rather spend the early evening exploring the nature of an intriguing and attractive man than lying in the tub trying not to scald her feet every time she had to add hot water by turning the hot tap on with her toes.

Her shoulder, she noticed, wasn't bothering her nearly as much as it had been back at the theater. Maybe it was frozen. Maybe she herself was frozen to the sidewalk, an icewoman, and dreaming of this mysterious stranger as her brain slowly shut down for good under the assault of the cold.

"Whew," she said as they ducked into the steaming, noisy heat of the coffeehouse. "Coffee, coffee, quick! I'm hallucinating, it's so cold out there!"

She pulled off her hat and shook out her short, dark curls, looking around with dismay. There was nowhere to sit; the place was jammed. She checked again, hoping she had just missed something. She did not relish the idea of going back out into the icy streets and trotting from coffeehouse to coffeehouse—the Village was full of them, after all, but it was also Friday night—looking for a place to sit down and pour something hot down her throat.

"Hell," she muttered, defeated. "Look, I'm not up for this after all, not tonight. If you could just help me flag a cab, I'll drop you wherever, Mr. Cragga, and go home to sleep, which is what I should be doing anyway."

His grip on her arm—light, but firm—did not yield. He nodded in the direction of a corner table far back from the draft of the street door, under a poster showing a Spanish beach. Three rough-looking kids in studded black leather and ratty furs were making a great to-do of getting up to leave, the boys stretching and swinging their muscular arms in big gestures that just missed the neighboring patrons, making them flinch and duck.

The girl with them, who had hair dyed flat black and arranged in sculptural points around her face and silver rings inserted through the skin at the outer ends of her blond eyebrows, watched their posturing with sleepy indifference.

"Arctic winters and barbarians everywhere," Ivo Cragga muttered contemptuously. "Truly, time brings back all things that were, if one waits long enough."

An odd remark, Jess thought, from someone scarcely older than she was.

As they approached the table the leader of the unsavory trio began to shove past. Cragga stopped him with his lightly curled fist thrust against the center of the boy's leather-clad chest. "Give way," he said calmly. "There is room to the side here."

"Room for you, pal," the boy said, snapping the edge of his palm hard against Cragga's wrist.

Cragga's hand did not move at all; it was the boy's hand that stopped, jarred as if by meeting with a concrete wall. The boy's face registered shock and pain. He recoiled, and turned instead to snarl at the two behind him, "Back off, you buttheads, you trying to run me over?"

Glowering, he sidestepped to let Cragga and Jess pass. The second boy made exaggerated, ridiculous bows to them, bobbing and grinning and tugging his moussed blond forelock like some British country bumpkin in a historical TV drama. The one in the lead hurried on ahead, holding his hurt hand to his chest and not looking back.

Then they were gone, and the uneasy tension in the room flowed back into busy noise. A thin girl with a red apron tied on over her black turtleneck and tight skirt came over with an order pad. She spoke to Jess, whom she knew from many evenings of stops here after rehearsal over the past weeks.

"I'm really sorry about all that—are you folks okay?"

"We're fine," Jess said, although she was trembling slightly in reaction. She had been close enough to Cragga to feel the aggression radiating from him and to see the taut lift of his head as his hand had shot out to the kid's chest, stopping him cold. She had known without any doubt whatsoever that if that sinewy boy in studs and fur had forced a fight, he'd have gotten more than he bargained for.

And maybe that was what she had let herself in for, too.

Two White Cats

◆

Jess ordered a cappuccino and Cragga asked for the same.

When the waitress had left, Jess leaned across the table and said to him in a low, angry voice, "I stop by here all the time, Mr. Cragga. I consider the staff my friends, and I don't show my friendship by coming in here and starting a fight, or by bringing people with me who are crude enough to do that. Those jerks were just showing off. It wouldn't have done any harm to let them go through their stupid little routine and be on their way without playing lion-tamer in front of everybody."

He looked back at her with a bemused expression. The silence stretched, and she flushed with unease but held his gaze defiantly.

"Lion-tamer," he said at length, with vast contempt. "You think those little ruffians are lions? You people have no understanding of violence at all. They were performing, just like you, Miss Croft, you and your theatrical colleagues, but for this audience of coffee drinkers. At home, do not doubt it, they practice their tough-guy nastiness and elaborate insouciance in front of the mirror, to the beat of their version of music. As for myself, I simply supplied a modicum of criticism.''

''All the more reason that you should be ashamed of yourself,'' she rejoined with spirit. ''Criticism is supposed to teach; pain just brutalizes people. You hurt that boy.''

''Not enough,'' he said, and his tilted eyes narrowed coldly. Had she found herself a Tartar, full of the casual brutality of the Golden Horde under his suave exterior? His next words did nothing to reassure her.

''I should have 'taught' him much harder,'' he said. ''Cowards are dangerous, unless you take care to make them very, very frightened of you.''

Outraged, Jess smacked the table with her palm. ''What are you, anyway—some kind of martial-arts nut who thinks he can get away with anything because he knows a few violent tricks?''

Why was she so incensed against him? Her stage training had taught her to analyze her feelings so that she could use them in her work. The intensity of his reaction to the bluster of the leather kids had alarmed her. Her fear translated into anger, now that the danger was past.

And, in fact, she was still a little nervous of Ivo Cragga, and very glad to be in a public place with him, a place where some people knew her and would notice if . . . if what? What exactly did she imagine he might do?

That was it: she had no idea. This man with the broad, strong face and the watchful eyes and the rich hair that gleamed deep copper was not just foreign; he was totally unpredictable. Talk about someone being dangerous!

Dangerous and beautiful, which meant doubly dangerous.

And, she realized, she had been a little afraid of him from the first moment he had appeared behind her in the theater, helping her on with her coat. How could she have sensed the danger in him without even seeing him, without his touch on anything but her outer garment?

"I have studied the arts and skills of battle, yes," he said, so quietly that she ought to have been unable to make out the words over the convivial din of the coffeehouse. But his voice cut right through the hubbub so that she heard everything as if he were speaking to her from the stage of a theater, and she were sitting in the front row. "Don't you find that such knowledge is valuable, in the world you know?"

This odd turn of phrase jarred her out of her mood and she asked with genuine surprise and interest, "Is there another world than the one I know?"

Now he smiled, but it was a small smile, and a melancholy one. "Of course. There have been many, many worlds before this one: the worlds of history, Miss Croft, the myriad worlds of the past, all of which you Americans are so quick to dismiss. You deliberately keep yourselves ignorant and pretend to invent everything anew. But those worlds were all real, and they have real consequences in the present, of which you are ignorant to your peril.

"And of the many such worlds I know, yours, this tight-packed world of modern New York City, is among the most fearsome and violent. I keep my guard up, and as you see, so far I survive in good health."

"Then you have more than your fair share of good luck," Jess snorted. "That boy could have had a knife or an Uzi under his jacket, for all we knew. You could have gotten a lot of people hurt besides yourself, you know."

"I thought you were worried that I had hurt him," he observed, eyebrows quizzically raised, "that little posturer with his pretensions of savagery."

"I don't like the idea of anybody getting hurt," she said, flashing back briefly to the exploding world of the car crash and all that had followed. There was so much hurt in the world already. Oh, the touchy aggression of young men! She hoped he did not see the flinching in her eyes.

"People get hurt no matter what, Miss Croft," he murmured.

"Look, are you really an antiques dealer, or are you some kind of gangster?" Jess said, pressing him with a willful anger that surprised and confused her. "You're beginning to sound like somebody out of *The Godfather*."

Again the quiet smile, rich with hints of complex thought hidden behind it. It gave Jess a very disturbing thrill to realize that the look in his eyes was one of appreciation.

She reminded herself sharply that dangerous tricks had been played on her backstage at the Edwardian; and she did not know this man, who had only been admitted to the theater—today at least—on the say-so of Lily Anderson.

Ivo Cragga inclined his head, a gesture of concession. "Please pardon my excesses; they spring from perhaps a harsher experience of life than you have had, if you are lucky." Cragga settled more deeply into his chair and steepled his fingers in front of him, contemplating her with thoughtful eyes.

"I will set your mind at rest about me, if I can. What Miss Anderson and I have been discussing is the design of a jewel motif for the scrim curtain that the audience first sees when the main curtain goes up."

Jess frowned. "But the 'jewel' of the title isn't really the treasure that everybody's supposedly fighting and betraying each other about; it's a metaphor."

"Really?" He blinked, suddenly nonplussed. "What sort of metaphor?"

"Lily didn't show you the script? Well, the emerald is a symbol for the true wealth of any family or country—its virtues and values, its honor and tolerance and forgiveness."

"That is a very heavily laden symbol." Cragga's understated sarcasm nevertheless brought defensive heat to Jess's cheeks. This stranger was criticizing Nicolas's work, after all. "I wonder whether any object, no matter how beautiful or striking, can carry so much metaphorical weight."

Jess deliberately produced a laugh instead of a riposte—

she thought she had his number now. His idea of flirting was to be provocative, to deliberately cause a quarrel, in hopes of turning the heat of conflict into other fires.

Well, let him try; she was not so easily maneuvered. She smiled sweetly. "That's our job as actors, Mr. Cragga—to convince you."

The waitress brought their drinks. Cragga lifted his cup and made the motion of a toast. Jess touched her cup to his, gingerly; who knew what this little gesture meant between a man and a woman, in his view? Other lands, other ways. And where did she want this strange meeting to lead, anyway?

"So what sort of jewel motif does Lily have in mind?" she asked.

Cragga's gaze changed. He seemed to withdraw in a curious way so that she felt watched—not critically but with a steady, alert, forceful attention—rather than simply looked at. It gave her a peculiarly chilled sensation, as if the weather outside had suddenly penetrated her flesh alone among all the people gathered in the warm room.

"I thought perhaps a cross," he said slowly, as if thinking it out as he spoke, "an antique religious object set with the rather crudely cut gems of olden times; or perhaps a large brooch or buckle, with the great emerald as its center. It must be something bold, even stark, Lily says, to capture the eyes of the audience. What would you suggest, Miss Croft?"

"I don't have any idea," she said, taken aback by this sudden attack. She laughed in nervous self-deprecation. "I'm an actress, Mr. Cragga, not Leona Helmsley. I don't come across much in the way of fine old jewelry. Have you thought of talking to the playwright? Nic—Mr. Griffin— might have had something particular in mind when he chose the metaphor."

He sat very still, his cup poised in the air. Then he tipped and emptied it in one swift swallow and set it down again, and he leaned forward with his forearms planted on the table. "I have indeed tried to see him, without success.

Perhaps he has been avoiding me. Do you know where I can find him?''

He must have noticed her recoil from the change in his manner, for he relaxed suddenly and cocked his handsome head, looking concerned and sympathetic. ''I don't mean to track him down like a criminal, but I would hate to do anything that would go counter to his own vision of the play. Lily said that if anyone can tell me where to find him, or give me some idea of what he would wish for this design motif, it would be you, Miss Croft.''

Jessamyn shook her head, suppressing an unkind thought about Lily, whom she ordinarily liked and respected. Well, if Lily had told this stranger the whole story—then there was nothing to hide, was there? But she could not help but resent the spreading of her private business beyond the limits of the theatrical crowd that she thought of as family, of a sort.

She said calmly, ''I'm sorry, Miss Anderson is wrong about that. Mr. Griffin and I have been out of touch lately. I'm sure Lily told you about the car crash: Both Nicholas and I have been preoccupied with putting our lives back together since then—separately, I'm afraid. You might try talking to Walter Steinhart, our director. He's the link between the company and the playwright, not me.''

''Ah,'' Cragga said, veiling his glance again. ''I see. Very well, then.'' He sighed and sat back, contemplating her with a self-possession that seemed far in excess of his years. ''Would you like something to eat, Miss Croft? I am hungry myself, and there is usually something on the menu of places like this that suits me very well. May I buy you dinner?''

Time out, Jess thought, with a small twinge of regret. Whatever he was really after, sparring with him was oddly exhilarating.

She smiled, accepted, and ordered a pasta Arabiata that she knew from experience was both spicy and sweet but not too heavy for evening fare. Cragga chose a double portion of carpaccio when the waitress told him that they got their aged, raw beef from an Italian source on the lower West Side.

"So," he resumed, watching Jess butter a piece of the delicious, warm bread the waitress had brought, "are you sure that Mr. Griffin himself doesn't have some sort of old European piece that he has used for—inspiration in the matter of this central symbol in his play?"

"Goodness, no, it's nothing so literal," Jess said, flooded with a mixture of relief and—*oh dear*—let-down as she finally understood. "Are you trying to find out if Nic has some precious old family jewelry of his own hidden away, something he might be persuaded to sell? I don't know for certain, but I think it's pretty unlikely. Nic's family is— well, it was, there's almost nobody left now—they were from England originally, not from the Continent."

"There is such a thing as booty brought home from war, Miss Croft," Ivo Cragga said, very softly, his eyes once again coldly intent upon her. He smiled, a mere spasm of the lips, more like a snarl, she thought uneasily. "Generations ago, of course; such events are too ancient to be considered *crimes*. They become mere 'accidents of history,' no more than interesting tales of the faraway past; fairy tales, almost. And yet there may be some truth in them."

Such dangerous depths of emotion! Whatever he was after, he was clearly not just a greedy European hustler. Jess sighed. "Mr. Cragga, believe me when I tell you, the Griffins made their money in this country and spent it on stocks and bonds, not on pretty gewgaws for ladies to wear. Nic says they were business pirates, not aristocrats; rather grasping people, really, to hear him tell it. One reason that he took to the stage was to break the family pattern of hard-driving commercialism."

She remembered that she hardly knew this man and drew back a little from him, embarrassed to have spoken so freely about Nic's family. "There's no point wearing yourself out chasing something that doesn't exist."

Ivo Cragga appeared to listen closely even as he attended

to the drizzling of olive oil and lemon juice on the thinly sliced raw beef on his plate.

"So," Jess finished, irritated to have had to explain Nic when Nic could have perfectly well explained himself instead of dodging the dealer, "I'm afraid that no matter how extensively you consult with Lily Anderson, she can't pay you with a tip on some fabulous piece of antique jewelry, only with a pair of comps."

" 'Comps'?"

"Complimentary tickets." *God, Lily didn't promise him a cash fee or anything, did she?* she thought with dismay. "We're theater people, Mr. Cragga, and we're Off Off Broadway at that. Can I give you a little economics lesson?"

"That would be most delightful," he said with a humorous quirk of his lips that was devastating to look at. "A businessman like myself can never have enough good financial information."

Sticking to a businesslike tone herself, she explained that the Edwardian stayed solvent, just, through subscriptions, contributions from supporters like the Whitelys and their friends, and in the case of mounting this play, some financial backing from Nic himself.

"Even people like Joshua Whitely will only plunk down so much. Usually, we have no money to spare for expert advice, and among ourselves the only jewelry we see is cheap stuff that our props and costumes person picks up at Goodwill or at a flea market. She works on other people's castoffs to make them look elegant, or she uses things of our own that we lend to a specific production. We do for ourselves as best we can. Most theaters do. Even good costume jewelry is expensive these days."

Cragga turned to signal the waitress with a peremptory gesture. He ordered aperitifs.

"Thank you for the very enlightening comments, Miss Croft," he said, turning back to Jess. "Naturally I am always on the lookout for interesting pieces. Perhaps I did entertain unrealistic expectations in this case.

"At any rate, now that the situation is clearer I think it all the more important that I speak with Mr. Griffin personally, to get his impressions of the kind of design he had in mind. It is not a light matter. Lily has suggested that whatever motif is used on the scrim can be used also in the printed program and in advertisements. When the play moves to a larger theater—"

"*If* the play is successful enough to move to a larger theater," Jess amended.

"—when the play moves, the use of such a device may become very important and go onto T-shirts, mugs, posters—who knows?" He smiled. "There are a few things that I already know about economics, you see."

Jess laughed, accepting the rebuke in the spirit in which it was offered. "I think you should talk to Nell Clausen; she's on the staff of the Edwardian, and she deals with anyone who handles merchandising work for them. She knows all about the details—terms and copyright and things like that."

His eyebrows arched again, all injured innocence, as if no thought of profit for himself had ever entered his head.

"You began," she reminded him, "by talking about 'commercial considerations'; the idea of payment must have crossed your mind."

"I have decided against it," he said. "I am honored to have a small part in presenting such an interesting exploration of the turmoil in my poor, war-ridden part of the world, and of the concept of ages-old grudges and revenge."

Was he in earnest? Her questioning glance found no clue in his calm, pale face. "Nell will be very glad to hear that," she said. "Maybe she can even put you in touch with Nic, if you still think that's necessary."

"I would prefer to have you introduce me to Mr. Griffin," he said. "You can explain to him the dubious nature of my initial interest, and also how you disabused me of my more extravagant and foolish assumptions."

Was he mocking her, or himself? She couldn't tell. He

was a very unsettling person to deal with, and on top of a grueling rehearsal session plus a small accident she was beginning to feel that she couldn't handle much more of his company.

"Look," she said, "I don't like to step on Lily's toes, or Nell's either. But if I hear from Nic, from Mr. Griffin, I'll mention your concerns."

"That is all I ask," he said. "You might tell him also that the themes of his play are of great and longstanding interest to me. I would welcome an opportunity to speak with him about how he came to tackle such a subject."

"I wouldn't bring it up with him, if I were you," she warned. "He doesn't like to talk about his work. He wants it to speak for itself."

"Then I will confine myself to the matter of the design," he said. "You see, Miss Croft, how helpful you have already been in correcting my rash impulse to trespass on forbidden ground."

He leaned forward and touched his glass to hers, his gaze ironic. Now she noticed that in the bright lights of the cafe his eyes appeared no longer dark but a clear, subtle green. It was the irises, black as wet basalt, that must have enlarged in the dimness of the theater to make his eyes look so black before.

She sipped her aperitif, a sweetish, acrid Amarro, and suddenly things seemed to come together for her.

"I didn't really understand before," she said with a rush of sympathy. "You're from Bosnia, aren't you?—or someplace in that area. Their terrible history of massacre and hatred is your history, that's why you're so curious about the play. That's why you talk about violence the way you do."

For an instant his eyes widened and she stared into dead black pits. These were the eyes of someone who sees plainly into the abyss and, having no hope whatsoever of escaping the long fall into those depths, neither blinks nor averts his gaze.

She was the one who blinked, and when she looked at

him again, he had lowered his gaze and sat sipping his own drink in that ruminative quiet that made him seem so much older than his apparent years.

Then he said, "Yes; that sort of history is alive to me in a way that it cannot be to you—to your good fortune, I might add. You could say that I am something of a barbarian myself, as people who suffer barbarism tend to become barbarized themselves. And will that make you get up and leave me here to end my meal alone?"

"I am not afraid of you, Mr. Cragga," she said boldly, although her heart was beating uncomfortably hard. In a strange, exciting way, afraid of him was exactly what she was; afraid, and angry at him, too—for frightening her, and for trying to use her.

"How reassuring," he said. "We never know how we appear to others, do we, unless they tell us?"

"Then let me say," she answered, "that I think it's a little 'barbarous' to come on to me with all this old-world charm, when what you really want to do is to get hold of Nic Griffin and talk Central European politics with him! Or did you have some more of your rather physical style of 'criticism' in mind? Does his take on what he witnessed over there run counter to your own? Maybe you want to knock some 'sense' into him, personally?"

He turned his glass slowly in his hand and said nothing, waiting for her to continue.

She did. "You didn't have come to the theater and take me to dinner to get to Nic, Mr. Cragga; and it hasn't done you any good to try it, either. I don't know what he's up to these days, or how long it will be before he shows up again in New York. And if I did know, I'm not at all sure I would tell you!"

"Because?" he said.

"Because I don't like this. You brazenly scraped up an acquaintanceship with Lily Anderson so you could get into the theater today and use me in my turn, to help you find Nicolas Griffin so you could try to pry something valuable loose from him, right?"

"If you think so," he murmured, "then I have been unforgivably clumsy. In fact, Miss Croft, I do not care about Nicolas Griffin. What I want is to ask you to come with me to an exhibition of antique jewelry next week, to look for something that might serve as the motif of the play. Lily has made some suggestions, but I am still looking for ideas.

"Oh, and of course—" He slipped from his pocket and held out to her a small velvet-covered box. "I meant to give you these, to wear in your performance in *The Jewel*."

He gently pressed her fingers closed around the box.

She guessed what she would find inside, and her guess was good: Nestled in the cotton bedding were two teardrop-shaped earrings, made of delicate black filigree that glinted with tiny silver stars and rosettes. These pretty pieces were obviously the complements to the pendant left for her in her dressing room.

She looked up, framing an angry refusal—what was he doing but trying to buy her complicity in . . . in something she couldn't even see clearly?—but he had risen and stepped around the table to her side with swift, catlike grace. He bent down and without putting a hand upon her or saying one word more, kissed her upraised face.

It was a strange, slow, thoughtful-seeming kiss, starting at the corner of her eye and drifting down along her cheek, a quiet, concentrated, browsing of his warm lips over her skin.

Astonished, she sat still, her eyes wide open in surprise. People were watching; she could feel their eyes on her and hear the sudden quieting of conversation nearby, someone whispering, someone giggling nervously—

She blushed, turning her face, and at once his mouth touched hers and hovered, and pressed her parted lips with the full shape of his own mouth. His unhurried tasting of her had a flavor of arrogance and privilege, as if in his mind there was no need to rush; all could be savored at leisure, for who would dare to interrupt?

Her whole body went molten inside with the silent expansion of the hunger that his somnolent kiss brought to bloom. She felt as if she were a new bud unfolding within the sturdy flower of her old self, opening hotter, bolder petals than showed on the outside, reaching upward toward a dark blaze of desire that stooped to envelope her.

What kind of flower blooms at night? she thought, and then it was over: he stood beside her, straight as a spear, his hand on the back of her chair and his face averted from her.

"Well, well," he said, so softly that she almost missed it. "Before, I was merely clumsy, but now? Willful, reckless, overbearing, perhaps?"

He looked down at her with unreadable eyes for a moment while she tried to find her breath and her balance and her cool. She noticed the thin waitress at the pastry counter, staring in their direction.

Cragga reached for his coat where it lay shrugged onto the back of his own chair. "I hope you will forgive me. If not, you have only to say so, and I will not trouble you again."

"I want to go home now," she whispered.

Messages

◆

The light in Jessamyn's window was out the next time Nic walked past her building. He wanted to stop and watch awhile, creating in his imagination a protective shield of invisible light that beamed from him up to her, safeguarding her night's sleep; or better yet, go up to talk with her, late as it was.

There was so much to say; but he could not trust himself to just say it, and leave. Like a lover in a ballad, he missed her so much that his heart was sore and sick. He felt too strongly to simply talk, not touch, not hold, not sink into and extinguish himself and all his fears and angers.

This was not a temptation to which he would allow himself to yield. So he turned his back on the wind knifing eastward from the Hudson and walked toward Broadway, his fists driven deep into the pockets of his overcoat, his chin and mouth buried in his scarf. The cold made his leg ache. He ignored the pain and headed downtown on Broadway, toward his hotel.

In his right hand he clutched the red stone, center of bad news, harbinger of doom. How he hated it, how he longed to go pitch it in the river! But who could tell now what the best course of action was, the wise course, the successful course? He could not count on impulse, not with this enemy. He must keep his options open, think and dare instead of just exploding with pent-up feelings.

Things had changed. He had sighted the enemy, he was sure—that smooth, leonine young fellow who had seen Jess to her door. Not tall, but broad-backed and solid on his feet, a formidable figure.

Who had kissed her hand; and dismissed the cab; and strolled away, but not until he had waited, watching, and seen Jess's light go on, upstairs, in the front room. Only then had he turned and gone, walking swiftly down West End Avenue.

I should have followed him, Nic thought. *He's the one, he has to be the one!*

But he had stayed, guarding Jess just in case the creature would be brazen enough to return and launch some kind of attack on her. Nothing of the sort had happened. Still, Nic was sure that this was his opponent. He was certainly no actor. This man had the odd, rolling gait of a fighter, keeping the center of gravity low and even. Nic knew men who had come back from Vietnam walking like that, men his uncle Rob had hung out with.

Christ, he should have followed the guy, confronted him!

But with what, for what? He was in no position to do that. He had had bad news yesterday, terrible news. His fingers convulsed on the object in his pocket, and he strode quickly through the crowd spilling out of Lincoln Center, shouldering his way past them.

Which of them had done it? he wondered blackly; which of his ancestors had destroyed any chance he might have— the chance any succeeding Griffin male might have!—to deal honestly with the enemy, and thus, perhaps, disarm him?

How had he miscalculated so badly? His plans were a

shambles, his future a ruin. He knew now that he had underestimated the demon whom he had baited out of hiding with his play, only to find that the damned monster was toying with Jessamyn instead of sniffing, as planned, along Nic's own trail.

Schoen had come up with some leads, but they pointed toward Europe. Could Nic leave Jess in the hands of an enemy she didn't even know was an enemy? (If it *was* him—but it had to be, it had to!)

Yet if he stayed and just waited for the Other to make the next move, what good would that do? Only going to the source could help. He must present a prepared response, armed with everything he could muster. Impulse wouldn't do it, cleverness wouldn't serve, and he could no longer simply depend on the reflexes of his athletic body.

Only action could save him and Jess. He must risk everything, leave Jess to fend for herself, and go trace the monster to its roots.

The idea made him shake with an ague of dread. Like father, like son—hadn't Eric Griffin done the same, bolting for Colombia in hopes of finding some way to bring the enemy down? And Eric Griffin had never come back. But he had not read the bailiff's story; he had probably never known nearly as much as Nic did about the enemy, and about the red stone.

Nic stepped into the steamy redolence of an all-night deli and went to the back to use the pay phone next to the stairs. She answered on the third ring.

"Lo?"

"Jess, I need to talk to you."

" 'S'late."

"I know," he said, closing his eyes and leaning against the wall. He saw her so clearly in his mind's eye, blinking and yawning amid the scattered pillows. Four pillows, five pillows—extras to elbow carelessly onto the floor, her endearingly modest idea of luxury. "But I have to talk to you. I don't want you to hear this from anyone else."

At once, her voice became alert. "Hear what? Are you in some kind of trouble?"

"Don't worry about me, just listen. Are you awake?"

"Of course I'm awake. I'm talking to you, aren't I? Nic, what's going on?"

He was silent for a moment, tongue-tied by the finality of what he meant to say. A waiter rushed past behind him, bawling a warning at the swinging kitchen doors.

Nic hunched the phone closer against the side of his face, cupping the speaker in his hand. "I heard you had an accident this morning."

"I was the target of a hostile little prank," Jess said. "Nothing important."

"Jessamyn." He stopped. She waited, breathing lightly into the phone. "I think you're in danger. Please, you've got to leave the production."

"I'm in," she said strongly, "whether you like it or not, Nicolas. You had your say, and I had mine, and the board liked mine better. It's pretty cruddy of you to come around now trying to wheedle me into backing down when we're two weeks into rehearsal."

Swallowing an angry retort, he stood clutching the phone in silence. Wrong approach, all wrong; he had blown it again. "Do what you like, then!" he said, savage with rage at himself. "You're on your own. I'm closing up the house and going to Europe."

"What? Where?" She sounded alarmed. "Not the Balkans again, Nic!"

"Lots of lame men there now," he said bitterly. "Nobody will even notice me. I'll get a chance to go places I never got to, see things nobody from outside has seen. There's interest from the *New Yorker* in anything I write from there."

"But Nic—damn it! They're *crazy* over there, and it's not your fight! You could get hurt, killed even!"

"The fighting's stopped," he said.

"The hating hasn't," she retorted. "The war could start again any day."

"There's no point in arguing," he said. "I've made up my mind. I just didn't want to leave Walter Steinhart the job of telling you." He chuckled. "He's not exactly the soul of tact, our Walter."

"I wouldn't say you were a star in that department either," Jess said in a muffled tone.

Nicolas sighed again. "I have nothing to do here. The play is shaping up, Walter's happy, without any help from me. I need to get moving again. Cabin fever is driving me out, if nothing else. But first I need to get through to you, Jess."

She was crying, he knew, though it sounded as if she had the mouthpiece partly covered with her hand.

He swallowed and went on as calmly as he could: "Somebody left some kind of jewelry for you to wear in the play."

"How do you know that? Nicolas, have you had people reporting to you about me? Trying to spot something you could use to get me thrown out of this production?"

"Of course not," he barked. "But I am worried, and that—that present is part of the reason. I can't explain the whole thing now, not over the phone, but it's a sort of—a sort of danger signal, all right?"

"No," she answered irritably. "Not all right. What the hell is this all about?"

How much could he tell her? How much would the enemy guess that she knew, and what would he do about it? "Look, this is going to sound strange, but you've got to believe me. God, I sound like an actor in a very bad play, don't I?"

She snorted. "Yup, a real stinker."

"Jess." Nic took a deep breath and plunged, trusting his instincts to put the proper limits on what he was about to say. "I've got an enemy. That is, my family has had a problem with somebody for a long time. It's like—think of it as a kind of a feud that crops up every now and then in our history."

"This sounds like the people in your play. Remember,

when Eva tells Marko that the family fortune is built on an old crime that has to be paid for?''

God, she knew so much already, without knowing that she knew it! He faltered, amazed to see that in fact he had mirrored the tale of the bailiff in the background plot of the play without having read the account at the Burch.

He shook himself back into the present (which smelled powerfully just then of fat corned beef and chicken soup). ''I'm talking about reality, Jessamyn. Listen to me, please. I never thought this old grudge would interfere in my own life, and I certainly never imagined you could be involved. My God, if anything happens to you—''

''Nic, stop it! You're scaring the life out of me! Are you in some kind of trouble with—with the mob or something?''

He knew his laughter sounded wild and desperate, and choked it off. ''No, no, nothing like that. It's a—a personal thing. It's to do with the car crash, Jess.''

He heard the little catch in her breath, and then the forced patience in her voice as she began to recite the old reassurances that meant nothing. ''The police checked that at the time, Nic. The brake fluid was low—''

''No, you don't understand.'' He leaned heavily against the scarred plaster, aware now of the pressing, odorous kitchen heat that was making him sweat under his heavy coat. He felt so tired. ''There have been—Some members of my family have died in violent and peculiar ways. Of course a certain amount of this is inevitable in any family, and you could say that ours went out of its way, sort of, looking for trouble. We've had more than our share of bastards profiting from other people's miseries, doing things that are likely to get you killed sooner or later. Still, when you look at our history you'd think there was some kind of bad luck dogging us—something willful and deliberate.''

''Nicolas,'' she answered, ''what kind of a completely credulous idiot do you think I am?''

''Listen to me!'' Someone spilled crockery and silver

somewhere in the kitchen, and muffled curses followed. "Before my grandfather died—Grampa Griffin, who started as a strikebreaking goon and ended as head of United Electrocom—he found a ring in his coat pocket one morning, a nasty sort of novelty piece. It had a tiny skeleton etched into the ringstone, laid out as if lying in a coffin, the most morbid thing—and there are rumors of other tokens, signatures of the enemy. Warnings.

"These things turn up, and then one of us gets hurt—" He couldn't bring himself to say, whichever man is current head of the family gets hurt. Gets killed. He hurried on, filling the silence. "Do you see why I'm worried? It sounds to me as if you've gotten one of the Griffin warnings."

"This is going much too fast for me," Jess muttered. She paused, then added rather plaintively, "What I got was a lovely thing, really, a sort of filigree locket, nothing nasty at all."

"I don't mean you're the target," he added quickly. "The warning is meant for me. The cowardly bastard is taunting me through you, because—well, it wouldn't be hard to find out that you and I have been close, in the past. So you have to watch out for yourself, Jess. Don't take anything for granted, don't take any*one* for granted, do you hear me?"

"I said, *hold it!*" she yelled into the phone. "Nicolas, are you telling me that you're running away from somebody you think is after you—this 'enemy' who's trying to get at you through me? Is that why you're going back to Europe?"

"Well," he said. "Yes, sort of. Look, I think he's just using you as a sort of message-drop, and there's no danger to you personally at all. But I don't like the sound of these pranks—marbles on your dressing-room floor and so on— and I don't want you letting any . . . any unusual sort of strangers getting near you, do you understand me? I don't know what he'll do. I don't know how to stop him. Damn it, Jess, I said I didn't want you in this show, but you wouldn't listen!"

"Unusual strangers," she said. She breathed quietly into the phone for a moment. Then she said, "God damn you, Nicolas, you *have* had somebody spying on me! Well, you can stop it, you can go off to Europe and leave me alone, you hear me? Oh, hell, I am too tired for all this now. I'll call you in the morning."

"I'll be gone by then," he said.

"You can't go!" she burst out. "What about your dogs?"

He groaned. "Softhearted Jess, you never change. I'll think of something. I'd give them to you if I could, to look out for you while I'm gone."

"Not with me in this little apartment, you don't," she said, "and I can look out for myself, Nic. I really can."

"Just remember what I've told you, will you? Be careful, for God's sake!"

He forced himself to hang up.

"About time," growled a fat little man in a huge tweed coat, shoving past him to get at the phone. "What a town, you can't even make a phone call without having to listen in on somebody's crazy soap opera first!"

Dining Out

**I**vo Cragga hunted with savage and single-minded intensity. He tracked a thin, weary prostitute, who wore a false fur coat trimmed with spangles, until nearly dawn. Then she collected her dole of crack in exchange for her night's earnings. He darted ahead of her as she hurried home, and called to her from the doorway of an abandoned and boarded-up tenement.

Already he felt better: steady, strong, and in control. This, he could deal with. It was his normal life, not like wild impulses to taste the mouth of his enemy's woman in a public place, like some love-stricken boy! Kissing, like a suitor, where for generations of his dark life he had only gone for food and had committed without compunction a swift piracy that involved him in no social aftermath.

What in the name of all his years had happened to him?

He shoved thoughts of Jessamyn Croft away and watched his chosen victim hesitate, trembling in the grip of her slavery to the drug in her pocket. Her face was turned toward him, whiter than salt, and he saw the tip of her tongue nervously moisten her lips.

She was a child really, but already the stamp of death was plain on her skin for those who cared to see. Without a doubt, she knowingly carried the infection that would eventually kill her. He recognized the dull sheen of despair in her eyes, the carelessness of despair in her unwashed hair, the neglect of despair in the droop of the ragged black tights showing below the shabby coat's hem.

Keeping silent, he watched her decide to turn one last trick after-hours, the payment for which she could secretly keep for herself instead of surrendering it to her pimp: something to buy breakfast with, later. Or drugs, more likely.

"What do you like, mister?" she said, standing close, her hands shoved deep into her coat pockets. She was shivering. She had ash-blond hair worn in a crooked French knot at the nape of her thin neck.

"Come close, I will show you," he said. "Twenty dollars—"

"Twenty-five," she said, with a spasmodic grin that must have been meant as a disarming smile. Two teeth were missing on the left side of her mouth. Her pimp was obviously not an easy boss. Someday Cragga would get around to him, too, maybe, and return treatment in kind plus a little extra.

But for tonight: "Twenty-five," he agreed. "Don't be afraid, I won't hurt you."

If she had been a little stronger, a little less sick and strung out, she might have wisecracked back, maybe saying something like, "If anybody could still hurt me, mister, I wouldn't be in this line of work."

And then he might have given her the money for the simple feel of her thin breasts under his hands, so that she would have cash in her pocket for a cup of coffee in the morning, and maybe that would lead her to something else—maybe out of the streets, somehow. It was a tale he could tell himself in such cases. But not in hers. She was too far gone. He was a skilled practitioner of his own form of triage.

She came closer without speaking, her thin face slack with resignation. So he turned her back against the boarded-up door, closed her thin and shuddering frame in his arms, drew down the matted collar of the fur coat, and pressed his lips to her throat.

A pinch on her cheek distracted her; she never felt his fangs break her skin, and then he sucked in such a powerful draught of her sickly blood that she at once collapsed in his grip, her consciousness leaving her in a sighing whisper.

Quickly, efficiently, he drained her. Then he hefted her cooling corpse in his arms and carried it across the street to the ratty little park on the other side, where he set her down on a half-broken bench. He tucked the coat modestly about the skinny legs and left the body there, pale and life-less; the girl herself he thought of as freed.

Bursting with new energy, he ran with great strides up West End Avenue where the good people of the city did not stray out late at night on foot. The dozing doormen thought a sudden wind had passed as he went by, if they noticed that much.

Once again safe in his own apartment near the river, he sat in the light of the special bulbs he had installed in his kitchen over three open cases of jewels. These were the fruits of his latest labors in Europe, on his last trip. He picked up each piece and studied it, matching it tentatively to a selection of names from a list of dealers and collectors on a long yellow legal pad at his elbow.

While he worked, he sipped strong red wine. His system had already cleansed the young whore's blood, but the taste of it had been foul.

Dark Mother, he called in his mind after a while, *are you with me tonight?*

Every night, the answer came. *You have fed on illness again, Baron.*

A lost, ruined, drug-wrecked girl, he said. *I ended her*

misery and filled my stomach at the same time. Isn't that what you intended for me, Dark One? That I should become a public benefactor?

I intended to help you find your property and take your revenge.

Well, I am close, I think. He scurries about, trying to find his salvation from me, and I wouldn't dream of interrupting his progress beforetime. Let it play itself out, that is always the best way. But meanwhile I must nourish myself, as you well know. Do you disapprove of my hunting?

Silence. He wondered if she had withdrawn, as she sometimes did for days at a time lately. He studied a handsome silver belt-buckle inlaid with jet, searching for cracks or chips in the stone. Often he obtained pieces under circumstances that did not permit close and careful examination on the spot—in bomb sites, makeshift cafes, and gloomy basements or alleys.

The setting needed polishing, just enough to give sculptural depth to the silverwork. But he didn't feel like laying out his cleaning kit. He was tired, as if the dead girl's weakness had infected him after all.

He sat back and toyed with his wineglass, turning it on its round base and wondering at how steep an angle he could hold it without losing a drop of the dregs.

What I disapprove of is not your hunting, the answer came at last, but as to that, with a little effort you could have taken sweeter blood.

He snarled, I do not want "sweeter blood"! I want no blood at all, and when my work is finished here I will gladly starve for lack of it. I have seen enough of addiction by now to swear that the last Baron von Cragga will not be bound to this world by an addiction to anyone's clean, hot blood!

So you deliberately choose to drink filth?

I drink filth so that I will not drink more than I must. And, he added with angry sadness, because for such creatures, the thrown-away ones of this foul society, no one else has any use that is not foul. These castaways sustain me, though, and for that I love them, in my way.

Who else loves them, Lady? What the world of men has become sickens and bewilders me. At least in my time there was the Church. The helping orders of monks and nuns, worldly and corrupt as they often were, did at least offer a little charitable love, even to lepers!

Again, a pause, and he could hear the faint pounding of mindless modern music vibrating in the building's walls.

Was she blonde, your prey of tonight?

Yes. And did she look like my lost Magda? No, she did not. I think not, anyway; I do not remember anymore what Magda looked like, you know that. But if Magda lived in this world instead of that one, she might have ended up on the streets like this girl, after my enemies were done with her.

This is an old pattern with you, Baron, sighed the voice in his mind. Are you not tired of it? Your pity, your love, your feelings of any kind have no effect one way or the other on these bits of human garbage that you release from their dreadful lives. I like to see you take pleasure in your meals. Perhaps this other one, this woman of the stage—

He did not answer, but turned and turned his glass and thought about a certain man he knew who would pay a pretty penny for that delicate intaglioed watch-fob in red carnelian, lying in the second box.

I see in your mind that she is beautiful, although marked by injury and suffering. Not like Magda, of course—

Nothing like Magda, he snapped, although as he said it, he realized it was not true.

Jessamyn Croft had a touch of what he remembered as a certain purity in Magda, not in the limited sense of chastity but the wider one of the quality of the soul. In Magda this had been the result of her devotion to God and all His saints and His angels; she had been an aggressively pious child, even for those days. But in those rough times piety had not been a bad defense for a young woman.

Sometimes he wondered if she had come to accept her abduction calmly, as simply God's assignment to her. She would have loved this dainty golden rosary cross with some saint—good God, he forgot which was which sometimes!—painted in the center in beautifully detailed enamel.

In Jessamyn Croft he also read a sort of purifying dedication. He could not tell what it was, but that it had drawn him he could not deny.

This actress loves the enemy of the house of Cragga, the Other said, interrupting his restless musing. You do know that she loves your enemy, do you not?

Angrily he shook his head as if ridding himself of a swarm of pests. Of course I know it! That is why she is of use to me: she will be my path to him, one way or another. As it is, I would only have to twist her hair in my fingers to have him come running to save her, right into my waiting hands. And when the time is right, I will.

Are you so sure? came the reply. I think you call her image to mind more often than befits a mere tool of your design.

He chuckled unpleasantly. So I should enjoy my feeding but not enjoy the hunt, is that your instruction? Why should I not toy with the woman who is the beloved of my enemy, before I attack that enemy himself? Did not his cursed ancestor use, abuse, and destroy the sweet one of my own heart, long ago? I take what is owed me, bit by bit; that is all.

Silence, broken by the distant wail of a siren that he could hear right through the windowpanes. He took another sip of wine and began turning the glass again.

You are not on your native soil now, Baron, came the answer.

He grinned and pulled up his sleeve to examine the design on the skin of his forearm—a dragon in dull red-brown. It was made not of inks but a solution of pulverized earth, the earth of his own castle keep, dug in permanently under the skin.

He said, Like the fairy-tale king who demanded that the world be covered in leather for the comfort of his walking abroad in it and whose servant gave him shoes, I have solved that problem brilliantly, don't you think? Where I am, there, too, is my native soil.

I mean, the Other said, there are so many distractions where you are, and too few reminders of your task. Take care that you are not drawn off your path, or it may be you who needs the pity and—the love, if that is what it is, of others.

Well, he said with a mirthless smile, that would be a new experience, at least.

But in his mind he saw the face of Jessamyn Croft, with its frank intelligence and its beauty subdued by suffering, and he imagined her smiling a pitying smile.

The wineglass broke in his grip, and the last drops shot out and spattered a fine necklace of inlaid Siamese silver, so that it looked as it had when he bought it from a weeping old man in the ruins of what had once been a music shop. Then, the necklace had still been stained with the blood of the old man's wife, shot by a sniper.

Accidents

On Tuesday Jess found Marie in the costume shop, huddled in a chair in the corner with a battered tin box in her lap. Half hidden amid the hanging racks of clothing basted and glued and Velcroed for quick changes, she was crying.

It's happened again, Jess thought with a clutch of dread; *the prankster has struck.* She pushed past the worn worktable with its aged sewing machines and bent over the woman. "Marie, what's wrong?"

The dresser mutely held out the box and pulled off the lid: It was the old lozenge-tin she had used to put the Berlin iron pendant and earrings in, to lock them inside the drawer in Nell Clausen's desk that served as the Edwardian's "safe." Now the jewelry lay tangled into a bizarre knot, held together as if by invisible welds, a useless lump of intricately worked metal.

"I don't understand," Jess said, staring at the mess in disbelief. So much for her plans to wear the pendant and earrings on opening night, and then give them back to Cragga with thanks, and—maybe—a sensible farewell. "Are they *melted*? What happened?"

"It's some kind of superglue," Marie gulped. "Somebody stuck them all together. When I tried to get them apart with solvent, it just took off some of the black finish—I've ruined them!"

"Marie, don't cry," Jess begged. "It's the prankster's fault, not yours. I can't believe this is still going on. It's like the behavior of some witless five-year-old with a childish grudge against me!"

And it was getting to her, she realized, breathing deeply to calm herself: she was on the edge of tears and suddenly unsure of the lines of Eva's biggest speech, which she was to work on this afternoon. Marie, of course, knew how important today's session was, and had tried to fix this latest problem without troubling Jess at all.

Poor thing, she would probably feel totally responsible if a performer she was dressing got hurt or scared off—

Unless Marie *herself*...? Suppose this was the extent to which Nic would go to get Jess's attention and warn her away from Ivo Cragga. Nic was supposedly gone to Europe; but he could have paid Marie, bribed her to do this, couldn't he?

Jessamyn felt dizzy for a moment, darkly dazzled by the possibility of treachery so close to home. But Marie did have the run of the theater, like most of the staff, and could work there at odd hours without being challenged.

I am really in bad shape if I can even think such a thing. Jess reproached herself angrily; but she was more furious with Nic, whose wild stories had planted the seeds of these paranoid speculations in her mind.

Damn the man, if he had to leave the country to get far enough away from her and from his play, now that her presence in it spoiled it for him, why couldn't he have just gone? Why call her up in the middle of the night to fill her head with nutty warnings and prognostications, like a ridiculous parody of the Three Witches in—in the Scottish play?

She became aware of the sagging lines of worry and the shadow of fear in the older woman's face as Marie hung on her reply, eyes shining with renewed tears.

"Relax, Marie, it's not the end of the world," Jess said, expelling Nic firmly from her thoughts. She pulled Marie to her feet and hustled her out of the costume shop. Once inside her own dressing room, Jess shut the door.

"We'll do without the damned earrings, and nobody will ever know the difference! As for Mr. Cragga, I never asked him for anything. If he wants to blame someone for what's happened it's going to be me, not you.

"Only it would help if you thought about this, Marie, while it's still fresh in your mind: Have you seen anybody hanging around the place who doesn't belong, anybody you think might have done this?"

Marie stood hugging herself and shaking her head dolefully.

"Think it over. I want to have a good grip on what we can say when we go see Nell Clausen and raise a fuss. Maybe we can use this to demand better security in this theater. It's pretty clear that we need it!"

The likelihood of money being available for this was minuscule, but she hoped that talking this way would help Marie gather her scattered wits.

Jess bent and peered at herself in the makeup mirror, wishing she could just go home and go back to sleep. She felt strung out, and she was not pleased to see that she looked almost as tired as she felt.

She sat down with a sigh in the swivel chair in front of the mirror. In a minute, she would be crying herself. The pressure of rehearsal against the deadline of opening night was tough to take at best; she wasn't sure how much more additional stress she could handle without cracking, which of course must be the prankster's goal.

This thought stiffened her determination not to buckle under the despicable attacks of her unknown enemy. But if things were to change for the better—to come under control so that she could give her full attention to making her performance the best comeback in history—it was all too clear that she was going to have to make it happen herself.

She tried again, turning in her chair and taking Marie's surprisingly soft old hands. She willed Marie to concentrate.

"Don't give up," she urged. "Think about it, Marie! Maybe you did see something, just a glimpse or a shadow—something you weren't even aware of noticing at the time. Think back—when you came to the theater, was there anything unusual?"

The older woman shook her head again, then paused, blinking. "Well, there was a man—of course there are always people around, but at three in the afternoon, in the stage-door alley . . . It did seem a little odd, someone standing out there in the cold like that, at that hour."

"What did he look like? What was he doing?" The wild thought occurred to her that perhaps Ivo Cragga had come around looking for her. Maybe he had sneaked in and ruined the jewelry himself, for reasons of his own.

"Just a guy," the dresser said helplessly, which pretty well clinched it: no woman could look at Ivo Cragga and say he was "just a guy"; not in the face of his confident stance and his arrogant and exotic beauty. "A tallish man, I think, but hunched down into his coat—it's so cold out, everybody's all muffled up. You wouldn't know your own mother out on the street these days!"

"Then he had a hat on? Gloves? A scarf, maybe?"

"A scarf," Marie agreed, but dubiously. Pushing out her lower lip in thought, she turned to combing out Eva's second-act wig, a lustrous black fall of curls. "And a hat, a regular man's hat, though I can't imagine why; it certainly can't give much warmth. I remember thinking at the time, his ears must be freezing! You see everybody in woolen caps like Russians this winter, or fur hats even, the men too."

"But what was he doing, Marie? Do you remember?"

Marie squinted, trying to see into her memory. "Blowing on his hands, that's what he was doing, so I couldn't even see his face: his hands hid it, and no, he had no gloves on, now that I think about it. I thought he was waiting for someone, standing there in the alley, but when I looked back to see if anybody else from the company was on their way in—before letting the door lock behind me, you see—he was gone."

"Listen, he was probably nothing to do with us," Jess said, hiding her disappointment at the meagerness of this report. "But if you do spot him again, you tell me right away, all right? Now, I would love a half-cup of tea before everybody else gets here. Something with a little caffeine in it and a wedge of lemon; my throat's dry as burned toast."

The dresser bustled out to the staff lounge with obvious relief. Jessamyn began doing exercises to open her throat and unlock the muscles of her neck, dropping her jaw and vocalizing from the diaphragm.

She needed to disperse her tension and get her thoughts focused on the tortured relationship of Marko, the head of a family steeped in centuries of profitable crimes and machinations, and Eva, the idealistic niece come home to make her claim on the fabulous family emerald, which she intended to sell for money to redress those crimes.

Marko had his own ideas about the emerald. He wanted to use it as bait, to bring vengeful family enemies to the treaty table where they could be slaughtered with the treachery he felt they deserved.

Perhaps she could use the increasing unease about the pranks (and now this prowler, if that was what he had been) to put a little extra edge on her character's nervous determination. It was something to try, anyway, and see how Walter and the others reacted.

In fact the rehearsal went splendidly that night: Anthony radiated a heightened degree of anxiety himself, infusing the character of Marko with an almost glowing quality of frenetic despair. He demanded that the enemy be repelled and punished, but it was clearly justified vengeance against him and his that he feared.

Anita MacNeil, playing his estranged wife, picked up on this and developed a quirky sort of murderous intensity that set off Eva's quiet insistence to admirable effect.

Jess did not go talk to Nell Clausen that day, although the slender blonde woman, in a casual but beautifully tailored suit, did look in on the rehearsal at one point.

It had occurred to Jess as she was trying on the first-act costume that if the jewelry had been in Nell Clausen's safe-drawer, it might just be possible that Nell herself was involved somehow in this latest stupid and destructive incident.

Not likely—why on earth *would* she? But she *was* an old friend of Anita MacNeil's, and had in fact originally suggested Anita for the part of Eva. Could the two of them be trying to shove Jess aside so that Anita, who was Jess's understudy, could take over the major role?

Now there was a nasty, paranoid idea! Not that such machinations were unknown in the competitive hotbed of theater work. But to even imagine that the gracious, unflappable Nell would stoop so low seemed demented. She was the calm, sound business head that kept the Edwardian afloat, unlikely to involve herself in a backstage feud even for a friend. Nor could she easily have been duped somehow by Anita; Nell was a smart lady.

But what about Anita herself? She was ambitious, and not young enough anymore perhaps to wait for success to be earned (which it mostly wasn't, as hundreds of New York waiters with stage resumés could testify). Maybe she was desperate enough to try to drive Jess out of the cast, counting on some kind of leftover weakness from the accident plus Nic's own opposition to Jess being in the play in the first place?

Jessamyn stared gloomily at her own reflection (noting in passing that Eva's dress still gaped at the neckline). She had never indulged in suspicion of her fellow professionals. (Well, not since she had been a very much younger, very much sillier girl just starting out.) She wasn't going to start now if she could help it. That kind of paranoia was poison to a production. You had to be able to count on your colleagues, and she was damned if she would let her trust in them be undermined by a set of dangerous jokes.

If they didn't trust each other on the stage, who in the world could performers trust? And their lack of trust could wreck the delicate balance of the play itself, as it was developing under Walter's careful attention.

Nevertheless she said nothing about the glued jewelry to anyone, and made Marie agree to keep it to herself as well. Jess wanted to mull all this over quietly and think about just who to approach about it, and how.

Despite her good intentions, though, she could not shake a lingering nervousness. When she started for home after the rehearsal she thought she felt someone watching her. She looked around, expecting to see—perhaps—Anita, smiling a secretive smile of satisfaction.

In fact, Anita was there, climbing onto the back of the motorcycle ridden by her boyfriend, while Anthony Sinclair mimed acting as her equerry, stooping with his hands linked for her to step into in order to swing up and astride some massive, imaginary horse. As the bike pulled out into traffic inches ahead of a UPS van, a yellow cab drew into the curb space and Sinclair stepped back out of the way of the opening door.

Something in his posture—a greyhound tension, keen and taut—made Jess stop to watch.

A woman got out of the cab and looked up at Sinclair— she was a head shorter than he—saying nothing as far as Jess could see from a distance of some twenty-five feet. It was Anthony who spoke, starting eagerly forward, reaching both arms toward the woman. She thrust out her hand between them, checking him, holding out—papers: mail, perhaps, or documents. She spoke; and slowly, the actor lowered his head and looked down at the proferred papers. He took them and stuffed them into his coat pocket without reading them.

She continued to speak. She was his wife, of course, it had to be Sally Sinclair, barely recognizable without stage makeup and costume and lighting. She was smaller than Jess would have thought—smaller than she had seemed playing the old lion's young wife in *Uncle Vanya* in a recent celebrated bare-stage production that Jess had seen. Smaller, but not less impressive: she was an olive-skinned woman in a fur hat and coat, exotic-looking as some princess out of an eastern folktale.

It looked to Jess as if she never took her eyes from Sinclair's face nor raised her voice; Jess heard only a rapid, low ripple of speech, passionate with intense emotion but not at all loud. The woman might almost have been pleading.

Except that Sinclair stood with his head bowed and his face averted, like some courtier taking a verbal lashing from his queen. There were no fireworks, no dramatics, perhaps because they were so deeply sunk in the intensity of their shared anguish that for once neither of them was aware of an audience. Nobody else turned to look; this was New York, after all.

Only when the woman had finished speaking, touched Sinclair's cheek ever so lightly and quickly with her gloved fingertips, and withdrawn gracefully back into the waiting cab, did Sinclair stir from his apparent paralysis. He lunged forward, grabbing at the side of the taxi, calling out in a hoarse voice. But the cab swung away from the curb and left him staggering in the gutter.

Afraid that he might fall, Jess started toward him. He steadied himself with both gloved hands braced on the hood of a parked car. When she anxiously spoke his name, the face he turned toward her was so bleak with desolation and longing that she stopped in her tracks. This was no moment for helpful intrusions.

She gave an awkward little wave and called lightly to him, "I thought we could share that cab, but no such luck! See you tomorrow, Anthony!"

He stared hopelessly at her, his handsome face as pale

as the papers sticking out the pocket of his coat. She had the feeling that he barely saw her and she suspected with embarrassment and pity that his eyes were simply blinded with tears.

My God, she thought fervently as she hurried away down the street, leaving him to the privacy of his pain, *Marie is right about those two! Any woman who thinks she can take Anthony Sinclair away from his wife is in for a hell of a rude awakening! That man isn't just in love with his wife, he's in thrall to her!* And then came a plaintive thought that she quashed quickly: *Was Nic ever that much in love with me? Could he ever have been, if things had turned out differently?*

If she got any deeper into that, she'd be in tears herself.

Only later, as she unlocked her own door, did Jessamyn remember that she ought to have been looking out for a stranger, the man Marie had seen in the afternoon. The man who might have gained entrance to the theater somehow, and gotten at the Berlin iron pieces in Nell's safe-drawer.

If he had done that, what else could he do?

Collectibles

◆

The reblocked scene was a problem. Jessamyn had trouble replacing the old cues with new ones. She was edgy and nervous anyway, and her continued blowing of two crucial lines was not improving her temper.

The theater was icy today because work was being done on the old boiler in the basement. Jess rehearsed in her coat, which made her feel heavy and clumsy where she needed to be light, almost ethereal: she was the idealist (and perhaps an ideal herself) in the grasping family; their salvation, if they had one. She needed to fly, but could barely clump around, flubbing her lines right and left.

Anthony Sinclair was little help at first. He had been touchy and absentminded all through this rehearsal period. The story of the glued jewelry had gotten out, of course, and he seemed particularly upset over it, although he clearly also had other things on his mind.

In the first break he went to the office to talk to Nell

Clausen, something about the payment schedule. Jess hoped he wasn't spending his paycheck wildly on something that was leaving him strapped and in need of advances on his salary. There were tales of Anthony hiring detectives to watch Sally when they were apart, but also of his suddenly buying her some incredibly expensive gift as a bribe.

Maybe he was just upset because the theater trickster had struck again that morning, filling Jessamyn's bottle of Evian water (kept handy for between-scene refresher sips) with ammonia.

Luckily Marie had discovered the substitution right away, but still, what a crazy, spiteful thing to do! Jess could hardly believe anyone could be so recklessly hateful.

Anthony returned looking worried. He came over to Jess at once and said, "I told Nell about the ammonia incident. My God, how childish! But dangerous, too. Are you sure you don't want to try rehearsing somewhere else? My place, Walter's, even, or over at Anita's apartment, just for a few days, anyway—to confuse this joker, if you can call him that!"

"Him *or* her," Jess answered evenly. "We need to start getting the feel of our moves here on the stage, Anthony. Johnny's watching everybody now; he'll catch the so-and-so sooner or later, which he can't do if we're working in somebody's apartment. Thanks for offering, though."

"This could be more serious than it appears," Sinclair said darkly. "The world is full of crazies these days."

"Oh, piffle," she said, more bravely than she felt. "It's a nuisance, and I have to peel Marie off the ceiling every time one of these things happens. I really appreciate your concern, but I can handle it."

He peered at her anxiously. "Coming through that car accident must have really toughened you up—made you brave, I mean. I know veteran troupers who'd bolt right out of a production rather than stick around for some nut to take potshots at them!"

Jess smiled, but she was reminded of the feeling she'd had all day that someone was following her, watching her every move. Marie's mysterious man blowing on his cold hands, maybe; she thought she had spotted a man trailing her on her way to the Laundromat this morning.

It had been an extremely creepy feeling, and had not improved the state of her nerves.

She walked through the scene once more, losing her place in the script and missing cues. She apologized to the others and began again. Walter helped, talking her from the arched cellar doorway past the broken sofa that had supposedly fallen through a shell-hole from the floor above, through the maze of trunks and boxes and discarded children's toys, to the crooked old wardrobe with its shattered mirror in which she could see her own pale, frightened face.

"We will never give up." Anthony Sinclair intoned Marko's lines. "We will wait out the worst they can do, and then we will turn the tables on our enemies and drive *them* underground, like rats!"

"To make rats out of human beings," Jess replied, whirling to face him, "*that* is the work of our family? And you wonder why I go away somewhere, anywhere, to get away from you all?"

" 'The *mark* of our family,' Eva," Walter corrected.

"I'm sorry, damn it—'Is that the mark of our family? And you ask why I go away—' Hell!"

"You're pushing it," Anthony said kindly. "Look, everybody else is still on book here." He gestured, indicating the other cast members with their scripts in their hands. "Take your time."

Then the stage manager called time; the Equity limit for the day's rehearsal had been reached. Jess stayed a little on her own, plugging away at her elusive lines, script in hand this time.

Of course she was distracted, wondering what Ivo Cragga would say about the ruined pendant and earrings. She had sent them off to a costume-jewelry expert recommended by the wardrobe mistress, but she did not know yet whether the damage could be undone. Meanwhile she was not especially looking forward to explaining the problem to him. But there could be no ducking the issue; he had probably already heard something from Lily Anderson.

Her remarks to Marie about insurance came back now to haunt her; what if Cragga held her responsible for the value of the pieces?

When she came out of the theater into the cloudy winter afternoon, he was waiting for her, studying the posters that flanked the entrance. He ran lightly up the steps and caught her hand, which he brought to his lips.

"Have you forgotten?" he said with mock severity. "The antique jewelry show! I invited you. You must come. Lily Anderson saw it at a special preview, and she says it is wonderful. I am sure you will enjoy it too."

"I've got something to tell you first," she said, steeling herself.

"Something troublesome, I can see," he said. "Let us step back into the lobby, then, out of the wind. Now, tell."

She told.

His brows drew together in a frown that turned his entire face into a grim mask which made him look much older.

"I see," he growled, when she had finished.

Her heart sank. "Oh, God—don't tell me they were priceless heirlooms, please! Why did you ever risk them in a silly stage play?"

"The play is not silly," he snapped, and then added more softly, "and the foolishness was indeed mine, not yours."

"I can't tell you how sorry I am," she said miserably, hugging her script case to her chest as if it could provide comfort. "I should have put them in a safer place—no, I should never have accepted them at all, not even temporarily! It's my fault, and I'll pay you back for them if it takes me years."

He shook his head. "You will pay me back by coming with me now to the jewelry show, Miss Croft. That is the sole reparation I demand, and you cannot say no."

Weak-kneed with relief but not inclined to buy into some sort of involved relationship of favors owed and owing, she tried to get out of it. "Oh, Mr. Cragga, I don't know—I did say yes, but it's been a long day—"

"The show is close by," he said. "You look as if some fresh air and a little stirring of the blood would do you good. Walk with me that far, and then if you still want to change your mind, I will fetch you a taxi and off you go. And it is time you begin to call me by my given name. I am Ivo, please, not this overbearing-sounding Mr. Cragga."

Before she had time to consider this proposition he had relieved her of the leather script case, tucked her hand in the crook of his arm, and was escorting her down the street.

How on earth could this charming young fellow be the cause of Nic's weird warnings? But who else had given Jess jewelry recently? Really, it was ridiculous!

No, it was sad, it was Nic's craziness rearing its head again, just like after the accident—the woman on the horse had been the same kind of thing. . . . She was pierced by a sense of loss, the loss of Nic as he had been, that took her breath away with its suddenness and strength.

"We go onto my turf now," Cragga was saying. "Is that the right word? So you must let me do the talking, and if you grow tired of listening, just say so. But you should know a little about this before we go in."

He proceeded to sketch a swift description of how until the nineteenth century, gems and jewels had been the possessions of the aristocratic wealthy alone, often by royal law as well as economic reality. Surviving pieces from those times were now so valuable, due to their rarity and tending as they did toward the elaborate workmanship and the showy encrustations of precious stones of upper-class pomp, as to be simply beyond the means of any but the richest of museums and collectors.

However, he said, decorative creations dating from the era of the Industrial Revolution, made with elements of machine manufacture as well as careful craftsmanship and thus handsome but also cheap enough for the middle class, were now eminently collectible. Made of more common materials and a good deal more commonly found, they were much more reasonably priced, and available to dealers like himself for trade.

"Then we're not going to see anybody's crown jewels?" Jess said. "You got me here under false pretenses."

"Crown jewels, and indeed all the many jewels worn by the royalty of Europe in the old days," Cragga responded, "were in fact savings accounts that could be cashed in at the money lenders at need. A crowned monarch or even a local feudal lord never knew when he would suddenly need to finance a campaign, or a quick escape from stronger enemies. Gems are small, valuable, and easily hidden away or carried in secret. Great families kept their accumulated riches in such a form. Indeed, many a warrior-knight wore his precious stones into battle."

"He did? But why?"

"To be sure they were not looted from his castle while he was away fighting somewhere for his liege lord," he said with a peculiar, ironic bitterness. "We turn here. . . . And to have wealth upon his person if he was captured and needed to pay a ransom. Also many gemstones were considered to have magical healing and protective powers as well, and the business of a knight often involved danger and wounds. And there was no penicillin."

They entered the lobby of a vast office building built around an enclosed atrium that was filled with plants, like a gigantic greenhouse. Cragga laughed with delight, pausing in the entry. "Why, it's like a garden in a cloister!"

He drew her to a poster on one marble-clad wall near a busy bank of elevators.

"You see," he said, "they have chosen this necklace as the emblem of the show. However, the necklace on exhibit here is not the real one, but an imitation that the family women wore in place of the truly valuable piece. That they kept at home, safe under lock and key."

Jess studied the blown-up photograph of an ornate golden chain with its pendant charms of pearls and intricately set emerald-green stones. "No kidding! I didn't think anybody did that until our own crime-ridden times."

He chuckled, a rich sound, and his eyes narrowed to humorous gleams. "All times are crime-ridden, one way or another. It's the human way, I think."

She looked sharply at him, chilled a little by this remark. "You're very cynical, Mr. Cragga."

"I am very experienced."

Jessamyn thought he was playing the suave, world-weary European with a becomingly light touch. A good thing, too; otherwise he might have seemed ridiculous. With his smooth cheeks and forehead, his eyes glittering with enthusiasm, he looked no more than in his mid-twenties and brimming with irrepressible life.

She turned back to the poster. "But why would copies be valuable?"

"The finest ones were made by a Frenchman named Tassie, who invented the best glass paste for imitating genuine gemstones. The workmanship and the results are so fine that Tassie's replicas themselves—and even those of his students—are now museum pieces. This particular necklace, however, is actually a more modern imitation of a reproduction made for the Duc de Chancey, shortly before the French Revolution."

"What happened to the real jewels?" Jessamyn asked.

Cragga cocked his head consideringly. "Smuggled out of France, broken up and sold to support the Duc's family in exile, I suppose; like so many others. As I told you, wealth in jewels provided emergency money for more than one noble house in hard times."

They walked up the wide marble steps to the mezzanine level, where the exhibition itself was mounted. "It must be very common, then," she said in a subdued tone, "for old jewelry to be connected with terrible stories of war and tragedy."

For an instant he checked, and she saw that he was staring at her with a focused ferocity that made her want to step back from him.

"What do you mean?" he said harshly.

"Well, nothing, I mean, only that—" She stammered. "Ivo, what did I say?"

He at once resumed his usual demeanor. "No, no, I was thinking of something else. What you said, Miss Croft, is precisely the case. If these objects could speak—" He waved his hand, indicating the entire exhibition floor with its drift of spectators who hovered at the locked glass cases, peering closely, murmuring to each other.

"If jewels could but speak, no one in this room would remain unmoved. Not even these grasping men with rocks for hearts."

Jess glanced through the wide doorway at a shaggy-haired older man with a covetous stoop worn into his back, deep in conversation with his companion, a bright-eyed young fellow in a checked suit who looked freshly minted and polished and vastly pleased with himself. The younger man saluted Cragga with a deferential wave of his hand, and spoke quickly to the older one, who glanced over his shoulder and nodded a sour-faced greeting of his own. Cragga nodded pleasantly in reply, as if he had not just characterized them both as heartless misers.

"Surely that's just an old stereotype, Mr. Cragga—the greedy hoarder of gems and jewels?"

He was quiet, and she turned to glance at his face again—a broad, almost brutally handsome face like a mask of pale, polished amber, with lambent eyes of clear green. At moments like this he looked agelessly remote, like one of those tensely peaceful figures sculpted on the tomb of some youthful knight of olden times.

He returned her look somberly and, taking her arm, strolled with her back and forth just outside the entrance to the exhibition, speaking quietly, close to her ear.

"Miss Croft, I have seen a beautiful woman—almost as beautiful as you, but faded with age and sorrow and fear—enter a pawn shop and with trembling hands lay out for valuation her last treasure, on which she depends to furnish money for food and rent. And the man behind the counter picks up and turns over with faint distaste the handsome brooch and the matching earrings and bracelet she has brought him, and informs her that they are cheap imitations, worth next to nothing.

"Perhaps he speaks gently and suggests she take her worthless hoard down the road to someone who deals in such trinkets, knowing all along that she will find no better answer there. But if he has been in the business for some time, he may speak with cruel abruptness because he is angry at her for being so foolish as to have believed that her dead husband's pathetic gifts to her have any objective value; and because he pities her, and knows he cannot afford pity if he is to survive in his chosen business. So perhaps he is brusque by design.

"And she leaves his shop with faltering steps and brimming eyes, Miss Croft, her last hope of security destroyed and all her fears breaking full upon her. While he shuts the door hard after her, relieved to have her and her budding tragedy out of his place of business and out of his life.

"These smoother men you see here today, they are only that shopowner's jumped-up relations, and at heart little different from him however finely they dress. And every one of them has been approached at one time or another by a wealthy customer now fallen on hard times, and has returned only half, if that, of the flat value of the materials in a piece, and none of the inflated value for which he sold it to that client in the first place. They all deal in the difference between dreams of opulence, grandeur, and love, and the cold costs of stones and settings.

"Gemstones are hard, and those who deal in them are harder or they could not endure."

She saw the bitter set of his mouth and ventured gently to ask: "Are you speaking of yourself, Mr. Cragga?"

"Perhaps I am," he responded. "And when you hear from others that Ivo Cragga has the hardest heart of all, remember that you heard it first from me. Now, let us go in."

Checking her script case and their coats, they paid a small fee and walked in past the two solid-looking and very obviously armed guards at the entry doors. Jess was thoughtfully silent.

Far from reflecting badly on him, his little story of someone else's misery belied his own estimation of himself. A hard-hearted man would surely never notice the pain a dealer's frankness caused to the poor woman whose hopes were pinned on worthless goods.

In fact what she felt was an increased closeness to him, as if in telling that little tale he had allowed her a rare glimpse of his own heart. His story and the manner of its telling had created a bridge of intimacy that she found unexpectedly compelling; more so than that lingering kiss, which in retrospect seemed like a dream.

Relax, she told herself. *It's just a walk around a room full of expensive old jewelry, not a cruise in the Mediterranean. And if he wants to kiss you again—so what? How many men are there in the world who know how to kiss a person, anyway? This is one; and Nic is gone, by his own choice; so enjoy yourself, you have a right!* The fact that Cragga was younger than she was only made his attentions more flattering.

The table-high cases and the wall cabinets held only a few objects each, set off on beds of lush gray velvet. Cragga pointed out a row of heavy men's watches with their finely engraved gold lids protected by outer cases in which the watches had habitually been carried; two long necklaces of Chinese cherry amber polished to a deep glow; buckles of cool gray gunmetal set with polished striped Scottish agate; gold-set cameo pendants and delicate cloisonné brooches; and he described, explained, and enlightened about each and every piece he spoke about.

Some of the pieces were for sale, and the prices surprised Jess; they ranged from just over a hundred dollars up to no higher than a few thousand at most. Cragga smiled when she said she would have expected much higher valuations on such beautiful things.

"These are simple jewels, Miss Croft, jewels without great luster or history, at least so far as anyone knows. Look here at this bracelet woven of human hair—yes, yes, the sable tresses of some beloved son or mother or sister who has died—held together with chased gold findings. It is a sort of memorial jewelry—see how the clasp is a locket, open to show the miniature portrait of the lost loved one inside?

"It is for some long-dead person's sentiment that a buyer pays in this case, the sentiment that financed this excellent craftwork with which to commemorate a loss that has left no other lasting mark. Like most of the pieces in this room, it is only worth what some collector is willing to pay to own it, and this figure varies from year to year, with fashions in collecting."

Fascinated, Jess barely heard the latter part of what he said. She stared at the woven bracelet of glossy black and swallowed. "How can you tell that's human hair? Couldn't it be horsehair?"

"Believe me, it is hair from a human head," Cragga insisted. "And you must understand, the hair in itself is worth nothing, the gold content is unremarkable, and though the enamelwork inside the clasp is exquisite, it is not of, or by, someone we know of in our time.

"Thus, the feelings and the care and craft of another era—qualities by their nature unquantifiable—confer a totally subjective value on this piece. Apart from that, it is a trinket, nothing more."

"But it was much more than that to the original owner of the bracelet."

"Of course," he said. "I only wish to make it clear to you that the pieces I sent you to wear in your play are of this kind: not expensive treasures, as perhaps you still believe. They are minor items in the world of old jewelry, but pretty enough, I hope, to meet with your approval—"

"They were exquisite, Mr. Cragga, and I am really so sorry about what's happened to them."

"—but not worth enough to create any sort of obligation to me. Let us have this very clear between us. Misunderstandings are so destructive of friendship, don't you find it so?"

"I certainly do," Jess said sadly, thinking again of Nic, and of how differently she would be viewing this exhibit if her companion were him instead of Ivo Cragga.

Cragga reached out and touched her chin, which was trembling, with a touch as light as a moth's wing. "Ah, you're sorry about a particular friendship that has been— hurt in this way?"

Jessamyn did not answer but turned her head aside. All she needed was a stupid, emotional outburst in public over a man who no longer felt anything for her!

"Look," Cragga murmured, drawing her attention to an- other case. "Here are objects which express what you feel, I think. All of these are also pieces of mourning jewelry, which became popular after Queen Victoria began wearing black jewelry upon the death of her prince Albert. See how finely the jet in this brooch is engraved with the shape of a weeping willow tree—a very common motif for mourn- ing pieces.

"What do you mourn, Miss Croft?"

He loomed very near, and suddenly his strong, square hands rested lightly on each of her shoulders and turned her toward him, so that she stood as if in a moment of intense privacy with him. The room, the softly lit cases full of jewels, the spectators studying and whispering over these jewels, might not have existed. Jessamyn felt the intensity of his concentrated attention like a cloak of warmth falling lightly over her and shielding her from outside scrutiny.

Except someone was looking, straight at her.

"Damn!" she whispered. "Who *is* that guy? I think he's been following me!"

The Ruby Tear

◆

Who?'' Cragga whipped around like a striking snake.

"He's gone," Jess said, startled by the sharpness of his reaction. "It's just some fellow I don't know—but I keep catching glimpses of him, or anyway I think I see him, and then he's gone."

"For how long is this?" Cragga took her upper arm in a painful grip and steered her around a corner of the room, out of sight of the doorway. His eyes probed everywhere, checking, she realized, for other entrances to the exhibition, or perhaps other watchers already in place.

"Well, for the past few days—"

"And he looks, how?"

"Tallish—I don't know. He wears a hat pulled down low, and those mirror-lensed sunglasses. I think he has a beard."

"What color?"

"Blond, or light brown." She was chagrined to realize

that she didn't really remember the follower all that clearly. "Sort of a hippie type, I guess. Look, Mr. Cragga, there's no need to get upset about this. I haven't; I've just assumed that he's an overenthusiastic fan, that's all."

"You are too casual," he said, looking searchingly into her face. "There are laws against what they call 'stalking' for a reason. Obsessive people can do harm, when they act upon their irrational fantasies."

Jess smiled wryly. "I'm not a shining theater star, Mr. Cragga, to be followed around by fanatics—" He gave her a small, quick shake as if to force a new focus on her vision, and this silenced her. His alarm had communicated itself to her directly through his hands and his narrow stare.

"You need not have such prominence to attract dangerous attention," he said. "How have you survived in this city with such naiveté? Did you not tell me, there has been a series of accidents in your theater? It seems to me that you may be the object of your 'unknown admirer's' unpleasant attentions already, and not even know it!"

She felt an impulse to step into the embrace of his arms and come to rest against him, enclosed in his strength and protected from all comers—

Which was first of all nonsense, and secondly, maybe just the effect he was after? Who was he to sneer about "unknown admirers" when he had given her jewelry before ever meeting her? It was even possible, she realized with a nasty jolt, that he was working for Nic, doing mischief at the theater himself as part of a plan to drive her out of the play. He had been there all morning with Lily, she knew, as a sort of unofficial colleague working on the scrim design.

With as much dignity as she could muster she pulled away from him. "The things you refer to are just ugly little incidents of petty harassment. They're the kind of thing that sometimes happens in a theatrical company because of jealousy. And I'm much better suited to judge the seriousness of what's been happening than you are, thank you very much.

"As for the man I saw just now, for all I know it's not the same person at all. I grew up in a small town in Connecticut, and I'm probably overreacting, if anything, to something unimportant. Frankly the city does still scare me a little. I may be naive, but I'm not stupid!

"Now, what can you tell me about all these pretty oddities strung on little chains?"

With an angry grunt he turned away, and she thought for a moment that he would leave her there and go hot-footing after the supposed watcher. But he seemed instead to calm himself, and rather stiffly returned his attention to her and to the exhibit. He explained that a chatelaine was a collection of useful items worn chained to a sort of belt-brooch that fastened at the waist, a pretty leftover from the days before ladies' handbags. So here was a thimble in an engraved silver case, and here a tiny scissors in a scabbard, a minuscule writing pad and a silver-cased pencil.

"They're like charms," Jessamyn said, "for a charm bracelet! My mother collected charms. She would have loved this."

"These items are all useful, though," Cragga said, "and the thimble is of course normal size. The 'chatelaine' of a castle, once upon a time, was its housekeeper, who kept all the great number of keys to the many doors chained to her belt. Hence the name of this assemblage of dainty tools."

"Noisy to wear," Jess said with a grin. "I bet the scullions and whatnot liked being able to hear the boss coming from the ringing of her keys!"

The last hint of sternness vanished from Cragga's face, and he favored her with a smile of peculiar youth and sweetness, touched with the oddest tinge of—was it regret?

"There are not many alive today," he said, "who would think of such a thing, or of such people—not the great and imposing men and women of the past, but the lesser folk who served them."

Jessamyn felt a faint flush warm her face. "Oh, it's just an actorly imagination at work," she said. "Someone like me is much more likely to play a servant than a noble lady.''

He caught her fingers lightly in his own and raised them to his lips. ''As I thought,'' he commented, his bright tenor voice turned husky, ''it only demonstrates the shortsightedness of those who do the casting. But tell me, is there nothing here you might like to buy for your mother?''

''Thank you for asking,'' she said, embarrassed by this Continental gesture and anxious to avoid another, more expensive one that might leave her even more indebted to him than she already felt. ''My mother died two years ago. She was in her garden, which she loved, and it happened very quickly. I think I'm over the worst of missing her— as much as you ever get over losing your mom, anyway. Are your parents alive?''

He shook his head curtly, and for the rest of their tour of the exhibit he spoke scarcely at all. She had forgotten that Europeans were much less forthcoming about their personal lives than Americans were, at least upon short acquaintance; and she wondered if he would ever feel comfortable enough with her to speak freely about his own family.

She wondered, too, whether she really wanted him to, and whether it was a good thing or an ill thing that his presence seemed to impinge so powerfully on her senses that she was always aware, now, of his body close beside her, lithe and vital.

When she admitted to being sated with looking at beautiful things, he took her to a quiet bar in a nearby hotel and bought her a Kir and told her tales of historic jewels, the legendary ones of popular fame: how the diamond called the Great Mogul caused the downfall of one high ruler in India after another; how a shah of Persia in ancient times was tortured with a crown filled with boiling oil to make him give up the Kohinoor Diamond; how the Hope Diamond was bought from a pawnbroker for what was then, in the mid-nineteenth century, a huge fortune, and may or may not be the same stone as a fabulous diamond sold to King Louis XIV of France in 1698; how a famous ruby in the crown jewels of England turned out at last to be not a ruby at all but a more common, look-alike red stone called a spinel; how zircons were passed off as diamonds, and how ambergris was for generations listed as a "marine gem" for its supposed curative powers.

His supple, velvety voice entranced her. She felt like Desdemona, bewitched as the exotic warrior Othello regaled her with stories of foreign lands.

"What wonderful, terrible histories," she said. "It's enough to make a person swear off wearing old jewelry forever! You wouldn't want to be haunted by all the wailing ghosts that must come with a stone like the Kohinoor, for instance."

"People will put up with a great turbulence of restless spirits to own gems of such fame and beauty," he said, pouring himself another small portion of Amarro. "If indeed there are any such spirits, influences, and curses."

"Curses," she repeated, suddenly remembering what Nicolas had told her on the phone about fateful jewels delivered to doomed men in his family. Had he really said such wild things? Two glasses of Kir had hazed her mind, in a pleasant way, but she did remember.

"I have a friend who says that someone in his family was given a ring, once, that might have been cursed. It had a skeleton on it, lying on its back as if in a tiny coffin, and not long after the gift was given, the recipient died."

Cragga sipped his drink and said nothing.

"Are there gems that carry real curses, that you know about?" she persisted.

"Oh yes," he said, in a bare whisper of a voice. "There are."

"In my line of work, we have plays that are considered cursed," she mused, "like poor old—what they call 'the Scottish play,' Shakespeare's tragedy with the three witches, you know? Look, here I am avoiding saying the title just like everybody else, as if I really believed it could be bad luck!''

She chuckled at her own credulity and made a rueful face. ''I guess I can't take any chances, when I've finally worked up the nerve to get back on a stage in front of an audience.''

''From what I have seen,'' he said, ''no one would guess that you are nervous about it.''

Ha, she thought; *caught you in a lie*! But it was a kindly falsehood, and instead of challenging him she said quietly, ''You have no idea how much working in *The Jewel* means to me.''

Then she felt her eyes brimming: this was something she should be saying to Nicolas.

''You do not believe in curses?'' Cragga inquired silkily. ''In superstitions?''

Jess pulled herself together. ''Not really. Even this nonsense at the Edwardian is just spite, not the ghost of some poor comedian bricked in alive behind my dressing-room wall.

''No, please—I've had more than enough to drink already, and I should be getting home. I need a whole night of good, sound sleep before I tackle a couple of big scenes off-book tomorrow.''

He looked baffled, and she explained that the script in her case was the ''book,'' and that she liked to begin memorizing lines early in the rehearsal process. ''Especially,'' she added, ''when I know the playwright isn't going to be revising as we go along and giving everybody new lines to replace old ones, which also means giving the actors fits.''

''Then I am glad,'' he said dryly, ''that I seem to have driven Nicolas Griffin away, with my efforts to get to see him and talk to him about the play.''

''That's okay,'' she said, ''I have plenty to worry about with switches in moves and timing from our director. If I didn't know that Walter Steinhart is first-class in what he does, I'd rebel, so help me. I'd march.''

''Would you? Your contract permits?''

"Of course not!" she laughed. "I'm joking. Even without a contract, I wouldn't dream of walking out." She sobered. "None of us would. It would mean letting everybody else down, too, and good colleagues don't do that to each other."

"Even when they are plagued with peculiar 'accidents'?"

"Especially then," she said positively. "Just how much do you know about that? Besides what I've told you, I mean."

"Everything. I have been talking with Miss Anderson," he said. "She is a very accomplished gossip, I think, very knowledgeable and pleasant to be with." An odd, shuttered look came over his face, and a faint and very private smile curled his lips.

Jessamyn remembered suddenly that this man was Lily's contact, not hers, and that in fact according to Marie—also a devoted gossip—he had been spending a good deal of time with her outside the theater. Odd, how that thought made her heart sink a little.

His eyes brightened again, fully alert and focused on her. "But also Lily is very professional, Miss Croft; very committed to this play, as you are yourself. I think you theater people are devoted to your work as some people were formerly devoted to their prayers, perhaps."

What an odd thing to say! Charmed, she could only smile at him.

He looked away from her and said in a more distant tone, "But before you go home to your well-earned rest, let me tell you the best story of a cursed gemstone that I know. One last story, is it all right? You will enjoy it, I promise."

Jessamyn shook her head helplessly. "You have softened me up first with beautiful jewels and wonderful tales and perfectly acceptable drinks; how can I resist? Besides, I still owe you for those ruined pieces you lent me."

With one decisive shake of his head he dismissed this problem as if it had never been. "No, that is finished, and you must speak no more about it. Let me tell you about a real gem, a stone without price, a treasure—and its awful history.''

He reached across the table and took her hands gently in his larger ones, like a medium creating a circuit of contact before summoning spirits. Was she imagining it, or did he feel a need to touch her this way—something more than an idle impulse?

"Imagine a time," he said lowly, "when the last remains of the great empire of Rome was broken and chaos replaced it—rather like this time, in fact, the confusion following the paralysis of your Cold War. Imagine a great commander, Charlemagne, pulling the shattered world that was Europe back together again by his intelligence, will, and armed might.

"Imagine that he rewards his faithful warrior-knights with fiefdoms and privileges, the standard spoils of the wars of kings. But there is one special treasure he seeks to lodge not with some armored thug with political aspirations but with a man of true honor; not, you see, a great noble who hungers to raise armies to support his own bid for a crown, but a faithful warrior of relatively low estate and no ambition other than to serve his sovereign truly and faithfully.

"He finds such a man among the ranks of his warriors, and after a great battle, he secretly entrusts to this gruff old fighter—a mere baron, a nobody—the keeping of a great and precious gemstone, known as the Ruby Tear.

"It was said that this stone was a tear of blood that fell from the eye of the dragon slain by Saint George; a great and holy treasure, you will agree. And it was said that so long as the Ruby Tear stayed safe in the hands of that Baron's family, peace would reign in Europe."

He sat closer, so that his knees touched hers under the little bar table, and he held her hands in both of his like a lover and curled and uncurled her fingers with his thumbs; and the voice in which he spoke was so rough with emotion that her protests died in her throat.

She felt as if he were entrusting to her something more precious than the jewels he had sent to the theater, just as the lowly Baron in his story had been singled out and honored by Charlemagne. She would not have given up that feeling for anything so she sat still and let him caress her hands in this curious, abstracted way that was both detached, and deeply sexual.

To lighten the spell—why did he always choose a public place for these breathtaking gestures of intimacy, for God's sake?—she said, "Then that didn't happen, did it? Because peace has never prevailed for long anywhere that I know of."

A great sigh seemed to lift his broad chest, and suddenly the eyes that looked into hers gleamed with sardonic humor. He lifted her hands and set them back away from himself matter-of-factly, and sat back in his chair.

"As you say, Miss Croft; if there was anything to that old tale, it has never come about. Far from it. That Baron went home to his little domain in Eastern Europe, where, as devout Catholic Germans, his family were on the front lines of the fight against the influence of the Eastern Orthodox Church and later the advances of the Turks.

"And in the wars that followed—for from the beginning, there was of course no peace—one of his descendants went off to fight and came home to find all lost. Foreign mercenaries, hired to protect the castle in his absence, had turned traitor, murdered his family, kidnapped his wife-to-be, and stolen the ruby given from the hand of Charlemagne. He went searching afterward, but in vain.

"But I have heard that the posterity of the man who plundered the Baron's castle has been afflicted ever since with strange and violent fates, which the hidden gem draws to them; because the young Baron who came home and found his castle destroyed and his family treasure taken and his honor defiled laid a curse against the offender for his treachery. And pursued him, and—they say—pursues him and his to this very day, with the help of the Devil, intent on revenge and reparation.

"And that is the tale of the Ruby Tear; perhaps you have heard it before?"

"What?" she said, filled with a strange sense of foreboding—surely just a product of fatigue, wine, and the company of this strange man, but what a roil of darkness seemed to churn below her heart! She went on, shakily. "I don't read very much history, Mr. Cragga—"

"Ivo," he said.

"Ivo. I don't know that story. Like most stage people, I don't have time for reading, except for some poetry sometimes, for the rhythm and the beauty of the language." There, that felt better—talking of things she knew and understood.

"Well," he said, cocking his head with barely disguised skepticism, "of course. I just thought that perhaps somewhere, sometime, you might have heard of such a story, and of this magnificent lost stone that the rightful owner has given away his soul to reclaim."

Jessamyn blinked at him, shaking her head to dislodge the velvety barrier his voice seemed to have raised against the music from the piano bar and the voices and laughter of other people at other tables in the low-lit, ornate room.

"No," she whispered. "Who would have told me a story like that?"

His smile was cold. "Who indeed, Miss Croft? Only some worn-out refugee from the Old World, trying with such laughable clumsiness to make his way in the new. Come, let me see you off homeward, after this most pleasant afternoon! I have worked up an appetite, but you look tired. I wouldn't dream of dragging you along with me to a late meal."

She glanced at her watch. It was after eleven, and she felt almost drugged with exhaustion. He kissed her hand and closed the door of the cab, and she nearly fell asleep before she was delivered to her door.

Later, soaking in her tub with script in hand, she saw very clearly that Nic's play was like a continuation of the tale of the Ruby Tear, told from the side of the robber's descendants. And she remembered also the warning Nic had given on the telephone, the story of the mysterious deaths among his forebears, and his command to be wary of unusual new companions.

She put her rioting imagination firmly on hold and made up her mind to ask Lily Anderson directly about Ivo Cragga the next day. It wouldn't hurt to find out more about him, if she could. Then maybe she could begin to make sense— *acceptable* sense—out of all this.

Besides, prudence dictated that she speak with Lily. One of the worst things you could do to a production-in-the-making was to deliberately provoke jealousy among members of the company. Enough such divisive currents arose spontaneously, even when people were trying their best to avoid them.

And here she had been more or less allowing Lily's contact, this attractive European with his seductively esoteric knowledge of ancient, beautiful, terrible things, to pay court to her; for surely that was what he was doing. How could she have just drifted into what was certainly a relationship, of sorts, with him? What in the world was she thinking of, anyway?

Of Nic, of course. Missing Nic, being furious with Nic, wanting to show that she didn't need Nic; that she could help make a hit out of his play, and find some other man, maybe a younger, better man, to take his place at her side, at least for a while. Being in a show often created a sort of time-out within which liaisons could form, mature, and end without any lasting effects on the ongoing lives of the people concerned.

Was that what she was doing, allowing this magnetic stranger to escort her around town, whisper in her ear, kiss her hand, kiss her *lips*, for God's sake?

Well, why not?

Because there was a very peculiar symmetry to the things she was hearing from him and hearing from Nic, and seeing, now, in Nic's play; but maybe if she pursued the matter, she could find out what was making Nic run from her, and put an end to it somehow.

Before things went any farther, though, she was going to

check with Lily and try to feel the situation out a little. No man, and no supposed secret, was worth fouling up a promising, smooth-running show for. Well, smooth-running except for these weird bits of sabotage. . . .

Could it be Lily, taking revenge for Jess's interest in Ivo Cragga?

Certainly the designer had plenty of opportunity. She was in the theater at all hours, working over her desk in a corner of the production office. But the "accidents" had begun before Cragga had shown up, hadn't they? Rehearsal time was in a way not real time, and Jess realized that she had lost track of the exact sequence of events in the early days.

She determined to get to the bottom of it.

But the next day Lily didn't show up. It wasn't her child who was sick this time, it was Lily herself, which Marie said was unusual: Lily had the constitution of a tough little Moor pony, she said, and this peculiar, anemic weakness that had struck her had come on very suddenly.

Lily returned two days later, in the course of which time Jess heard nothing from Ivo Cragga. Jess found her working in watercolor at her desk, on a tracing of a design drawn in ink in a firm, bold hand. The designer looked pale, with big circles under her eyes, but she greeted Jess brightly enough. "For the scrim," she said. "Handsome, isn't it?"

It was. The design showed a jointed bracelet of golden rectangles, very bold and rough in outline, and boasting large gemstones in the center of each plaque that were set about with smaller stones in a sunburst pattern.

"It looks like a real piece," Jess said.

"Well, it better not be," Lily said. "I told Ivo it should be a composite, so we don't get hit with some kind of permissions problem for using the image!"

"Ivo Cragga gave you this design?" Jess said with what she hoped came across as total innocence.

Lily smiled wryly. "Yup. And yes, I know he's interested in you. In fact I saw the two of you go into the jewelry show together the other day. I went again myself; professional interest. Look, Jessamyn, I am not anybody's idea of a beautiful woman and I know it perfectly well—let me finish, okay?''

Jessamyn swallowed her protestations.

''Thanks. What I mean is, I don't compete with the stage people for partners, you know what I mean? If somebody shows an interest, that's very nice, very flattering, and I'll go along as far as it stays pleasant and fun for me.

''But when a guy has satisfied his curiosity about going out with a person who is not very tall and not very pretty but very talented in a business that sets 'pretty' on a very high pedestal, I start letting go again. There's no use setting my heels and dragging back if he prefers a woman with looks like yours.''

She shrugged her small shoulders. ''Believe it or not, there is an up-side: a certain kind of freedom. And I think everybody should have as much freedom as possible when it comes to feeding the needs of their heart, you know what I mean? So if he's interested—and it sure looks like he is—and you're interested too, then go for it, and good luck to you both!''

''Lily—'' Jess stopped, her heart full. ''Hey, can I hug you? Maybe some of your wisdom and sweetness will rub off on me.''

''You've already got more of your own than most,'' Lily said soberly. ''You've had to fight hard, against real problems. I wouldn't talk this frankly to most actors; they'd just get all huffy on me. And by the way, one more thing: He's an odd one, so keep on your toes with him. It may be just that he's foreign, but maybe not.''

''What do you mean?'' Jess said, her heart beating hard.

Lily shrugged again, pursing her lips. ''Damned if I know, but there is something—I can't explain, really. It's just a feeling. Pay no attention, I'm just thrumming with slightly psychic vibes, that's all; it happens once in a while, but you can't live your life by that, can you? Come on, here's your hug, if you still want it.''

But Jess guessed from the designer's parting glace at her—a wistful, melancholy look, quickly veiled when she saw that Jess had noticed—that however odd or unusual Ivo Cragga might be, his attentions were not to be given up without some regret.

Jess shivered with an exhilarating mixture of apprehension and delight. Perhaps Nic had not totally ruined her for other men—very special other men—after all.

Legends

◆

**N**ic walked in a graveyard, hunched into his coat. The morning was raw and foggy. Fresh new mounds had been squeezed in among the older plots, neatly decorated with the plastic flowers which were all the mourners could afford these days. At night someone might come and steal the days' tribute of flowers to resell; he had seen it happen in other towns.

He stumbled over a crumbling headstone and the fear of taking a fall jarred a curse out of him.

"Swearing in a graveyard," someone remarked in a gravelly voice; "it's bad luck, even for foreigners."

The figure looming out of the fog resolved itself into a bent-looking man with a cane. He was wrapped to a false fatness in an old quilted coat with who knew how many additional layers under it. His neck was swathed in what looked like strips of blanket and on his feet he wore cracked dress shoes with tapered toes. More blanket strips were wrapped around his lower pant-legs, like old-fashioned gaiters. From under his rather rakish tweed cap, he studied Nic with gleaming eyes set deep in nested wrinkles.

"I'm sorry," Nic said contritely. "I thought I was alone."

"How could you be alone here?" the old man said, indicating the field of chipped and discolored markers with a roll of his eyes. "This is the busiest place around here. In the worst of the fighting, so many bodies were buried in backyards, in empty lots and behind sheds; they must be taken up again and put here, for reasons of the public health, they say. Today we can bury our dead here on an open hillside without being picked off by snipers in the hills as we stand over the grave. Tomorrow, who knows?"

"I'm sorry," Nic said. He said that a lot, here.

"Sorry? For what?" the old man said. "It was nothing to do with you, was it? No, no, for years on end, it was nothing to do with you. So why do you come now?" He peered more closely at Nic. "You are Mr. Griffin, from America? I see now. You come to find out about relatives, ancestors, people dead a long, long time already. Lucky ones."

"Come on," Nic said sharply, "I don't see you cutting your own throat to join those 'lucky ones,' and I daresay you dodged the Chetnik snipers as briskly as everybody else, or you wouldn't be here now. And you'll do the same again if you have to, won't you?"

"What would you know about it?" the old man muttered, looking gloomily back toward the town.

"You know my name," Nic said. "What is yours?"

"What do you care what my name is?"

"I don't," Nic said. "I'm trying to be civil."

"This is not a civil place that you have come to." The old man shot him a fierce look. "You choose a strange time to come searching for your 'roots,' young man."

"I'm a journalist," Nic said. "I want to write a history of this area, but with a tight focus on one family, to try to understand what's been happening here from a more personal point of view that readers can get caught up in. Besides, the personal point of view sells, and maybe people will learn something, too.''

''Oh,'' the old man said. ''A family saga, like *Gone with the Wind*?''

''Nothing so ambitious; just an effort to throw a little light on things, maybe, for outsiders like myself.''

''So who are you looking for? What family name?''

''Von Cragga.''

The old man gazed steadily at Nic, his expression intent and closed. Without a word, he began walking away down one of the aisles between the graves.

He was not the first to have turned his back on Nic when the name of von Cragga came up. Nic had come out this morning expecting to meet no one. He had nothing with him to offer, no bribe for something besides silence. He stared helplessly after the old man, silently cursing his own lack of forethought.

Cursing in a graveyard; bad luck.

The old man looked back over his shoulder. ''Aren't you coming? It's this way.''

Hastily Nic followed, and soon they came to a cracked stone sepulchre with its carvings worn smooth, its gate torn off, and its low doorway nothing but a gaping blank. There were no other graves immediately around it, although the rest of the cemetery was crowded with tilting stones and broken monuments.

Above this lone building leaned a single tree, thick and crooked. It reminded Nic uncomfortably of the oak at the junction of the shortcut with the Pie Corners road.

''That's it,'' the old man said, swinging his stick out in an arc to indicate the structure. ''In the pit under that little death house lie the dust and bones of generations of von Craggas. The barons were plain people, they didn't give themselves airs but went to rest here close by the common folk.

''Which is not to say they were particularly beloved, you understand; always off to this war or that, the barons, like

all the men of their class. Every time they went they took
men from the villages round here to be soldiers for them,
and many of those didn't come back. But there was always
a baron to live in the castle in those days. They're gone
now too.''

Nic had seen the ruins of the castle and made some
sketches, there, on the hilltop that was fog-shrouded today.
There wasn't much left, just broken walls and hollow-worn
steps that led nowhere but up empty sky.

''Of course we are so much more civilized now,'' the
old man added, looking down meditatively at his aged
shoes.

''Much more civilized,'' Nic agreed. ''We do our killing
from further away.''

''They were Christians,'' the old man murmured, ''those
men of Craggenheim. Like the Chetniks today. I am Muslim myself. We all are, now, in the town. The others, our
Serb neighbors, left, to gain that very distance, Mr. Griffin,
from which to comfortably shoot down old people and children for being not-Christian. They still have their barons,
too.''

''So what are you doing here in a Christian graveyard?''
Nic said, giving in to impatience with this needling, justified though he knew it to be. He also knew that there had
been atrocities on both sides; but the score was far from
even, and the total cost of the combined savagery was in-
calculable. He had seen the ruins of once-beautiful Sarajevo, the result of years of bombardment while the rest of
the world stood by and wrung its hands unwilling to risk
anything but words to end the shelling.

The old man shrugged faintly. ''I thought perhaps you
have something to give for information, so I followed you.
Everything is very costly these days, Mr. Griffin. Maybe
you can cross the street without being shot, but when you
get to the other side you find you can't afford to pay for
meat at the butcher's. I have a grandchild who has not
tasted sweets since she turned three, at the start of the fighting.''

Nic bit back a mumble of sympathy, a useless offering of comfort: more words, not the kind of any use to the old man. Instead he said briskly, "I have money, back at my room in the town. I'll give you what I can, if you'll walk back with me later."

The old man nodded and stood quiet, head cocked attentively, eyes hooded.

"Von Cragga," Nic persisted. "Anything specific you can tell me about that family?"

"They say you already know about the present baron," the old man murmured, plainly already well-informed.

Nic said sharply, "I thought you said there were no more barons of that name." His leg ached with the damp and he was beginning to feel hungry. Breakfast had been scant, though probably not so scant as this old man's breakfast, or his grandchild's.

The old man propped his hips against the lip of the tomb, planting his cane between his knees. "Not here, no. And in any case there is no *line* of von Cragga," he said. "Someone goes about with the name nowadays, doing business here and there like a merchant, like a peddler— well, there are plenty of people who are glad to see him, I suppose. He doesn't blow your house up when he has to hand it back to you again, just to keep you from using it. That's a recommendation these days."

"You're saying this man has no right to the name?"

"They once held the whole valley," the old man said, lifting his chin to indicate land now patched with snow and mud and obscured by drifting fog. "And two more besides, when the barons won their wars. There has always been fighting here, always; plows still bring up bones from before the last war, and next spring they'll turn up brand-new bones. A great deal of blood swells this soil. People used to say that blood made it fertile, at least so long as some priest or holy man blessed it."

"I have to sit down," Nic said. He had seen the officials searching for hidden graves, mass graves, men who walked slowly and thrust thin metal rods deep into the ground, then pulled them out and sniffed the ends for the reek of rotting flesh. God, his leg hurt.

"Why are you so weak, so delicate, a young man like you, with years of good meals packed on to his bones?" the old man inquired, coldly looking him up and down.

Well, he was entitled to his resentment. He must have once foreseen a peaceful and respected old age for himself, not years of dodging sniper-fire and struggling with war-time poverty.

Nic said patiently, "I have an injury that bothers me sometimes."

"Well, don't sit *there*," the old man said with sudden shrillness, pointing sharply at the great gnarl of tree root that Nic was about to settle on, under the single tree. "I thought you were an old traveler in our poor part of the world! Why do you think that tree is still standing, when we have had no fuel to burn in our homes all this winter?"

"Because it's too far from the town," Nic said, sitting anyway.

The old man sighed, pushed away from the tomb and came to sit on the root by Nic, rubbing his hands together and blowing on them. "We could break off some branches and make a fire," he said wistfully, "except it would bring bad luck, and we certainly don't want to risk that, not with all the good luck we bask in around here. But we can imagine a fire."

"Is there a story about this tree?"

"Yes." Up close, the old man was redolent of sweat and smoke. Soap was hard to come by, and expensive. "A bad story, the kind of story most people want forgotten. But what harm can it do for an old man to rest here a moment and talk about old days? What else is an old man good for?"

In this remark and the old man's bleak eyes Nic read the guilt of being alive when so many children were dead, so many strong young men and women, so many more robust and promising souls. He said nothing, because there was nothing to say.

After a moment the old man began quietly, "It was said that long before the Christians and the Muslims started fighting each other over this territory—before the Christians fought each other, too, one church against another—there were older beings worshipped here. Certain places had special spirits living in them. There was a daemon of this grove—what used to be a grove.

"She was a thirsty darkness, this daemon, sprung from a crack in the stone of the hills that goes down to the very heart of the earth. They say it was the blood of feuds and wars, slipping down that crack, that brought her up to the surface, hungering for more."

Nic licked his dry lips and shifted uncomfortably on the thick, warty root. His heart beat fast: this, just this, was what he had come all this way to hear, he was sure.

The old man cleared his throat and turned his head politely to spit on the ground. "They say dead bodies were buried around here first to appease her appetite. Only later the ground was sanctified, and a church built over the mouth of her cave, just over there a little distance—you can't see it, it's been shelled to rubble. She took to the forests she had come from, but most particularly she stayed in the grove.

"Now, this Dark One was respected by the barons, Christians though they were. They were Germans, you know, originally, or anyway they came from what was to be Germany later on. They were conquerors, occupiers, but smarter than the Nazis of the last war, and much smarter than the Chetniks of this one. The barons were clever enough to use superstition to help win the support of local people. They built their family tomb here, under her tree, as a mark of respect for her, and wouldn't let the priests cut the trees down."

"A daemon," Nic said, staring at the cracked and discolored walls of the von Cragga tomb. "You mean, from the Devil, from Hell?"

"From the days when forest covered everything," the old man said. "Before there was a 'Devil,' or a 'Hell,' or a church, or a mosque. All lands have such daemons, don't you think? Blood feeds them and makes them strong. Blood draws them, and blood can bind them; or so those old heathen people believed.''

"You are saying," Nic said slowly, sidling up to it, not wanting to hear but knowing he must hear, "that such a daemon came to life here? And what happened then?''

"Nobody knows, it was a long time ago," the old man said.

"I told you, I can pay," Nic said shortly. *Don't stop now, you can't quit now and leave me hanging!* "Tell me what happened.''

"Nobody knows," the old man repeated, staring into the fog with a squinting, abstracted gaze that deepened the furrows around his eyes. "But what I've heard is that the daemon—she has several names, but I don't know them and if I did I wouldn't speak them here—the daemon made a pact with the last Baron, when he was dying of some treachery or other—"

"Wait." Nic stopped him and asked a question that filled him with dread. "Was there someone else involved, someone like me—a foreigner, who did the Baron wrong somehow?''

"Not that I heard, but it's an old story; who knows what details have been forgotten? It could be as you say. On the other hand, we have never needed to import treachery from other lands. There has always been more than enough of the home-grown variety to go around.''

Nic grunted, grinning despite himself at the other's mordant humor.

The old man shifted his feet—he must be cold in those thin-soled city shoes—and went on. "So the Baron dealt with the daemon to assure vengeance on his enemies. Therefore, although he died, he came back again, this time living as a creature of such a daemon must live: on the blood of ordinary, mortal folk. They say he still walks the earth and calls himself Ivo von Cragga.''

"Still," Nic said, feeling light-headed. He could see

every wild, greasy hair winding out from under the edge of the old man's worn woolen cap, every liver spot on his wrinkled skin. "But he did actually die, have I got this right? How long ago?"

"Generations," the old man said, but did not elaborate.

"He died," Nic said doggedly, "but he's still walking around, as if he were just one of us."

Walking around; hunting my ancestors down; stalking us like deer in his baronial forest—no, like bears or wolves.

The old man breathed deeply and hugged his bulky clothes tighter around his body. "Well, it's only an old story, a foolish story. But it's about revenge, you see, and we bathe in stories of revenge here. We eat and sleep and drink them, so of course such stories stay alive."

"Is there more to it?" Nic said.

The old man looked up at where the sun shone palely behind the drifting fog. "Probably. Our stories of vengeance never end."

He stood up.

"Tell me everything you know; please. It's important." Nic grabbed the trunk of the tree to keep his balance, rising in turn to his feet.

"Of course, I can see it's important," the old man said. "But I am hungry, and my granddaughter is hungry, and you say your money is back where you are staying. I have already earned some of that money, don't you think?"

It could all be lies, Nic told himself, turning to look across the crooked, bullet-scarred tombstones. *Everything he's told me so far and everything he's going to tell me. But why would he lie? And the more fantastic it is, the truer I will know it to be. Maybe if what he gives me is good enough, I'll tell him that I've seen his daemon with my own eyes, and what she looked like, and von Cragga too, and then he can scoff if he likes and play the superior man of reason.*

"Who told you these stories?" he said as they walked down toward the pitted remains of the road. "Did you hear them from your grandfather, your grandmother?"

The old man grinned, flashing two gold teeth. "My grandparents? No, no, how would they know? They lived in Mostar, I grew up there; we were city people. None of the people from around here would tell you these tales, not even for soap and candy and fresh fruit; they're still afraid of the Baron and his daemon, they don't talk about them.

"No, I came out here to study folk music in the countryside, and people told me these things after a while. Also there are references in some of the older songs, if you know what to look for. I married and stayed."

"Was she a Christian woman?" Nic asked gently. "Your wife?"

The old man nodded. "She isn't here, but in another burial place. Muslim women they raped. Christian women who had married Muslims—they did worse, to punish the treachery of such marriages, you see."

They walked a little in silence. The old man dragged one foot slightly at each step, the edge of his shoe turning over pebbles that made a wet sound in the mud.

Nic said, "You could leave this town." He didn't say, go back to your own family, your former home. He knew how seldom there was anything left for such people to go back to, and it was no surprise to him when the old man shook his head in answer.

"No, I'll stay here."

"In spite of the Baron who died but came back to life?" Nic said, glancing back at the crowded graveyard, the shabby sepulchre, the leaning tree.

"Why should I fear him?" the old man said. "He doesn't come here. He travels, Mr. Griffin. I don't think he will come around here and bother me; and how much more bother could he be, anyway, than a pack of Chetniks dug in on the slopes up there and shooting at us in the ruin of our streets?"

Nic had to restrain a laugh, a surge of energy, a cry of triumph: at last, he was *doing* something; not sitting at home waiting for the Baron—the enemy—to come after him, but going onto the creature's own turf. And this filled him with hope as he hurried through the dissolving fog after the old man who had come from Mostar to study folk music.

Advice

That was not wise, the Dark One murmured. You are careless, to take your meal again so close to your quarry. What if the little gnome-woman remembers more than she should about your time with her?

You are mistaken, von Cragga thought. He stood on the street corner and watched the plate-glass window of the Two White Cats, where Jessamyn Croft could be seen taking coffee with two of the other actors, the older "lead" and a younger one. She did draw men to her, but how could it be otherwise?

The other would not let it lie, but asked him, How, "mistaken"?

Jessamyn Croft is not my quarry. Nicolas Griffin is.

How strange, Baron. You seem to spend all your time with her, and none looking for him. Naturally, I conclude that the one you seem to be stalking is your quarry.

Nicolas Griffin loves her, Cragga replied, digging his fists deeper into his coat pockets. He will not truly go far away from her for very long. Old as you are, do you know nothing of love? Why can you not understand this? If I stay near her, eventually he will come back to me.

Do you still want him to?

Of course, he thought. But perhaps not too quickly. I am in no hurry, Lady.

Two of the young leather-clads he had dealt with on his own visit to the coffeehouse stomped by him in their heavy boots, not noticing him where he stood under the awning of an all-night Korean grocery. Now, that is where I ought to be feeding, he thought, following their progress down the windy street with burning eyes.

This is true, came the soundless words in his mind. They are full of drugs and sickness, exactly what you like best, or so you tell me.

He shrugged irritably. Not always. I drank from the little theater woman, and she was clean; not even the taint of tobacco.

You liked it?

He did not reply. His attention was trained on the threesome at the window table, blurred as they were by the vapor on the inside of the glass.

If you liked it, you could go back and finish. This person would welcome your complete attentions, Baron, do you not think so? She has a poor life, in the corners of a world of appearances that despises and pities her for her stunted stature.

No, he answered. You are quite wrong, Lady, or are you deliberately testing me? Lily Anderson enjoys her life, despite dark passages of self-doubt and regret and envy of others. But who doesn't have these? In addition, she also has a child she loves, and she is respected for her talents. She gets lots of work, good work because of it. Also because she functions well as part of a team, I think. Her life is strong and centered, against great odds. I do not care to destroy such a person. There are too few of them in the world in any century.

Like this Jessamyn Croft? Is she one of them too? Is that why you spend your time looking at her, even at this moment when you came out here to see if you could entrap the one who follows her?

Instantly, he pounced: Who is it, Lady? Is it someone involved in the accidents at the theater?

Why do you care?

Feeling unfairly harried, he smiled angrily, baring his teeth—not fangs, not without the hunting lust to draw them down. In his quiescent state he did not fear to smile like other men, living men.

I like to know who the players are, before I risk high stakes in the game, he answered finally. You can tell me, you can surely see from where you are: Who is it that attacks her at her work with such cowardly slyness, and tracks her in her own city's streets?

I might see, came the dreamy reply, but I have no wish to. These petty intrigues are uninteresting, Baron. You indulge yourself, but I am not indulgent by nature. I await the full flower of your revenge, which was the purpose of your extended life, remember.

He squinted, watching the leather boys giving the waitress—the same thin, fragile blonde as that other night—a bad time. He thought of commenting on the mindless devotion to revenge that provided the feast of blood the Dark Lady had fed on lately in his homeland, but the remark died in his throat.

After all, he himself could consider with pleasure the prospect of demolishing those youthful savages—as payment for what? Mere discourtesy; but their crude arrogance had left lodged in him an inclination to teach them a hot, red lesson.

And his Lady was correct: revenge on Nicolas Griffin was certainly his purpose in pursuing first Lily Anderson and now the actress Jessamyn Croft; wasn't it? Vengeance offered such a full, rich flavor to the palate of the imagination! No wonder most people—even an "undead" person like himself, with a long, long memory—never lost a taste for it.

Certainly not with the Dark One attentively hovering to remind him of the sweetness that he sought: Griffin blood, Griffin screams, Griffin spasms of terror and agony—a parade of men in various stages of extremity passed before the eye of his memory; men he had driven to reckless desperation, to outright madness, to suicide, or whom he had dispatched personally and with pleasure.

Why shouldn't he enjoy this? They were wicked men, stubborn men, greedily withholding from him what he knew and they knew was rightfully his.

Through the plate-glass window of the cafe Cragga watched Jessamyn laughing at something one of her companions said. She threw back her head so that her thick curls sprang with life. But he knew that in her eyes the shadow of sadness still lurked, if you looked deeply enough. It was something worth searching out. This shadow provided the power behind her delicate features, for it was the stamp of her awareness of her own mortality and that of others she loved, the awareness of the passage of time and all things that lived in time.

Even now, as she sat enjoying herself with her colleagues, he noticed that she glanced occasionally at the leather boys, who crouched over their drinks at a nearby table and leered. She was wary of them, and rightly, having learned the treachery of time and flesh; he respected her for that. Denial in all its many forms was so much more common.

No, more: He admired her, for looking into death's face and willing herself to survive, and climbing back into a real, living life with all its risks. In her work she multiplied the experience of those risks manyfold, like a great warrior charging again and again into battle, and this intrigued and impressed him.

He knew from the rehearsals he had seen that in the role of Eva, as in others she must have played, she inhabited many triumphs, many failures, many griefs—in aggregate more than any one life could hold. She dared to act out these shocks and changes, she dared deliberately to subject herself to them and show the results to the world.

In his own way, of course, he, too, led many different lives—but successively, moving through centuries of time, and his performances were designed to be convincing, not enlightening. Also he had a single, driving purpose throughout, a purpose old and deep and not linked to anyone's entertainment—except, perhaps, his own, and the Dark One's.

Jessamyn's performances were true, in the deepest sense, although they were fictions. His were all lies.

If you do use her, came the distant murmur, as you say you will.

I mean to, he replied. But I do not inflict my vengeance on the innocent, as you well know. I never have, and I never will. It is not the Cragga way.

After a moment, in which a number of revelers bustled past wrapped to the ears and making a great deal of tipsy and irritating noise, the answer came: There was your uncle Georg, after the siege of that walled town in Hungary, remember—certain extreme things were done to punish the townsfolk for their resistance. Yet surely those people were guilty only of wishing to survive with their families and goods intact?

Ivo chuckled deep in his throat. Well, then, it is not my way, and as I am Cragga now—there are no others left, you tell me—it is entirely up to me to determine the definition we seek. If I do not do it, then it is not the Cragga way. What I do, is.

Then you may fail, Baron, for a whim.

He shut his eyes tightly and stood there, his shoulders bowed, his fingers clenched on one of the cold metal rods that supported the outer corners of the grocer's canopy.

A man whose history has passed away and left him behind has little left to him but whims, he answered bleakly. Apart, of course, from the thirst that sustains me. But my whims are trivial compared to yours, Lady, as you well know. The history of my homeland is made up entirely of your devouring whims, I sometimes think. It seems to me a considerable achievement, given your example, that I manage to hold to my purpose despite the lure of my whims, or the command of yours.

Well, you are young yet, Baron, and full of fancies. But I tell you, this woman is the cause of your restlessness. She puts you in more danger than you know. Do not imagine that Nicolas Griffin is a flimsy opponent, to be lightly cast down. Do not imagine that you can overcome him without effective tools. This actress is the best tool you could have, and your attentions to her will indeed bring him to you in the end. But it may be as you yourself suggested: that she needs to be in obvious danger for him to come out of hiding and face you in the open.

Leave me, Lady, he gasped in the lightless heart of his being. Leave me to my own needs. Griffin is lawfully mine, like all his line, and I do not give him up for anything. But the woman has held to her own life against heavy odds; she has won it back from death's hand with her own strength. It is true, she is more than just a weapon against my enemy, and in any case I am not careless with fine weapons. She is not simply mine to do with as I please. Not even for your amusement.

But there came no reply, and when he let go of the pole and opened his eyes and turned around, Jessamyn and her two friends had gone. Only the leather boys sat hunched over their plates, sniggering together like evil apes.

One of the store clerks had been eyeing him for some time, and now came purposefully toward him from inside the store.

Cragga felt the peremptory stirring of hunger. He turned and strode away uptown, a muscular young man with his hands in his pockets and his burning gaze avidly probing the night world before him.

Costume Call

Jessamyn's dress for the second act looked splendid—a silk gown with the skirt cut on the bias so that when she turned, it swirled like an opening flower. The fabric was a subtle shade of slate blue, embroidered at collar and cuffs with small flowers in delicate touches of pink and orange. The costumer had found the dress in a thrift shop and had cut and trimmed it for Jess's slender figure.

The costume was only basted, not yet firmly sewn, but already Jess was thinking about what kind of offer she could make to Wardrobe to buy it after the production closed. She hadn't dreamed that her first costume since the accident would be so beautiful, and she articulated her delight at every opportunity. You could never go wrong by openly appreciating work of the people on whom you depended for support onstage.

Anthony was less pleased with his gray suit, primarily because he hated the tie they had found to go with it: a hideous blast of clashing colors intended to express a degree of vulgarity that he said he preferred to try to get across with his acting, if they would be so kind as to credit him with being able to do so.

He looked terrible, haggard and yellow in the face. He said he hadn't been sleeping well: "Nerves, that's all. I've just never been able to loosen up properly on the way into a play, not since that awful night in *Ghosts* when I cracked my poor head on that damned table. And I can't help thinking about all these weird little afflictions, the Edwardian's secret demon, you know."

"Demon, shmeemon," Marie muttered under her breath as she worked on a troublesome snag that made Jessamyn's dress gape in back. A mouthful of pins didn't even slow her down. Jess wondered how many she had swallowed in her career, and if she had a magical method of popping them harmlessly out again. "He's got more trouble with his wife. Poor Mr. Sinclair, you can't help but worry about him."

"How could there be more trouble?" Jessamyn whispered. "Don't tell me she's found some serious new guy! Anthony would be heartbroken."

She glanced fondly at him, feeling a small twist of regret that she hadn't helped him to be the one to break free first, if that was what was going on, by being "someone else" for him even if only for a short time. He was a lordly-looking man even in the offending tie, and she sometimes felt a stab of regret when she saw him flirting with Anita MacNeil.

"Oh, it's been 'new guys' all over the place for both the Sinclairs," Marie grunted, half in disapproval, half admiration. "It always is, when they're going through one of their quarrels."

Jess shot a mischievous grin over her shoulder at the dresser. "So it's rupture or rapture with them, is that it?"

Marie sighed. "Never mind; they've been one of the best, longest-lasting teams in the business. No matter how bad it looks, nothing's serious for those two but each other."

No, it's a professional problem: her show is closing, she's out of work starting next week. Haven't you heard?''

"Oh no," Jess said.

Marie made a wry face. " 'Oh no' is right. Sally Sinclair is a—difficult person, let's say. Roles don't just come rushing up to her begging for her to do them, you know. Oh, here—these got back yesterday." She fished a little velvet box out of her kit and handed it to Jess.

The pendant and earrings were nested inside, cleaned up and parted from their gluey tangle.

"Are they okay?" Jess said, stroking the pendant with her finger. "I don't think the finish has come out exactly the same."

"Turn," Marie said. "Little bit to the right; that's it. Of course it's not exactly the same, but close enough. Nobody except an expert would ever notice."

"But Ivo Cragga *is* an expert, Marie!"

"An expert maybe, a damn fool for sure," the dresser said, her hands nibbling at the back of the dress like persistent mice. "No sensible person would have sent you those pieces in the first place. Of course he's a young fellow, and you never know what they'll do when they're smitten with a girl; the young ones and the old ones, they're very much alike that way.

"Now, if I were you I'd get these things back to him right away. Or give them to Lily; he's been looking in every day to see how the scrim painting is coming along. She'll see him sooner than anybody else around here."

"I'm not letting that jewelry out of my hands until I can give it all back to him personally," Jess said firmly.

"Well, I'd lock the stuff up someplace until then, if I were you," Marie said. "And I mean someplace safer than Mrs. Clausen's office. Johnny spotted our Mystery Watcher—at least we think it was him—hanging around a three-card-monte game up at the end of the block this afternoon. I went over to get a better look, but he slipped away into that bookstore across the street. I sent Johnny in after him, but it's a rabbit warren in there, you know, with all those floors and stairwells and things."

"You're sure it was him?"

"Nope, but I think it was. All *furtive* looking, if you know what I mean. Up to something. And he looked familiar, somehow, even though his outfit was different this time—a big duffle coat, camouflage pants, high-tops, one of those Maine wool hats with ear flaps."

Jess frowned at her anxiously. "Be careful, Marie, you and Johnny both. We still don't know who we're dealing with here. I hate to think of you running after some character who could turn out to be really dangerous."

"Oh, I can take care of myself," Marie said airily. "I know a few disappearing tricks of my own, if you know what I mean."

Jess caught her hand. "Just don't get overconfident, okay? I'm not sure stage magic is enough to handle a real villain, if it comes to it."

"A real villain?" Marie jeered. "In a hat with *ear flaps*?"

It was useless. Jess could see that the dresser had actually enjoyed her escapade. Why not? It had drama, after all.

"Come on, now," Marie said, "that's enough gossip and rumor for today. Let's get this finished. Nancy's beginning to lose focus; you know how she gets. This sleeve is kind of crooked, isn't it? Right side, toward the back."

"At least you don't have to cope with shoulder pads," Sinclair grumbled, coming over to scowl at himself in the mirror.

Nancy, the costumer, was a dreamy-eyed woman who somehow never heard criticism, let alone showed any sign of being wounded by it—at least not so far as Jess could see. *It must be nice,* she thought, *never to get rattled by things.*

"A little short in front," Nancy murmured, obviously talking to herself as she turned Sinclair first to one side and then another, like a mannequin she was studying in the glass. Actually, she stared at the suit that he happened to be modeling at the moment, not at him.

He snapped into a robotic imitation, swinging stiffly and all of a piece at every guiding touch. Nancy worked on, talking to herself, oblivious. Sinclair's glance met Jess's over the costumer's bent head and he offered a comical moue of resignation.

He really did look wrung-out. Jess couldn't help thinking that he might be on the verge of getting really sick. Her stomach gave a little lurch of anxiety.

She could manage with Sinclair's understudy, of course. New readings and new business, some as good as or better than what they were doing now, would undoubtedly crop up in the play, given a new actor playing Marko. Change could be invigorating.

But she had come to depend on her rapport with Anthony Sinclair, as she depended on his warmth and professionalism to carry her over her own fears about the play. Face it, she had become very fond of the older actor, and grateful to have his shoulder to cry on if she needed it, especially today.

She had come in to find xeroxed pages of the script, stained with what looked like real blood rather than a stage mixture from the prop shop, glued to the makeup mirror in her dressing room. The reflective surface was completely covered. The effect had been truly horrible, a sort of menacing threat of obliteration aimed directly at her in a most personal way, through the play itself.

Jess still felt trembly with shock. It was particularly upsetting to consider that the person who had committed this weird, ugly assault might well be the mysterious watcher. The idea of Marie and Johnny chasing after somebody with such a sick mind scared her. She could just about manage the idea of danger to herself, but danger to other people around her as well was too much.

She found herself sneaking glances at the other cast members, particularly Anita MacNeil in her slinky beige gown, and wondering how they really felt about it all. On the surface, anyway, everyone had adopted the tactic of more or less ignoring the incidents, or at any rate refusing to discuss them.

This had been Anita's idea, actually.

"If it's somebody around here," she had said, "let's not give them the satisfaction of seeing us fluttering like a flock of panicked parakeets over their asinine behavior."

Yet Jess still could not completely discount the possibility that the culprit could be Anita herself, angling for a chance to take over the part of Eva. Jess had not missed the understudy's assessing look at Eva's costume, obviously judging how the cut and color would suit her in Jess's place.

It could be any of them, that was the frustrating thing. There were always members of the cast and crew wandering in and out of the Edwardian at odd hours. Johnny couldn't be on the lookout all the time; he had other duties. They were just going to have to withstand the attacks and soldier on through.

I weathered the crash and, worse, the hospital and the therapy afterward. I can weather this, she told herself grimly.

Walter hurried in late, fighting with the jammed zipper of his old bomber jacket. While Nancy fluttered at him, fixing it, he checked the look of the costumes, praised Nancy, and still managed to make several fairly radical suggestions for changes in her handiwork. As usual, the costumer blinked, adjusted her inner vision, and sailed off on these new tacks with scarcely a tremor.

Hell, maybe *she* should be playing Eva!

When the session was over, Jess found Walter in her dressing room, watching one of the apprentices work on the defaced mirror with rags, solvent, and a razor-blade scraper.

"It's almost worth getting a new mirror," Walter growled, "but I put some money into a lock on the costume-shop door instead. Nobody has keys but Nancy and

me. I don't want any of this crap going down in there, now
that the costumes are started.''

Jess bit her lip, turning away from the mirror. The un-
sightly clumps of glued, stained paper made it look as if
something had been killed there, leaving dried and crusted
traces of the carnage. Her fear came rushing back, double
strength. For the first time, her heart quailed.

''Walter,'' she said lowly, ''do you think I should drop
out? If my being here has become a threat to the whole
production—''

''Equity contract,'' Walter said at once, ''you can't. And
anyway, I can't think of anybody else I'd accept in the
part.'' Then he grabbed Jess in an irresistible bearlike hug.
His sympathy was so welcome Jess almost burst into tears.

''Don't let it get to you, Jess.'' He patted her back clumsily. ''Listen, I'm driving you home tonight. Just as a kind
of signal, you know? We take care of our own, and any
creep who messes with you has all of us to deal with. So
me or Jack Nelson will take you home from late rehearsals
from now on, and I don't want any arguments.''

Nelson, the lighting chief, lived on the Upper West Side.
Jess thought of objecting that Jack would have to drive far
out of his way every night that he took her home. The
sound of the scraper juddering across the encrusted mirror
stilled her.

Walter rocked her a little, muttering into her hair, ''This
moron is a real glue freak, isn't he? Or she. Whoever it is,
they better watch out; if I catch them, I'll personally glue
them shut all over and then come and laugh at them every
day they get to spend in the hospital afterwards.''

Rehearsal went rockily. They were doing the big quarrel
scene in which the two major factions in the family come
to blows over conflicting claims to the emerald, while the
enemy bombardment increases. It soon became clear that
the fight choreography had become too complicated, re-
sulting in one broken chair and a nasty bruise on Anita's
knee before they were finished.

In a somber mood, Jess climbed into Walter's beat-up

Dodge, which only made it into town on very rare occasions. It smelled of cold smoke, plastic, and metal, which tonight she found oddly comforting.

"Heard from Nic?" the director said, as they swung out of the parking lot into Friday-night traffic.

"No," Jess replied, too quickly. "I've been concentrating so hard on Eva, I haven't even checked my messages or my mail."

"Well, I've heard from him." Walter sounded troubled.

Jess glanced aside at his blunt profile. His gleaming eyes were fixed on the sea of flaring brake-lights ahead. The traffic stream had to negotiate a maze of heavy machinery, striped warning cones, and temporary steel plates in the street that made a vast obstacle course of this stretch of Eighth Avenue. He did not seem inclined to expand on his news without prompting.

"Okay, I'll bite," Jess said, over the thumping of her heart. "What's he say? Where is he?"

"Well, this is a little awkward," Walter said. He was scowling, but it might only have been frustration at the cab that had just cut in front of them with inches to spare.

"Don't tell me he's got revisions to suggest, two weeks into rehearsals!" she exclaimed, in an attempt at lightness. "Nothing doing. If he wants changes at this point, he can play Eva himself."

"I told him to get in touch with you directly," Walter said, "but he said no. He called from Zagreb. It's not about the play, you see. It's more—personal."

Zagreb? A sudden suspicion dawned. "If you're going to say something scurrilous about Ivo Cragga, Walter, I don't think I want to hear it."

"You and Nic should get married right away!" Walter exclaimed. "You're reading his mind and he's not even here. Look, this is kind of—You want to stop for a drink or something?"

"And park where, for heaven's sake?" His hesitation was pushing her to the limit of her patience. "Keep going, this is fine. So what's he got to say, our shy playwright who can't even stay in the country to see his own play mounted? And how does he know that Cragga's been hanging around, anyway? Has he been checking in with you, Walter? Asking about me?''

Now Walter glanced at her, his homely face sagging into a reproachful expression. "Nic always asks about you. As for Cragga, his name came up in connection with the scrim design. I told Nic how great it's looking, and he said who did the design, and—''

"But how does he know Ivo's name in the first place?''

"Because he's heard about him," Walter said with a sigh, "over there. In Europe. Our generous consultant has a reputation, it seems, but I'm sorry to say, Jess, it's not for generosity.''

Jess slumped against the passenger-side door, bowed under a weight of dismal foreboding. She had been having odd, uneasy dreams lately, which she had always been prone to when a role really began to take hold. Her sleep suffered. Probably she looked almost as worn-out as Sinclair did, but nobody dared say so. One thing was sure: she was too tired for this discussion.

The heater in Walter's car was broken. She kept her hands stuffed into her coat pockets, and her nose and ears felt numb. She wished she had taken a cab.

Virtue would of course refuse to listen to whatever dirt Nic had dug up on the foreigner. But it wasn't Jessamyn's staunch and virtuous side that was engaged by the mention of Cragga's name; it was something much more primitive, and less concerned with ethics—something fascinated. If there were things to be known about Ivo Cragga, she had to know them.

"Well, spit it out, then," she said. "Just what kind of a reputation are we talking about here?''

"Ever see a movie called *The Third Man*?" Walter asked.

"Walter, *everybody's* seen *The Third Man*. Postwar Vienna, nice Joseph Cotton gets tangled up with rotten blackmarketeer Harry Lime, played by Orson Welles before he got fat. Harry Lime is scum who deals in penicillin and other critical stuff for his own profit.''

She stopped and stared straight ahead, feeling a flush of anger rising in her neck. "Come on. You're not telling me that Ivo Cragga is a modern-day Harry Lime!''

"Well, maybe I wouldn't go that far,'' Walter said, drumming unhappily on the steering wheel with his thick fingers. He peered ahead at the Columbus Circle traffic.

"But Nic would?''

"Sorry, Nic what?''

"Nic thinks Ivo Cragga is some kind of war racketeer, like Harry Lime?''

At the next red light, which was always a long one, Walter sat back with a sigh. "Nic said to please talk to you, because I told him Cragga's been coming around the theater so much. Folks are saying Lily's really gone on him, poor thing. But people with their eyes open know it's you Cragga comes for, not Lily. Did you see him watching you rehearse today, from the back of the theater?''

"So what did Nic say, exactly?'' Did everybody in the theater today but her know that the damned man had been watching? She flashed on the touch of Cragga's muscular fingers, and his explorative, arrogant kiss in the coffee shop. No wonder she had felt nervous doing that scene today— as if somebody besides the familiar members of the company was studying her performance and registering every misstep and every verbal flub.

Damn Cragga anyway, for insinuating himself into her work situation like this! It would serve him right if—If what? If she found out that he was some kind of crook, a war criminal, even? But that would be a problem for her, not for him, surely! He must not mind being a Harry Lime, if he was one. The knowledge would only be painful for her. Did she really want to know anything that Nic had deliberately gone and dug up on him, anyway?

She felt swamped by a wave of resentment, not against Cragga but against Nic. How could he stoop to sniffing around in another man's past, out of jealousy over someone he didn't even want for himself?

He couldn't. It was impossible, at least for the Nic she knew.

. But what Walter said next reminded her forcefully of the Nic she didn't know.

"People talk about Cragga," Walter said, driving east on Fifty-seventh with the hair-raising élan of an old-time cabbie, "all along the borders of the old Eastern bloc countries. According to Nic, they say he's a—a sort of scavenger, a parasite. He makes trips over there looking for desperate people with old family treasures to sell. Then he buys cheap and runs the stuff out to high-end Western markets, where he sells at inflated prices and pockets a huge profit.

"Nic compared him to some kind of South American tomb-looter, trading in the national heritage of people who don't have a dime. All they have to sell are priceless antiques and art objects that were frozen under communist rule for decades. Even ikons and church vestments from inside Russia itself—well, what used to be Russia—are up for grabs."

Jessamyn said heatedly, "And everywhere Nic goes people come running up to him and telling him these stories, right? About somebody Nic has never met. Walter, I don't know much about what's going on here, but what I do know is pretty disgusting."

Walter shifted his big hands on the wheel. "Look, I've got nothing against Cragga. As far as I'm concerned, he's done the production a big favor, donating his time and his talent for the scrim—Oh, drive your damn car, will you up there?

"But there's more. Nic sounded really worried, and to tell the truth, he's got me worried, too. There's some other stuff that's more—well, scarier, Jess. He just wants to make sure you know."

"So," she said with a bravado she did not feel, "you've gone this far. Don't stop now. Tell me."

Once he had turned off into her street and double-parked outside her building, he told her.

Baron Ivo von Cragga was said to have had a hand in the disappearances of several people, among them three young women from Budapest. The Baron had been seen poking around at the site of a particularly gruesome, ethnically motivated massacre on the Albanian border two years ago; and many people along the western margins of Russia clammed up completely at the mention of his name.

Except one old man in a graveyard who had had a good deal to say.

"Nic says this old guy enjoyed telling him this stuff. It's got to be, oh, you know, just a tall tale trotted out to thrill the nosy foreigner. But a few other people say they've heard similar things, and some of the locals that Nic has run into seem to really believe it. Which says as much for the stresses they've all been under as it does about Ivo von Cragga, obviously."

What they said was that Cragga was the last of a noble line that had died out four hundred years ago, and that he roamed the world vengefully searching for the descendants of a man who had injured his family in those ancient days.

No, not just his family: he pursued the descendants of a man who had harmed *him*. Word was that Cragga himself was hundreds of years old, that he was the man who had been wronged in the first place. They said that Ivo von Cragga was a monster, a relic, a living dead man from ages past.

They said he was a vampire.

Jessamyn laughed, producing an unlovely squawk. "Walter, I hate to spoil this fabulous story, but Ivo Cragga walks around in daylight, he casts a reflection and a shadow, and I've seen him eat carpaccio at the Two White Cats."

"I'm just telling you what Nic has heard," Walter said doggedly. "And carpaccio is raw beef, right, sliced very thin? Bloody, even?"

"So now he's a ghoul, or a werewolf or whatever, as

well as a vampire? Or maybe a cannibal? I think I'll go upstairs, Walter, this is too much for me. Thanks for the lift, okay?'' Jess grabbed the door handle.

Walter caught her arm. "Wait, Jess, please. I *told* Nic he should talk to you himself. He may believe this crap, a little bit anyway, but I know delirium when I hear it. Vampires, I ask you! The point is, what kind of a guy must this von Cragga really be, to inspire rumors like these?''

"Oh, balls," Jessamyn snapped. She began to struggle with the doorlatch, which like everything on Walter's car was only intermittently functional: and not at the moment, it seemed. But she had to get out of the car. It felt like a padded cell. It felt like a funeral coach. It felt like a coffin.

She giggled, helplessly.

"I know; it sounds crazy to me too," Walter said. "To tell you the truth, Jess, I'm afraid Nic's lost it again, like when he told that story about some woman he saw in the road before the crash. It scares me that he's over there wandering around by himself." He looked at her with pleading eyes, half his face luridly illuminated by the glare of the streetlight overhead.

"Walter, that's crap," Jess said wearily. "There was nothing wrong with Nic's mind then, and he's not crazy now, either. You think a crazy man could have written *The Jewel?*" Here she was, defending (as she had been for months after the accident) someone who, capital A, didn't even love her anymore and, capital B, might really be cracking up for all she knew.

Walter cleared his throat diffidently. "I know, I know, it doesn't make sense. But I can't help worrying. If I didn't have this show on my hands, I swear I would get on a plane and go over there right now, and drag him home myself."

I have got to get out of here, Jess thought. *I need to think.*

Her breath misted in front of her. Her toes felt frozen. Her mind felt frozen. Her heart thundered, hot and heavy, in her chest.

"Walter, I—" I what? What in the world was she supposed to say in response to all this? And in the light of what Nic had said to her before he'd left—in the light of the tale Cragga himself had told her, about the cursed gem called the Ruby Tear—in the light of Nic's play about a besieged family whose virtue and honor was compromised by an ancient crime—what in the world could she think and believe, and what could she say to solid old Walter?

She said, "Thanks, Walter; good night," and left him before he could say any more.

It was only after she was upstairs in her own kitchen, heating a can of chicken broth and scraping the disgusting blue mold off some venerable cottage cheese, that she allowed herself to consider the question: What if Cragga was indeed the saboteur at the Edwardian, not to help Nic force her out of the show, but out of some mad spite or vengeance of his own? People didn't have to be vampires to be evil, manipulative, and deranged.

How big a step could it be for an arrogant young man like Cragga (she believed without question that he was an aristocrat, at least) to go from maneuvering desperate refugees out of their pathetic possessions to trying to sabotage Nic's play? Maybe Nic had made an enemy of this man somehow, years ago in Bosnia when he was writing about the war there.

Sunday was an Equity day off. Cragga had offered to spend the afternoon and evening running lines with her to help her perfect her memorization of Eva's big speech in Act One. Was she brave enough to confront him with any of this? How about merely being in the same room with him, after what Walter had said?

She took the earrings and the brooch (which she kept at home now, where they were subject only to the dangers of simple burglary) from their velvet case. She laid them out on her pillow where she could look closely at them by the light of her reading lamp: each piece was a masterwork of fine black iron wire twisted into vinelike curlicues, a model of painstaking craftsmanship.

If Ivo von Cragga had wheedled these lovely pieces out of the hands of some impoverished refugee who was only trying to buy safety from one brand or another of "ethnic cleansing," then he was damn well going to give them back.

Or at any rate, he couldn't make her keep them!

But as she lovingly handled the lovely, delicate earrings, she noticed how quickly her heart beat when she thought of Cragga.

A man who might be—a vampire?

Ridiculous!

Delicious, thrilling, amazing—ridiculous.

She surprised herself with the depth of anticipation she felt for Sunday.

Thugs

—◆—

You can only run lines for so long before you start training in your repeated mistakes instead of the corrections. Besides, Jess found the difference between Cragga's dry, accented locution of Marko's lines and the way her mind had recorded Anthony Sinclair reading the same lines very distracting.

Sinclair's reading—beautifully paced and shaped, like a singer's delivery of a poetic lyric—was of course much better suited to a stage, or rather to an audience that must hear words delivered from a stage all the way to the back of a theater balcony. But Cragga's approach lent an attractive level of ironic self-awareness to the material. Jess didn't want Eva to start responding to that quality, and then not get it to respond to in performance with her actual leading man.

And she wanted to be outside, in public, when she asked Ivo Cragga about the rumors Nic had picked up about him in Europe. Well, about some of them; there were limits.

She was not about to ask the man if he really was a *vampire*.

The weather had turned warmer. Jess enjoyed the brisk walk downtown alongside the low stone wall that edged Central Park. The air was moist and rich-smelling, almost as if spring had arrived.

It was an illusion, of course—there would be more storms and freezing days before the winter was over—but meanwhile the air was bright and bracing without that raw winter edge. People moved about on the streets with the buoyancy of cave-dwellers unexpectedly let out into the sun.

"A week and a half till we open," she said, swinging energetically along at Cragga's side. "That's why I'm burbling today! I hope you don't mind—it's the tension, a good tension really—you can't make a show go without a little bit of terror gnawing at the actors' hearts, you know—and of course this break in the weather—"

"I understand," he said. "I feel it also. Did Miss Anderson tell you, she will have a small credit printed in the program for me, for my help with the scrim design? You will see it soon. Little as I did, Miss Anderson is very appreciative."

Jess said that appreciation was due, she was sure; but she couldn't help thinking how pallid Lily was looking lately. Yet here was this manifestly corporeal young fellow, broad-shouldered and robust, matching her stride-for-stride in full daylight.

He could have been a champion European footballer, a precocious EC tycoon, a charismatic and vibrant leader in some ex-Soviet region hustling for a prosperous Western-style independence. In a word, he was nothing like those shadowy creatures of myth you saw in the movies, screaming in sunlight and melting to sludge on the spot.

Poor Nic, crazy Nic! And to use Walter to carry his loony messages!

How was she to ask? What was there to ask about, really? She was damned if she would be distracted from the delights of the day by rumors of legendary monsters and hints of doom.

Instead she talked about the play and the character of Eva. She was by now deep into thoughts of how this woman, raised in her family's atmosphere of self-righteous greed, power, and privilege, had been shocked by her travels (and a tragic affair with a man of the enemy party) into a very different view.

Cragga offered little comment. He listened. He bought her coffee and little shrimp dumplings from the street vendors whose metallic carts, clustered on the corners along midtown Fifth Avenue, emitted mouth-watering steams and smokes. She leaned side by side with him on the railing of the sunken ice-skating rink at Rockefeller Center while she ate the greasy, delicious street food. He said he had already eaten.

She sighed gustily and licked her flavorful fingers, watching a girl in tights practice swift little jumps under the eyes of a skating teacher in a striped parka.

"What a life," she said, grinning at Cragga. "You do whatever you like all day, look at pretty jewelry, go to the theater, stroll in the city—is that all there is to being a dealer in collectibles?"

"No," he said. "As you guess, that is not all."

"I thought not." There was something profoundly sad about the set of his mouth; she backed off at once, angry with herself for having given in to her newly sharpened curiosity about him. Briskly she went on. "I think you're homesick. Why else would you keep looking in on rehearsals of a play about your part of the world that's not even written by a native?"

"Oh, homesick—" He made a dismissive gesture. "The home I had is long since gone and I am a practical man, Miss Croft. I do not hanker after what no longer exists. Everything has its natural term and then is replaced by something else; how else could the world move along? But it is a strain sometimes, living in such a different place, at a faster tempo, and making a new life here as I go along."

"That's what people do in America," Jess said. "This is a country of stories and dreams."

He smiled. "Oh, yes. There is that youngster down there, dreaming, no doubt, a story of skating in the Olympic Games. And you, Miss Croft," he added, turning to study her with a sleepy, cat-green gaze, "what do you dream for your own future? Let me guess.

"I foresee a move with the play to a grander theater, and a long run, and then perhaps a part in the movie, and another film beyond that. Then comes relocation to California, protestations that the stage is still your first and last love, an award or two, a marriage or two, a child or two, and then maybe a secondary career as speaker for some worthy charity. Last comes an increasing number of quiet days in a rose garden in Pasadena, between sessions at your computer where you write your memoires."

She was speechless; he had described her mother's ambitions for her, and somewhere beneath her own grander flights of fancy, a more realistic version of her own hopes, too. Something must have shown in her face—surprised recognition, chagrin at being seen through so easily, embarrassment at how paltry it all sounded.

"Not so far off the mark, I think," he said, and she frowned and turned away. He had no business sounding so smug and amused about it.

"And not so hard to come up with," she said with spirit, "considering all that you know about me."

He backed up a step and bowed slightly. "Forgive me. I only made a speculation. I'm sorry—is it rude of me to ask about your own expectations?"

"No," she said dubiously. "But it takes my breath away to have a whole future laid out for me like—like a recipe!" Come to think of it, she hadn't liked it much when her mother had done it, either. Now she smiled with wry fondness at the memory.

Cragga laughed, a rolling, purring sound, like a lion laughing. "I am forgiven?"

"Maybe."

"You are annoyed," he said, "because I omitted the most important thing, or so all your songs say. I left out the love."

"So what about these two marriages of mine? Serial ones, I hope, not side by side. Bigamy is a crime in this country."

"Serially, of course; and in my summary, you marry for the stability a successful life in the arts requires, and because these husbands are strong and sympathetic, and you think you love them; serially. Beginning perhaps with your leading man, Mr. Sinclair—"

She rolled her eyes. "Not Anthony, thanks, not even if he weren't married already."

Cragga was silent, leaning over the railing and following the progress of a tubby man in a topcoat and a woolen beret who skated flawless circles with his hands clasped behind his back. "See that little old man, who learned to skate in Europe, I am sure? Soon he will retire to Florida, perhaps, or Arizona, like so many others like him. Meanwhile yet another wave of refugees will creep up onto these shores as Europe descends into deeper divisions and harsher wars, I am afraid."

"You can't know that," she protested.

"I am part of the beginning of that wave. But to return to you, my first American friend—Can I regard you in that light? It means much to me—to return to you: no old history binds you. You may go another way than the way of my 'recipe.'

"There is a man you love, a man you have loved for some time, a man for love of whom you might allow your life to be changed in any number of directions and be grateful for them all—wherever they might lead."

"What?" she said, blinking up at him in surprise. She managed a rather hollow laugh. "And you call yourself hard-hearted! You're a wild-eyed romantic, Ivo, and you're letting your imagination run away with you."

"Bravely said," he responded, "but I know better, and I can prove it, if you will permit—?"

"*Permit*," she thought, charmed by his exotic courtesy. She was supposed to be asking him questions about his past, to lay to rest certain wild suspicions and tales. Instead he had sailed into this breathtaking voyage across her future, and of course she would "permit." She had no idea of just where she would draw the line, and what she would *not* permit. And she only knew one way to find out.

Could he read in her eyes and the language of her posture her impulse to lean against him and drink his breath and his warmth and his scent? Did he, too, feel the pull of the strengthening threads of attraction between them?

Well, why fight it? She was no one's property, she reminded herself with a flash of anger, and no man's fool, to be scared off by lurid tales from dubious sources.

Cragga took her hand and began drawing off her glove. Laughing, she pulled back. "Wait a minute, woah. I admit that it's an unusually warm day for winter, but it's still too cold for taking off any clothes."

"Like most Central Europeans, if you are to believe what we claim," he said suavely, "I have gypsy blood. Let me read your palm. You will not deny me the chance to show off my poor, small talent for you?"

So they ended up sitting on a bench in a vest-pocket park on Fifty-seventh Street where the cutting edge of the breeze couldn't reach them, while Ivo Cragga pored over her extended hand. "Here, see, the linkage of the heart line in love, true love that is deep and lasting and that overcomes all shallower involvements, with someone very close—close, I think, in work, in profession. You have already met the man who could reshape your life—long, oh long before I came along; sad for me.

"I make no pitch for myself, Miss Croft. What am I, after all, but a bit of wreckage that has floated this way on the tides of struggle washing out from my poor homeland? I make my little living, I can afford a gesture of appreciation toward beauty now and then when my heart compels, but in the long run I have little to offer someone like you.

"No, I only envy this fellow, who—it shows here—

seems to have no sense of his own good fortune but hides away from it, leaving you to the eager claims of others.''

She had an almost irresistible urge to reach out with her free hand and touch the burnished richness of his hair, as vivid and luxuriant as the thick coat of a fox. Her other hand lay lightly in his broad palm, half covering an old scar she saw there in bitter white.

"There is someone," she murmured. "Or there was."

"The author of your play, I think," he said. "Nicolas Griffin."

She pulled her hand away. "Why do you keep asking about Nic?"

"Please," he said. "The hand shows love lines in the expressive zone, something to do with the arts, so I thought, a writer—"

"Like hell," she said. He had touched nerves so raw that she couldn't help lashing out at him. She felt caught off-guard, invaded and used. What in the world had she been dreaming of? Some of what Walter had said about him must be true. She felt like a fool, an infatuated girl betrayed by a sophisticated foreigner, the quintessential American naif who was putty in the hands of a smooth, Old World rogue.

"You're up to something, something to do with Nic," she accused. "I'm just some kind of—of pathway to him for you. All this help and friendliness is just a ploy. I've heard about you—I've heard enough to quit playing the patsy in whatever scam you're running here."

He stood, thrusting his hands deep into his coat pockets, and stared at her, suddenly steely-eyed and haughty. "So, you have been asking questions about me? Why not ask me to my face?"

"Good," she snapped. "I will. Is it true that you're a—a smuggler and a profiteer, preying on refugees and war victims?"

"It is true," he said coldly, "that I am in a position to help many who need a conduit to people with money, so that they can trade pretty objects for the necessities of life. Is this a crime?''

''Probably not, but it's not particularly nice, and the opportunities to cheat and abuse people would be tempting to a saint. Frankly, I'm beginning to think you're a pirate, and a liar, and a very slick operator, *Baron* von Cragga!''

She was transported with outrage, a burst of emotion that obliterated the smaller bloom of fearful questions deep in her heart: was he also Nic's enemy, and maybe her enemy too, and maybe—maybe the other, unthinkable thing as well?

She had an unreasoning urge to run away from him, but felt that if she allowed her fear to show she would be lost. Predators are excited by their prey's fear, hadn't she read that somewhere?

He said in a low voice, ''These are matters you know nothing about—the wretchedness that displaced and besieged people live in; what it means to be what you call me, 'Baron,' and go-between, and peddler. All of which I am, since you ask it—to my face, finally. But *you* have no idea what any of this means.''

''Good-bye, then,'' she said, standing abruptly and finding to her dismay that her knees were ridiculously shaky. ''I'm sorry, I don't have time to stay around while you enlighten me. I have a play to prepare for in my own foolish, inadequate way, so you'll just have to excuse me.''

She rushed away toward Fifth Avenue. The winter sun was setting and not many people were on the streets. No buses were in sight, and the cabs were few and all fully occupied. She looked over her shoulder, afraid he would be following her, afraid he would not. She didn't see him. Bursting with confusion and warring emotions, she walked quickly across town, longing for the simple, dependable walls of her own rooms.

Close to home, on a quiet side street grown blustery with evening wind, she passed the mouth of a delivery alley between her building and the adjacent one. A tall iron gate usually blocked the mouth of this service entry.

Tonight the gate hung open, and as she hurried by, quick hands reached out and snatched her into the darkness with a suddenness and violence that left her sucking vainly for air to scream with.

Someone pinned her against his chest, with his arm tight across her throat. Another closed in, breathing hard, hissing breaths as he fended off her frantic kicks. Something flashed from his upraised fist: a blade, keen and pale.

She uttered only strangled gasps as she twisted in her captor's grasp with the convulsive strength of panic. The knife whipped harmlessly past her face, but hard fingers dragged her head back by the hair, immobilizing her. The man behind her snarled, "Take it easy, you want to cut my damn ear off?"

"Hurry up, somebody's coming!" came a whispered warning from nearby—a female voice. With incredulous horror Jess saw the glint of silver eyebrow-rings as the lookout at the mouth of the alley turned her head. It was the girlfriend of the two leather boys who held Jess trapped between the high, blind walls where no one could see or hear what happened.

Jess croaked wildly and kicked with all her might, snapping her knee up into the body of the boy with the knife. He turned and blocked the blow with his hip, and the blade swept up again, toward her face. Flooded with fear too strong for thought, she writhed and strained to turn away despite the agony of her hair that the other held fast.

Impossible things happened, one right after the other. Close in front of her staring eyes, the hand that held the weapon seemed to explode open with the fingers splayed wide. She heard a guttural cry of pain, and the blade flew into space and hit cement with a faint ringing sound.

The other man gasped and shoved her forward, reeling away from him. Jess staggered to the opposite wall and turned, breathless and stupid with shock.

A figure dense as ink stood holding her captor overhead at the full stretch of his arms, gripping him at belt and collar. For an instant, the suspended punk threshed arms and legs in nightmarish slow motion. He uttered a gargling wail as he was swung through the air and released as if from a catapult. Out of sight in the darkness, he landed with a crashing impact.

Jess gaped, excited and terrified, her body tingling and her mind wide and uncritical like a child's.

She knew Ivo von Cragga by the sweep of his brazen hair, the glint of his tilted eyes, and the swaggering swirl of his coatskirts as he backed a step and swung one foot forward. There was a terrible, ripe sound of impact. She saw the lift and the flopping arms of the figure sprawled below him on the floor of the alley: the one who had had the knife.

Von Cragga stooped over him, destructive energy evident in every line of his body.

Jess found her voice. "The lookout's gone. She'll bring people."

He glanced at her, a flash of tigerish teeth and eyes, and bent deeply over the writhing punk. All doubt of his true nature vanished. She thought he was going to feed right in front of her. She gagged silently and clutched at the bricks behind her for support.

But he only slapped the face of the leather boy with a wide, hard swing of his hand, and spoke to him harshly: "Who sent you against this lady? Tell me now, or I rip the face off your skull. Hurry up."

Jess heard a whimpering reply, a plea, sobs.

"The name," Cragga snarled. "Quick!"

More whimpering, faint sibilants in words Jess could not make out. She felt dizzy and sick, and almost fell, but someone caught her, someone held her up. *Shock*, she thought, deeply disappointed in herself. *I am going to faint*.

She was walking, half carried by a companion, toward her own building. The vampire—what else but a supernatural monster could have taken on and beaten two thugs armed with knives, and thrown one of them bodily through the air?—the vampire von Cragga knew where she lived.

Sensations washed over her in rapid succession: headlights passing, a dog barking somewhere, hands seizing her purse and rummaging impatiently through it, the stale warm smell of the foyer, the steep, steep stairs. She thought the stairs would never end. He fumbled at the apartment door, suddenly, oddly clumsy.

"Let me." She took the keys from his hand that was smeared, she saw, with dark blood.

Somehow she opened the door but could do nothing further—her legs would not obey her.

Without turning on the light he picked her up and carried her, held tightly to his broad chest, over to the big chair by the living-room windows. He groaned a little, straightening up. She blacked out.

When she woke, there were still no lights on in the apartment, but she knew he was still there.

"Ivo? What happened?"

"One of your colleagues, unable to drive you away with stupid tricks, hired those savages to drive you off."

"A knife," she gulped, shivering violently. "Jesus! They came at me with a knife!"

"It was a straight razor."

She gasped involuntarily and cried, "They tried to cut my face!"

Silence.

"Who would do that?" She punched the arm of the chair in impotent rage and pain. "I don't know people who would do a thing like that, I don't work with people like that!"

A creaking sound came as he moved, shifted his weight.

"What time is it?" she said.

"Late," he murmured. "The bitch-thug has of course not gone to the police. She is off saving herself, no doubt, so I think we are secure here for now. Jessamyn, she hurt me. I must lie down awhile."

"Hurt you?" She squinted woozily, seeing more than she had before now that her eyes were used to the scant illumination from the streetlights outside, the dim reflections of headlights gliding across the ceiling. "How could she hurt you?"

A beat of silence went by, two beats. "She had an ice pick."

"My God," Jess croaked, shoving herself up out of the chair with fierce energy. He was just a man, of course, what else could he be? And he was wounded, he needed help. She wondered if she wasn't sliced up herself but too numb to know it, and at the thought she was afraid she would be sick to her stomach.

Be like Eva: toughened by crises, able to drive beyond her own needs and even her limitations when necessary. No: *Be* Eva. She tottered closer and let him take her hand and guide it to the torn place on his shirt. A kind of thick welt throbbed on the hot skin beneath. "Here," he said.

There was no blood. His shirt was dry. How could there be no blood?

She led him into the bedroom. He leaned on her now, and he was heavy; the bed creaked loudly when he sat on it. She turned on the bedside lamp and helped him get out of his coat, jacket, and shirt. His torso was smooth-skinned, thick with muscle, and tracked with the red weals of old wounds.

A fighter, she thought; barons led soldiers to war, in the days when the title meant something functional. No wonder he talks confidently about violence: he knows it well, its stories are written all over his body.

She wanted to run her palms over his chest and along the strapping of muscle encasing his ribs and down the plates of his belly. This was not the sculpted musculature of the gym or even the dojo, but the coiled, packed power of a body that had been tested and strained in hand-to-hand fighting from an early age. It was beautiful the way heroic statuary is beautiful, but poignant, too, because it spoke of a life without anything resembling true childhood and the freedoms of childhood that modern people took for granted.

He had probably had a sword in his hand from the age of six. She wondered what rage and embarrassment it must cost him, to be hurt like this by a work-tool in the hand of a mere girl!

But there was no blood. Looking down at that war-marked torso, she thought wonderingly, *So it's all true? Can he really be a man out of another time, preserved by some unbelievable, dark magic?*

"What can I do?" she said, out of her infuriating helplessness and ignorance. She was not Eva after all; she had never witnessed violence worse than a boy knocked off his bicycle by a delivery truck on Third Avenue.

And her own hands, flayed by flying shards of Nic's windshield. Nic should be here, he knew more about such things. He had been on battlefields himself.

"I need more light," she said, and when Cragga did not reply she snapped on the table lamp beside the bed.

His face looked bluish white. Dark stains of exhaustion and pain seemed to spread slowly beneath his closed eyes. Exploring gingerly, she found again the ugly puncture wound under his lower left ribs, sealed now as if with swelling but bloodless still.

"Ivo, what should I do?" she whispered, sitting beside him on the bed. "Does this need bandaging, or disinfectant? Something?"

He shielded his eyes with his forearm. "Make it dark again, please," he said. "Just sit with me a little."

She snapped off the lamp and sat there, her hands folded uselessly in her lap and tears sliding silently down her cheeks. "Can I get anything, bring anyone?"

"No."

"Are you dying?"

"No."

"But you should be," she said in a strained voice. "There should be blood, you should be begging for a doctor, asking to go to a hospital . . ." Her voice died away. She heard only her own panting breath. "Nicolas says there are people in Europe who think you're a vampire."

He sighed. "This makes things easier for me. What they

say is true, even though they are mistaken about many of the details.''

"She really hurt you," Jess said stupidly. She couldn't free her thoughts from some sort of slow, sludgy thickness that made them feel clotted and coiled. "She really stabbed you, that punkette. But you're a vampire, so you're not going to die."

"I will heal. At least, I always have before. But I am weakened. No one must come, no police, no little leather-armored vermin with razors and ice picks. So we cannot stay here."

"But—"

He caught her wrist in his powerful fingers. "You have an enemy, and the enemy knows where you live; but not where *I* live. In a little while, we will find a taxicab, and we will go to my apartment."

She had an enemy. Ivo von Cragga admitted to being a vampire. One of these things she could face right now, but not both.

"What enemy?" Jess said. "That kid told you who sent him after me. Who was it?"

No answer.

"Ivo, they were going to cut my face, or maybe worse. I've got to know: Who sent them?"

"Don't ask me this."

Nic didn't want her in his play, but Nic was in Europe. Nic was crazy, or not crazy, or half crazy and half sane— could it be him? She couldn't live another moment without knowing, one way or the other.

"Tell me the name."

After a long moment of silence he said quietly, "Anthony Sinclair. I am sorry."

The knot of tension in Jess's chest finally dissolved, and with it the solid sense of community she had always felt in the theater. Away drained all of the good, warm feeling of belonging where her talents fitted her to be, among people who understood and respected her work, among equals all dedicated to the same cause; all selfless, when you came right down to it, in service to the play itself.

All that solicitude, all those suggestions that she think about getting out; now she realized what Sinclair had been doing. All those nasty tricks, most of them not really dangerous but designed to cut the ground from under her feet until she had no firm place left to stand.

She could almost despise Sinclair for the paltriness of the means he had chosen. Why not just murder her at the start and be done with it? Didn't he have the guts?

Apparently not, at any rate not until her stubborn refusal to flee from his secret persecutions made him desperate. And all the time he had been so sympathetic, so supportive, so full of fond concern! Taking her to his apartment that night after Whitely's party—would he really have slept with her if she'd invited him, knowing what he was doing to drive her out of the play?

Well, he was an actor, wasn't he? Someone capable of behaving very differently from the way he really felt, someone who could throw himself into any part. Someone able to take her in completely.

But *why*?

Though she could not begin to piece together a motive for Sinclair's attacks on her, it never occurred to her to doubt the truth of what Cragga said. Once the words were out, she was sure it was the right answer: a monstrous answer from the mouth of a wounded monster.

She couldn't understand where her path had veered into this eerie, sinister territory of shadows and betrayals. How would she ever make her way out again into the plain light of day? Worn to her limit and stretched too tight to bear, she began at last to sob.

The man who was a vampire said nothing, but lay still and held her hand.

The Vampire's Lair

$\blacklozenge$

His apartment was over a carpet dealer's on Madison Avenue, in a stolid building with a plain facade in clay-colored brick. There was no doorman, no awning, no marble-floored lobby. This was a commercial building on the ground floor, its unimposing entrance a locked plate-glass door set between two shops. The foyer held a wall of mailboxes, a table for packages, a tiny elevator, and a fake marble urn next to the bottom flight of the fire stairs.

They took the elevator up, cramped together in very close quarters. Jess was horrified by the trembling she could see now in his lips, his hands. She refused to think about the prospect of his collapse there in that coffinlike space.

But he lurched out of the elevator under his own steam, and moved painfully down the carpeted corridor to his door. Leaning on her shoulder, he unlocked the deadbolt.

"It came furnished," he said, "and I rarely entertain."

He was apologizing for the unexceptional breakfront and

dining table, the sofa and the leatherette armchairs in the living room with the low teak coffee table. The small kitchen was spotless, clearly unused except for a wine rack in the corner and bottled water in the fridge. A thin layer of dust filmed the bare countertops.

Geraniums crowded in leggy clumps from two pots on the kitchen windowsill. All the other windows had dark, floral-patterned drapes, drawn to cut out the sun.

Flowers. The vampire kept pots of flowers in his apartment. *This is crazy, crazy, crazy; I am dreaming or out of my mind.*

"You expected Gothic furniture," he remarked as he sank onto a long couch in the living room with a grateful groan. "You want to see dusty tapestries and lugubrious portraits, maybe a suit of armor in the corner? You are a hundred years too late. It took me that long to grow out of nostalgia for the past, but I did. It brought great freedom, to learn that I need only functional shelter, an occupation, and the appearance of a normal life. You have no nobility in this modern world, and if you did it would mean nothing, so one might as well live as others do."

"Why flowers?" she said, wandering into the kitchen. The dirt in the geranium pots was satisfactorily moist. He took care of his plants.

"We had gardens in the old castle at Craggenheim, terraced gardens with mossy steps. I spent much time in those gardens, recovering from wounds, fevers, bellyaches from eating bad food."

Jess came back and perched on the arm of the sofa. "You had a castle? An apartment must be quite a comedown. Do you miss that life?"

"Jessamyn," he said in a small voice, "I am cold."

She got up and drew his overcoat over him, tucking the collar around his neck. Eyes shut, he added faintly, "I don't miss the wounds, the fevers, no. But I miss the sense of certainty. Can you understand? We knew who we were, and what God wanted us to do, and where we would go when life ended, depending on how we had lived and whether we were shriven or not just before death. Not a bad life for people who for the most part did not live long enough to truly mature."

She was quiet, considering the painful irony of his situation: a man who had enjoyed the sort of circumscribed, short-term existence he described had been drawn into a tremendously prolonged lifetime. He had already had more time than anybody could possibly need, to mature and grow old, very old indeed.

"How old were you?" she said. "When that life ended for you?"

"Oh, seventeen, eighteen," he sighed. "I don't remember. Only that it was a shocking disgrace that I was not long since married and a father! But there had been a break with one family after endless negotiations, and another bride chosen for me died suddenly, so there was nothing to keep me at home. I went off to war when I could, while my parents cast about for some other suitable match for me. It was hard in such tumultuous times, though."

"Weren't you lonely, if all your friends were already married and had families?"

"All my friends were soldiers, and we shared the 'love life,' as you call it now, of soldiers when we were in the field together. Don't ask for the details, you won't like them. Suffice it to say there was plenty to be forgiven by a priest, when we could find one. Are you shocked?"

She hesitated, then admitted, "Yes, I am."

"I was an arrogant roughneck in those days. But at least when I killed a man, it was hand-to-hand and for serious reasons."

Jess stared angrily at him. "What reasons? Better ones than ours?"

The long, thick lashes rested for a moment on his cheeks; then she saw the glint of his open eyes again, and he said wearily, "The same ones: property, privilege, religion. But it was not so—so calculated as now, or so complex. Jessamyn, in peacetime we farmed and hunted. When enemies left their own farming and hunting to threaten us, we fought them. Then all those who were left thanked God to be still alive and returned to farming and hunting, for the living must eat or die.''

She felt tears in her eyes. ''You must have been older. You don't look seventeen, Ivo!''

He checked a motion that had been intended, she thought, for a shrug. ''Well, I have lived a long time since. I have been—seasoned, if not exactly aged. You cannot see all that I have seen and show nothing in your face, I think.''

Her mouth was dry and she felt her muscles tense to flee, but her terror had a blunted edge. She was getting used to the idea of what he was, though her body still wanted to escape. She intertwined her fingers and made herself sit still. ''A vampire is supposed to be a—a revenant, someone who dies and comes back to life. Did you really die?''

''Yes, I died.''

''What was it like?''

''Not like what the priests had threatened and promised.'' He laughed, coughed, groaned. ''Do you know the effects of the anesthetic gas used by dentists? It was something like that: a tingling feeling, a sense of suspension, weightlessness, and distance, but at the same time a very close, sharp awareness of the throes of the body. But it just didn't matter enough to try to do anything about it, even if there had been something to be done.

''And then some drifting, darkness, confusion—and waking again with the soreness in the limbs of having been trampled by warhorses, and the beginnings of a hunger that has been with me ever since.''

She sat mute, shivering.

''I saw no dark passages, no angels, no pure white light, if that is what you are asking,'' he added, ''but then, this was no normal death. I worry now and then about how it will be when I come to truly die. I pray sometimes still—in fact I have spent several periods since in monasteries, finding them quite congenial. But for the most part now I think religion is a waste of time.''

Jess got up again and moved restlessly around the room,

bending to read the titles of the books on the shelves by the false fireplace: auction catalogs, issues of collectors' magazines, books on gems and jewelry; a few volumes on arms, armor, and the history of warfare; a half-shelf on horsemanship.

She sat back down across from him, feeling light-headed and dazed. "How long have you lived here?"

"Some three or four years, now. But I travel often." He gazed unhappily at her smudged fingers. "I use a cleaning service, but they are unreliable."

She leaned forward, resting her forehead on her palm. "Ivo, what am I supposed to do now? Have this nice, insane conversation in your living room and then go home and forget it ever happened?"

A chessboard sat on the coffee table, set up for a game. His right hand fumbled weakly among the pieces, adjusting them to sit neatly in the centers of their squares.

"This is a nice conversation, isn't it?" he said. His voice had sunk to a thready whisper. "I hope we can keep it a nice conversation. I have trouble sometimes, getting back on an even keel when there has been violence. It shakes my—my balance. Hatred always disturbs me."

Jess shook her head. "I'm sorry, I think I'm still in shock. What are we talking about?"

"About Ivo the vampire, of course. Ivo the murderer, too. I think that one I flung away, I may have killed him. I hope so, and I am not in the least sorry."

Jessamyn made as if to rise, impelled by an unbearable mixture of disgust, revulsion, and savage exultation.

He watched her. "I was a soldier in a time when men were either slaves of the soil or slaves of the sword. I went first into battle when I was fourteen years old, and younger men fought with me, or against me. I have no patience with these modern punks. They have no true toughness, no discipline, no skills to speak of, and no reason beyond quick thrills for anything they do."

"Maybe you hate them so much because you were like them," she said.

"I saved your life," he said in a shocked tone. "Are you deliberately trying to insult me?"

Jess bit her lip and pressed on, heart pounding. Weak as he was, she was sure he could throttle her one-handed if he chose to. "You've spent centuries hunting down Nic Griffin's family. That sounds like gang vengeance to me, Ivo: an eye for an eye, one drive-by shooting for another."

"I watch the news on your television," he said curtly, "and it is nothing like that. I have pursued my quarry, as I am sworn to do. I have killed, or caused the deaths of, many men of the Griffin line, but I had to keep trying because I never found what they took from my father's castle. They are a clever clan, which makes the hunting more interesting."

"Maybe you haven't cared as much about your lost treasure as you think," she said. "Maybe you got to like being a secret persecutor."

"Then I am a lost soul indeed," he murmured, tipping over the white bishop with his finger. "Nearly a devil of Hell already, and irredeemable forever."

Jess knew she was in over her head. How could she answer a man from a time when people believed in Hell? Did he really still believe? What should *she* believe?

"I think," he went on thoughtfully, "that it is the scarlet of fresh blood that I have sought most, not so much this cold red gem I am supposed to be pursuing. That would explain why I have hunted it so ineptly, don't you think? I, who was a champion huntsman in my father's woods."

She saw the flash of his eyes in the light from the window: wide, glaring eyes, keen as a hawk's. She knew herself to be in frightful danger. She had to bring his focus back from realms of speculation where she could not follow, and down to now, to this life, this world, this real person sitting in his real apartment with her.

"You're not a hunter or a soldier now," she said strongly. "You're a vampire, living on people's blood. You drink from other people than Griffin men and their families, right? From Lily Anderson, for instance."

"Yes." His eyelids drooped, veiling that terrible glare.

"Does she know? I mean, does she remember, afterward?"

"No. I can put suggestible people into a sort of trance with my voice, my eyes—no, not you, Jessamyn. All your suggestibility is inward, from yourself to yourself, in the service of your art. You are not vulnerable to me in that way."

"And she's not—changed? Because you—" Her throat closed on the words: *bit through her skin and sucked blood out of her veins.*

"She is unchanged. I have never had the power to pass my condition along to others; neither that, nor any illness in the blood of anyone I drink from."

She closed her eyes, shuddering. "You'll need to drink soon, won't you? People need nourishment to heal."

"Even undead people, yes," he said. "And for something that isn't going to kill me, this injury hurts a great deal and has weakened me alarmingly."

There followed a short silence during which she watched helplessly while he dealt with his pain in his own way. Jess hugged her knees, thinking of all the scars on his powerful body, all the pain that must have come with each of them. Her own scars from the crash tingled in uneasy sympathy.

At length he said, "Don't concern yourself, Jessamyn. When I can get back on my feet I will go out and serve myself, as it were. You are not involved in that."

"You'll kill somebody."

"Possibly." She heard the dangerous distance in his voice. In this territory she clearly was not welcome, let alone influential.

"You should have drunk one of those bastards dry on the spot," she cried, with a wrenching shudder of dread. The flashing blade, the grip on her hair—her scalp, she realized, was still aching from it.

"God damn them!" she raged. "I didn't go through all those operations and therapy and nightmares just so a pair of creeps could—could slice—Jesus! You know who cuts up women's faces? Pimps. Greasy crooks working for the mob do that, to prostitutes who give them trouble! I can't believe—''

She blotted her nose on her sleeve. ''Shit. I'm sorry, I can't believe I'm raving like this. Surviving that car crash— you know about that, don't you? Along with everything else.''

''I know about it,'' he answered gravely, watching her.

''Living through that should have made me stronger, not hysterical and maybe completely crazy. God, suppose I'm still in the hospital, hallucinating you the way Nic hallucinated a woman on a white horse? No, no, never mind, that's just the theatrical imagination running overtime. Isn't it? Say something, damn it! Don't just lie there listening to me snivel and rant!''

His hand hovered above the chess pieces. ''He did not hallucinate. That visit of the Dark Lady is paid to each of the Griffin men when the time draws close for him to meet me.''

''But who—what *is* she?''

''A spirit, a demon, a witch,'' he said, catching up the black queen and turning it in his fingers. ''Who knows? Perhaps only a dream the Griffin men dream in the extremity of their guilt and fear; or a cultural idea, an ethnic myth. An old story, an ancient being from a time before mankind. Forget her. You will never have to deal with her.''

Jess's mind could find no foothold in this. Her thoughts shunted aside, back to the play, to Eva, who was as much a spirit of idealism as a character. Jess sat up straighter, thinking hard.

''It's not an emerald, it's a ruby,'' she said. ''The gem in Nic's play. He put the whole story in his play. It's his gesture of defiance to you, isn't it?''

''The red flag to the bull, as it were,'' Cragga replied. ''I think so, yes.''

''But *why?*''

''He knows he cannot fight me, nor can he escape. Perhaps once he saw the Lady, he decided to get it over with instead of living his days in fearful anticipation. Some of these Griffins have shown courage in the past."

"But that makes no difference to you," she said. "Whether they're brave or not."

"No, that makes no difference to me."

"You're going to kill him."

His hand dipped, giving the white king a sharp tap that flipped it off the edge of the board onto the carpet.

"Oh, no. Ivo, *no.*"

He offered only silence, that terrible silence that felt like withdrawal down a corridor of centuries. From outside came the screech of tires and a siren much farther off, and they were like sounds in a dream.

"Listen," she said desperately. "I could have left you there in that alley, I could have gone for the police and told them everything."

He snorted. "You could barely walk at the time, if you'll take the trouble to remember."

"I've helped you. I got you to my place to rest, I even got you here!"

He raised one finger. "One: you took my gifts and were careless with them, and they are ruined."

"You said it didn't matter!" she cried, outraged at his duplicity. "You said the earrings were just trifles, and it was your own fault for giving them to me! I never *asked*—"

"Two: I have saved your good looks, your career, probably your sanity, and possibly your life tonight. This certainly cancels any debt I may owe for your assistance."

"Don't be so sure about my sanity," Jess groaned, rubbing her eyes. This wasn't happening, it couldn't be.

But despite what he said, she felt a lifting in her heart, a surge of energy. He wasn't out hunting Nic right now, he wasn't boasting and threatening; he was here dealing with her instead. He had kissed her once, and he had attacked those thugs like a tiger, exuding fury, when they had done *him* no harm—as if angry on her behalf. He cared; and while he cared, Nic still had a chance.

"Three," he concluded. "I have discovered for you the identity of your cowardly persecutor. It seems to me, Miss Jessamyn Croft, that *you* owe *me*, not the other way around."

"And I can repay you," she said. Now that she understood, she saw her only course. "What would you say if I brought you the Ruby Tear?"

He became very, very still and for a wild moment she wondered if he had died after all. Would he crumble into dust right in front of her?

"This is a trick," he said at last.

"Trade me Nic's life for the Ruby Tear."

"You do not have it to trade."

"I'm telling you, I can get it!"

Silence again. Then he said, "I am listening."

She took a deep breath. "Nic is out of the country, running from you—"

"More likely he has gone to see if he can find some way to fight me," the vampire interrupted.

"He and I were going to be married," she went on, quelling an onslaught of tears. "I still have keys to his house in Rhinebeck, security system and all; and his dogs know me, they'll obey me. I know where the safe is." She stopped in heart-dropping consternation. "But I never learned the combination! Can you crack a safe? It's an old-fashioned one, no fancy electronics."

"Are you trying to fool me?" he demanded. "The stone isn't there. He must have put it in a safe-deposit box somewhere. You continue to think of me as hopelessly back-ward-looking. I do know modern ways, Jessamyn."

Jess shook her head hard. "Nic hates banks and bankers, he doesn't trust them; not since his mother's trust fund was mishandled. He'd stuff valuables in a mattress before he'd turn them over to a bank."

He sighed and thought, rubbing his palm over his jaw with a dry sound.

"You don't know what to think, do you?" she said kindly. For all his proud claims to sophistication, she knew that he was at a loss for the moment. "Ivo. Think of me as somebody who has always loved Nicolas Griffin very much—"

"Enough to betray him by handing over his most precious possession to his worst enemy?" Cragga inquired dryly. "That is devotion indeed."

"He won't see it that way! Nic knows—" But who knew what Nic knew or believed these days? "Well, if he hates me, he hates me, that's my problem. I want you to let him off the hook, him and his descendants. If helping you rob him is what it takes, that's what I'll do."

"What if it takes more?"

Her heart hammered dizzyingly. She tried to ask him what he meant, but her throat was too dry for speech.

"Come over here," he whispered, "and lie next to me for a little while; there's room on the couch, if we press close together. I am very cold, Jessamyn, always very cold at the core. The heat you feel in my skin is generated from the blood that I drink, but the center of my body and the center of my soul are always cold.

"I was a living man once; I still crave warmth, your warmth, Jessamyn; the thought is not foreign to you. If you are honest, you will admit that I ask for nothing that you have not considered giving me. And remember that I know you are honest."

She hugged her arms about herself, dumb with terror, trembling with a desire to assent. Maybe he was doing to her with his voice what he said he could do, deviously sapping her will to resist him. If she obeyed, he might take not just her body's heat but her blood, even her life, and then go on to murder Nic after all. The risk was huge, its allure all but heart-stopping.

He went on, softly. "I will heal faster with your vibrant life next to my skin, and the feel of your heart that beats so full of trembling determination."

She had felt his lips press tenderly on hers, and had seen his phenomenal speed and strength bent to her support and protection; and since she had first met him, she had never been free of a powerful attraction to him. He had followed her tonight, and perhaps other nights, watching over her, a demonic predator-turned-guardian angel. Who wouldn't hug an angel, given a chance?

As for living men, what were they? Noble-looking Anthony Sinclair, who had tried to wreck her confidence and her career. Even Nic, who had kept his darkest secrets from her and left her here alone at the mercies of this terrible, unimaginable enemy.

Worse, she was sorry for Ivo von Cragga, dragged through history by his single-minded search for a stone, a bright bauble that could never in a million years really replace all that he had truly lost. And he had been the one to speak of objects that couldn't support the weight of the symbolic meanings that people forced on them!

Besides, he was right: he asked nothing that she hadn't thought of herself. She had thought of more.

She got up and crossed to the couch.

"Make room for me, then," she said.

His arms took her in, and his face pressed against her neck. She felt the cool exhalations of his breath on her hair and skin, and the rousing of his body that was so full of vital strength that it could overcome death. The tension of passion tightened his sinews, folding her closer, as if he would take her into himself forever, swallowing her whole into his sturdy frame.

"What do you want?" she gasped. "What do you really want from me?"

"One sweet, healing sip of your health and vigor," he said almost soundlessly, his lips against her ear. "One joining of two bodies into one being. Don't be afraid: I have no living blood, so I carry no disease, and no seed to start new life."

"Oh God," she said faintly, staring out into the dimness of the monster's living room with its rented furniture. *You would think a canopied bed at least, a desecrated altar, a soaring flight together in the icy moonlight.*

"Listen," he said, going suddenly still, "you don't have

to. I would not force you for the world. Say yes or no, I still trade Griffin's life for the Ruby Tear, as we agreed. I am not a soldier now, a brutal boy with a sword, to take love as loot. I want more than I did then. Give me that, willingly, or I will do without.''

He lay holding her without force, all his powerful, muscular frame bound taut in an agony of deliberate inaction. His restraint freed her to acknowledge her own appetite for him, the hot urge that heated her blood and made her breath come quick and shallow.

"Jessamyn?" he breathed. "What is your answer?"

"My answer is yes," she said, and she uncoiled and opened, offering herself as willing plunder. His hands covered hers at the buttons to her blouse. She sank into the bottomless pit of his longing like red-hot gold through ivory wax, like soft lightning striking down through eternities of time. She felt this man out of the Dark Ages reach up in response, his ancient and deep-banked fires flaring to ravenous life. His skin was fire against hers, his hands slid over her like molten steel.

He nuzzled her throat with greedy, grunting breaths. His lips pressed the skin taut, and two points like needles of ice pierced her there and seemed to spread an exquisite chill deep into her veins, drawing the heat from her as his sex built heat inside her. She became one half of a ring of flowing fire and cold that he completed with his own body, sealed to hers at throat and groin.

She burned and flared and burned again with the heat of ice and the heat of flame. He sobbed and groaned as his body surged and shuddered against and within hers.

At last they were extinguished in each other. She lay dreaming in his ageless arms, against his unbeating heart. But what she dreamed of, she could never remember after.

Gems

**H**e had a car, a very unremarkable Toyota. He asked her to drive while he slept, still recuperating from his injury, on the back seat. A plaid blanket from L. L. Bean shielded him from the brilliance of the sunny morning. Dull daylight was no problem for him, but prolonged exposure to the full, bright face of the sun made him dizzy and weak. Incredible: that part was true.

Jessamyn, a sometime driver like most New Yorkers, kept pulling off the parkway to check the map. She played the radio, softly. The music steadied her and kept her anchored in the present. Now and then she slid a finger under the silk muffler she had taken from Cragga's dresser drawer and she touched the two scabbed punctures on her neck. They itched slightly, but were too tender to scratch. Apart from this, she was unmarked and unharmed. Except that her skin still tingled at the thought of embraces that had seemed to uproot her spirit from her body and send it winging freely through time like a soul unhoused by an ecstatic and lingering death.

No, that was a dream generated by the fever of sex, she told herself all the way to Rhinebeck. She felt wide awake and energetic. She felt completely herself, sharply alive to the day and its uncanny dangers.

But what did it mean that she had spent a night in a world of blazing, magical sensuality with a vampire? That she was reckless, vengeful against Nic, starved for the hungry embraces of love? Mesmerized by some crazed hope of catching immortality from a monster?

Wasn't an eagerness to grasp what life offered, no matter how weird, a sign of reengagement with life after the accident? An adventure had come breathing hard on her heels, and she had turned and embraced it: Hell, she would do it again.

Would she?

She glanced at the blanket-swathed figure curled in the backseat like a big cat (lion, leopard, purring into her skin that vibrated in resonant pleasure, breath cool and moist like the spray from a waterfall on her cheek . . .). She had really done this mad thing: she had made love with a man with a mind from the Middle Ages, an ageless body cabled with warrior muscle and laced with scars, a mission born in legend and lies, and a need for nourishment that he drew from the veins of living folk.

She had given herself as that nourishment and more to a not-man-any-longer, bronze-maned and stronger than any human who ever lived, who owned a Toyota and preferred that someone else drive because he was tired and injured and it was a bright day—but most of all, she suspected, because he was a little afraid of cars, and of traffic, and of a world that moved so much faster than his medieval instincts and reactions could.

So what am I? Jessamyn thought, swinging out to pass a truck full of baled hay. Mistress of a demon, the bloodsucker's girlfriend, the monster's comfort and convert to his plans.

Making my comeback not on a stage at all, but playing the lead in a lurid, impossible, erotic horror story!

She couldn't let it alone. Her mind kept circling, swooping and hovering over the blurred, fantastic events of the night before. If only he had been cold to the touch, or smelled like decay; but he had tasted like rain-wet stones, he had smelled like hammered copper. Thinking of these things, she ached to sink back into his arms again and twine around his body like a flowering vine, blind and mindless with terror and delight.

Nic saw a woman on a white horse; am I delusional too, thinking I've been to bed with a beautiful vampire? Maybe we're a pair after all, two crazed minds that would have been better off wiped out in that wreck.

She watched herself indulge in rationalizations, fully aware that they were not true. The thing had happened; the scabs on her neck and the irritating, melting sensitivity of her breasts and her sex were irrefutable, delicious, embarrassing evidence.

In Rhinebeck she parked in the shade and went into the Inn for a cup of coffee, sitting by a window so she could watch the car. Daring and curious (what was beyond the rashness of a woman who let a vampire suck her blood and plumb her body with his transformed flesh?), she asked the waitress who was watching the Griffin house for Nic while he was away.

"Paddy Garrow," the woman said, recognizing her. "He'll be surprised to see you, Miss Croft."

"Nic asked me to check on the old place when I had the chance," Jessamyn lied grandly. But on the way out to the house, she worried. Suddenly this whole thing began to seem not only foolish but dangerous. What if Paddy Garrow had a gun?

And if he didn't—if no warning shots brought neighbors to investigate, if everything went well—what then? Success now seemed even more fraught with perils. Once Cragga had the stone, what if he laughed and went to hunt Nic down anyway? When had going to bed with a man meant that you could trust him?

There was a car parked behind the low-slung double garage adjoining the house, a rusty Chevy with a trailer-hitch in back. She drove on past, then swung around on a dirt track that wound its way over to an unused dumping ground. There, as they had planned together, they waited for dark parked in the shade of some scrawny evergreens.

At some point in the long afternoon he reached for her again, and they fell together in a slithering tangle and lay interlocked until he took his lips from her throat and buried his face in the short curls at her temple.

"This will weaken you," he panted, "and make me heavy with satiation. But you must be strong and sure, and I must be lean and quick, Jessamyn. We must stop. Help me to stop."

She moaned a little in protest as he withdrew from her, and then they said nothing for a time, while they retrieved and rearranged their disordered clothes. Combing her hair, Jessamyn looked at her face in the rearview mirror and hilarity bubbled in her throat: making out in the backseat of a car, how quaint! A few bloodspots on the upholstery instead of just the usual stains—she shook away wooziness (how much had he weakened her already, how much had he drunk?) and handed him her comb.

"This may sound naive in the extreme," she said, watching his foxfur hair flatten and spring up again under the passage of the comb's teeth, "but I'm not exactly the first, am I?"

He turned on the seat to look deeply into her eyes. "No, of course you are not. But you are the most special, Jessamyn—"

At that she gave way to gusts of laughter, and when he pressed her anxiously for an explanation she could only shake her head helplessly and wave off his questions while mirth shook her till her stomach ached and her eyes teared.

Vampire or no vampire, right now he was a man in the backseat of a car with the woman he had just made love to, saying what any such man would say: "You are the most special . . ."

She took her comb back and tucked it away with a sigh, serious again. How easy it would be to lose herself in these aching, sweet embraces and fathomless driftings. With no effort at all, she could become one more plaything in his long history of such toys, loved, no doubt, until they grew shapeless and frayed at the edges with use and time, or until one more attractive and challenging came along. So it might be with any partner, of course; but so it *must* be, with this one. Time stood between them, centuries past and centuries still to come.

Time, and death. Killings, many killings. He wasn't just a soldier. He was a killer, from a time when men killed easily and vengeance was a rule of conduct for gentlemen.

She looked at her watch. "It'll be dark soon, and we'll go. But, Ivo, you have to promise me one thing."

He looked at her warily out of the corners of his slanted eyes. "If I can, Jessamyn."

"The kid house-sitting at Nic's—I know him. He's a local boy, harmless and not too bright. I don't want him hurt."

"He is someone to you, or to Nicolas Griffin?" he said. "No."

"If he doesn't make trouble for me, I have no reason to trouble him," Ivo said; and she saw she would have to be content with that.

Paddy Garrow was lounging in front of the living-room TV set; they saw him through the window, holding an open beer can on his T-shirted stomach with one hand and lazily channel-surfing with the other.

Jessamyn unlocked the back door, eased it open, and chirped softly to the dogs. They did not bark, but rushed to lick her hands and step excitedly on her feet. Mac had a sniff of Ivo, who stood very still and did nothing, while Beth lay on her back waving her paws in the air and wouldn't get up until both her armpits had been scratched.

Jess whispered to the dogs to lie down on the back porch

and stay. Cragga brushed past her down the passage and vanished around the corner of the doorway into the living room. The television sound, which had been loud enough to mask their approach, clicked off abruptly, and she heard curtain rings slide and clash sharply together.

She reached the doorway within moments. The young man slumped half-naked on the sofa, eyes shut and breath noisy. Cragga knelt, mopping up spilled beer with the boy's T-shirt. The drapes were drawn, and only one standing lamp still burned.

She noticed the smear of blood on Cragga's chin with almost clinical detachment; the moment for misgivings was long past. (This must be how it began, the necessary distancing of yourself from the unthinkable deed, the first layer of callousness necessary to a vampire, or a vampire's lover.) She must hope that Cragga had kept his word and done no serious harm. Quickly, afraid the boy might wake and require rougher silencing, she led the vampire down into the cellar of Nicolas's house.

"It looks like the set at the theater," Cragga murmured, staring around. "For your play, *The Jewel.*"

Jessamyn turned on the light and saw his pupils shrink instantly, catlike. Her scalp crawled. *Keep going, don't turn back now.* Yet some part of her longed to kiss the lids of those strange, tilted, animal eyes.

"There," she said, pointing to a spot between two joists near the back of the cement-lined chamber.

"A fuse box?" Cragga said with a frown.

"The real fuse box is upstairs." Jessamyn opened the lid and pried out the plate under it, with its dummy circuit-breakers. Behind this lay the safe.

"Is there an alarm?" Cragga said.

"I don't know," she answered with some asperity. "I'm not a burglar usually, so I never thought to inquire."

Cragga smiled. He ran his fingers over the box. "I can manage this, I think," he said. "Perhaps you should go and see to the dogs, that they don't become restless or change their minds about me."

"What about Paddy?"

"Paddy?" His narrow-eyed stare made his face look totally alien. She forced herself not to turn and run.

"The kid upstairs, Paddy Garrow. Is he likely to wake up anytime soon?"

The smile again, a small shake of the head—of course not.

Now she thought she saw fangs. Her stomach lurched. Maybe he was going to take his prize and then kill her. Maybe he made love to impressionable girls all the time and then drank them dry on his way out.

He had sung to her in a wavering, oddly nasal voice what he'd said was an old love song of his country, sometime during their long, flowing coupling of the night before. She couldn't remember the tune, only the strange minor key and the exotic, slightly oriental tone. He had licked the sex-sweat off her scarred eyebrow with his tongue. She could not believe he would kill her.

"I'll go keep watch upstairs," she said.

He nodded, fiddling with the safe like a character in a French gangster movie. She ran upstairs. All seemed quiet, except for Paddy's stertorous breathing. They were going to get away with this. She could hardly believe it; her blood fizzed with incredulous exhilaration. She stepped outside for a deep breath of cold, sobering air.

The dogs were gone from the porch. She thought she heard them moving quietly out in back and she called them, gingerly. No one would hear, no one lived close enough. But still—"Mac!" she whispered, as loudly as she dared. "Beth!"

"It's bad luck to name the Scottish play," someone said from the murk beyond the porchlight's glow. "If you have to call them, try Beth first, *then* Mac."

"Nic!" She rushed to intercept him as he walked out of the darkness with the dogs at his side. "Oh my God, what are you doing here? You're supposed to be in Europe!"

"You're supposed to be in the city," he said, looking

down at her. "What are *you* doing *here*?" He caught her in his arms and crushed her hard.

She smelled the good warm scent of his skin and his hair and melted against his familiar long torso, enchanted to recapture the easy fit of her temple to his cheek.

Flesh that would age with her flesh, blood that beat to a finite time, heat of the surface as well as the core—his humanity roused her to a giddy edge of desperate, inopportune lust.

"Nic," she whispered, "don't let go."

But he stepped back and looked past her at the house. "Go get in that car and drive like blazes, Jess."

She seized his hand. "What about you? Nic, what are you going to do?"

"I'm going inside. Don't say anything; it's what I've come back to do."

She glanced in horror at the house, then back at him. Planting both fists on his chest, she willed herself as strong as a fieldstone wall. "You can't! Come with me. We have to talk; I'll explain—only you can't go in there!"

"How's he doing, do you think?" Nic said, caressing her hair. "That safe is old, but it's strong."

"I don't know, but he could come back upstairs any minute, and I can't be sure—We have a deal, but if he finds you here—Nic, please"

His long-fingered hands closed around her wrists. "I know what you're trying to do," he said against her cheek. "But it won't work. Don't you think I thought of it myself? He won't find the ruby, Jess. He'll find something, but it's not what he's looking for. He'll be angry, and we both know what he can do when he's angry."

She pulled back and peered at his face in the gloom. "You saw? In the alley last night?" And what else had he seen, then?

"No, I was at the theater. I had some business of my own with that bastard Sinclair—"

"How do you know about Anthony?"

"I caught him fiddling with the wiring in your dressing

room yesterday." Nic grimaced. "Setting some newer, nastier trap in case his hired thugs missed you last night. Persistent swine. Don't worry, I didn't break his arms or bust up his face, but it was a near thing. Anyway, heading for your place later I saw the ambulances at the alley. It was a mess, and I guessed that it had to be about you. About *him*."

His grim expression made it clear that he meant Cragga, not Sinclair.

"I saw Sinclair with those two guys before I left the country, and I saw what somebody did to them last night. It wasn't hard to put two and two together. I want you out of here, Jess, before you get hurt. Take the dogs, they'll protect you. Beth! Mac! Stay with Jess!"

He folded her into one more enveloping hug—she felt his heart pounding—and kissed her forehead, and then he strode to the house and vanished inside.

Jessamyn stood paralyzed, her face wet with tears. How could she have thought him a coward on the run from his enemy? How could she have imagined he had stopped loving her when she still loved him so much?

She ran after him, afraid to call out. The dogs followed at her heels.

"I'm Nicolas Griffin," she heard him announce at the back door to the house. "And I see you've found the Griffin luck."

She stepped cautiously up onto the porch. Nic stood in the hallway facing Cragga, who had just come up the basement stairs with a small brass box in his hands.

Cragga was shorter, broader in the chest and shoulders. His aura of restrained fury was terrifying. He must see Jess, but he paid her no attention as she hovered on the porch, horrified and helpless. His eyes, black now with the enlargement of the pupils, were fixed on Nic.

"I found this," he spat in a tone of utter contempt. He opened the box and took something out of it: a gold-set stone, shining crimson in the glow of the overhead light, and a swag of golden chain that hung down along the back of his hand. The box he tossed into the living room where Paddy Garrow snored on, oblivious.

Cragga held up the pendant. "This stone is not a ruby, Griffin. It is a triplet. Someone took two polished and faceted slices of a cheap mineral called beryl, and sandwiched a layer of red glass between them with invisible cement. It's worthless, a clumsy fake."

He closed his fist in a convulsive gesture, and Jessamyn heard a tiny cracking sound. Bright fragments fluttered down when he opened his palm again. He slung the chain to the floor at Nic's feet. "Did you think you could fool me with this rubbish? Where is the gem that your ancestor stole from my family? Where is the Ruby Tear?"

Nic—her Nic, as she remembered him but stronger, more solid and steady in the face of this blast of focused rage— lifted his head. The light shone through his unruly blond hair like a halo. *Saint George and the dragon*, Jess thought wildly, *like Ivo's story.*

"Well, it fooled me," Nic said, "and others before me. I never expected it to fool you."

Cragga's lip curled with disdain. Jess saw his body tighten in preparation for an attack.

"Ivo, wait!" she cried. Nic risked one wild glance over his shoulder, then turned back to face his enemy. "You promised!"

"And *you* promised *me* the Ruby Tear," Cragga retorted, his eyes blazing at her, "not a composite of crystal and red glass!"

"Your business is with me, not her," Nic barked. "You killed my father, Baron von Cragga."

The vampire threw the charge off with an impatient shake of his burnished head. "Your father ran from me into the arms of his death. The men who killed him make their living in drugs, Griffin. Your father had had dealings with them before. His real interests were not in emerald mines but in more common treasures—cocaine, to be precise."

Nic's shoulders slumped. "I believe you," he said in a weary voice. "I always suspected." He took an audible breath and announced, "Well, then, Baron, there is no other business outstanding between us, so let's conclude this. Your demand is justified. In spite of all the misery you seem to have caused my family, I owe you an answer, and you'll have it. But first, I want your promise that you won't harm Jessamyn, whether I'm alive or dead, now or ever."

Cragga's glance did not waver from Nic's face. "You have my word. And now I will take what is mine."

Nic held up his hand. "I'll give it to you in my own way, sir," he said, and with a dramatic gesture he opened his duffle coat and whipped the gray silk scarf from around his neck. It was enough to check Cragga, who stared with narrowed eyes, his nostrils flared as if to catch the scent of trick or treachery.

From where she stood, Jess could see Nic's hands shaking; but his voice was steady.

"Baron, the stone you call the Ruby Tear was long ago cut into smaller stones and sold, to mend the fortunes of my family after everything had been gambled away by a particularly worthless uncle. That's why none of the Griffin men who came before me ever tried to buy his life by simply giving the ruby back to you: each one in turn found that damned imitation in the box, and realized he had nothing to bargain with."

My God, Jessamyn thought, *he's playing this like a heroic stage role, and very well too—with authority and flair.* Now she saw the man who had walked through battlefields and written with passion about what he had seen there. In his own way, he was a warrior like his opponent.

Nic folded his scarf and set it down carefully on a small side chair by the hall phone. "What's more, I owe you a new debt," he said grimly. "Jess was in danger. I misjudged the situation and left on my own business before Sinclair was discovered and neutralized."

He glanced over his shoulder at Jess, his pale face full of love and pain. Then he turned back to Cragga.

"Well, you guarded her better than I could. You probably saved her life last night, and I'd trust you to do it again if you had to."

The vampire said in a low, deadly voice, "Why did you come here tonight, Griffin? Why do you talk about this small matter, instead of the wrong your ancestor did to me and mine?"

Nic spread his hands, placating. "Look, when I knew what this was about, I wanted to do what Jess has tried to do—just give you the damn stone! That was my plan when I did the play: it was supposed to lure you to me, so I could offer you what belonged to you. I was going to pay you accrued interest on the value as well, at least as much as I could afford.

"Then I had the stone appraised." He shook his head and sighed gustily. "*Big* mistake. They told me it was a fake. I was left literally empty-handed. So, since the only alternative was to fight you, I went looking for a weapon. In Europe I collected all kinds of stories about Baron von Cragga, but no practical advice on how to deal with you.

"So I came back. I followed you both here tonight to end this once and for all, the only way I know how."

Cragga folded his arms, elaborately patient but implacable as granite.

Jessamyn stood in the back doorway, one hand on the collar of each of the Dobermans. They quivered against her legs, nervous now and alert from the tension in the air. What could she do? What did she *want* to do?

Nic shrugged out of his coat and threw it on the chair seat. "I can't restore your lost treasure to you, but I can help you finish your quest."

He squared his shoulders and his raised voice, an actor's voice trained for the stage, rang in the hallway. "I am the last adult male of my line, and I have no children. The ruby that my ancestor stole from you is gone, destroyed. In settlement of that old debt, I offer you rubies that I know that you value even though they aren't made of gemstone."

He slipped a penknife from his pocket and with a lightning movement jabbed himself once under the jawline.

Blood sprang down the side of his neck, a beaded line of brilliant red. Jess bit her lip to keep from crying out.

Cragga started forward intently, and his gleaming hair seemed to lift menacingly like the hackles of a wolf.

"Take what's yours," Nic said, tilting his chin up slightly. The knife he tossed down on the floor. His voice cracked slightly, but he stood his ground, his back rigid and his fists white-knuckled at his sides. "I won't fight you. Take all you want, drink your revenge!"

Jessamyn screamed, "No, Ivo—I'll set the dogs on you!"

Nic wheeled, his eyes wide with horror. "Jess, don't—"

Cragga laughed. "Do you think your dogs could stop me, even if they tried? One jump and their backs would be broken before they hit the ground again. But I wouldn't dream of punishing them for your impulsiveness.

"Dogs!" he cried, and the two animals bolted from under Jess's hands and sat down flanking the vampire, licking and sniffing eagerly at his fingers.

She flung herself past Nicolas, evading his desperate hands, ignoring his shout. "It's not Nic's fault, you can't do to him what you wouldn't even do to dogs!"

She sank on her knees, looking up into Cragga's hard face with a passionate gaze. "If you have to punish someone, take me! Leave Nic alone; can't you see that he's not like his ancestors? He's a decent man! He deserves better!"

"And you love him."

"Yes," she said. "I love him."

Cragga said, "Not me?"

She glanced back over her shoulder and saw Nic's stunned expression, the anguish of comprehension bright in his eyes.

"Not you," she said softly to the vampire. "You were a dream, Ivo, an indulgence. And that's all I am to you, too. You say 'love,' but I can only be one more passing dalliance for you, and you—I think you would be an addiction for me"—odd, she saw him flinch at that word—

"not my lover. I don't regret a damned thing, and I hope you don't either. But it's love we're talking about, and I love Nic. I've loved him for years, and I'm asking you to let him go, him and his sons, if he ever has sons."

"Jessamyn," Nic began, moving up behind her to grip her shoulders. His voice was ragged with emotion. "You're making things worse. This is between the Baron and me."

"The hell it is!" She stood up on wobbly legs, covering Nic's hands with her own trembling ones. She stared into the vampire's eyes, which were nearly level with her own.

"If you hurt him you'll have to kill me, Ivo," she said with the full conviction of her bursting heart. "Otherwise I'll tell everyone about you, over and over and with everything I've got, until somebody believes me and they go hunting you and bring you down somewhere, somehow—"

"Hush," Cragga said. A thin, sad smile curved his mobile mouth. "You stage people have no sense of moderation. Can't you see that the scene is done? You win, Jessamyn."

He stepped closer to her, and his voice sank to a husky whisper. He might have been alone with her, speaking to her only, with no one else nearby to overhear. "You win your brave knight, and he wins you. Brute or not, I was raised as an aristocrat. I know nobility when I see it. I see it now."

His right hand darted out past her and she felt Nic flinch and heard him gasp. But he stood his ground and made no move to defend himself.

Cragga brought his crimsoned fingertip to his lips and licked the shining moisture from it. His eyes glittered. "So I accept your offering, Nicolas Griffin, in settlement of our old, old debt. Your offering, and one other."

As they stood together, stupefied by the unexpectedness of his judgment, he reached out again, and this time it was a tear from Jessamyn's cheek that he brought to his lips, his gaze intent on her face.

Then he sighed, stepped back, and dusted his palms together. The light caught a faint, luminous drift in the air, falling from his hands—the last breath of the false ruby.

"Now call these fine dogs of yours, or they will follow me and be lost to you for good."

The Baron von Cragga turned and walked down the hallway, threw open the front door of the Griffin house, and stepped into the night without a backward glance. Darkness swallowed him up, sight and sound and the disturbance his passing left in the air, in what seemed like an instant.

Jessamyn, her vision blurred and her voice raw with released tension, had to call the dogs back from trotting out after him. They came bounding in again, all jolly eagerness to please, pink tongues lolling. She sank down to hug them both and release a great burst of weeping into their coats.

Nic sagged against the wall, strengthless and white-faced. He held his hand pressed to the cut he had made in his own flesh, from which the vampire had snatched and drunk a single scarlet drop.

Opening Night

◆

 The audience sat silent as *The Jewel* ended. Jessamyn stood poised in front of the shattered mirror with the door open behind her on a menacing—promising?—slash of darkness and brightness beyond. Her pose was a question, the open door was a possibility.

She couldn't breathe. She was afraid she might pass out as the curtain slowly descended. There was always the chance that they were not awestruck by the power of the play but indifferent, or asleep.

In the age-spotted glass she could see the reflected swags of heavy velvet rippling toward the stage, blotting out the blurred sea of faces.

What could they be thinking? In her own mind, her final costume, a tapestry dress in deep jewel-tones, seemed suddenly old-fashioned, garish, and unflattering. The scar on her eyebrow felt raw and hot, blazing out from under a pathetic mask of sweat and makeup.

They hate the play, she thought despairingly. *They think it's ugly and stupid; and they hate me. I've lost everything I thought I could bring to this; I've made a fool of myself and let the others down.*

Applause began like distant surf, rushing with supernatural speed toward the shore on which she waited at its mercy. Gasping with gratitude, she turned to give herself to the tumult of clapping, cries, and whistles.

Nic stepped forward from his position downstage to join her. He dragged his damaged leg a little—he admitted freely that the role of Marko was longer and more tiring than he would have made it if he had known he would be playing it himself. But his eyes shone with elation.

"We did it, Jess," he crowed. "We did it!"

The curtain rebounded and Jessamyn saw people's hands held high as their palms smacked enthusiastically together. Thrown flowers landed helter-skelter among the footlights. It wasn't a very big theater, but for these moments it was bursting at the seams.

"Author, author!" they yelled.

Nic stepped forward, and how they cheered! No one out there knew why Anthony Sinclair had dropped out of the production, but Nic's agreement to take on the role of Marko himself had sealed the success of the production. It was a double comeback: Griffin and Croft, returning together. The audience loved it.

Walter Steinhart ran onstage to take his bows with the cast.

"Jess!" he said, taking her hand in his broad, strong paw. "You were wonderful!"

"Damn good thing," Nic said out of the side of his mouth, "considering what a lump she's got for a leading man."

The director laughed. "Lump, schmump—what are you talking about? You'll grow into the part, Nic. You're going to have a nice long run to do it in, too."

Jess drew the two men's hands together in her own, smiling from one of them to the other and then raising their hands high, offering her colleagues for the crowd's adulation. Meanwhile, her gaze searched among the excited faces out there for one face that she both hoped and dreaded to see.

But if the brazen-haired vampire was there, she couldn't spot him. She could not have said whether she was more disappointed or relieved.

There followed a half-dozen curtain calls, and then a rush backstage to prepare for the whirl of celebration as friends and well-wishers came to congratulate the cast. Jessamyn, swiftly shedding her costume and makeup with Marie's help, toweled off and put on her green silk dress. With a woolen paisley shawl drawn over her shoulders for warmth (the theater boiler was still not working properly), she signaled Marie to start letting in the mob from the corridor, a few at a time.

Kisses, hugs, extravagant declarations, damp handshakes, and clumsy compliments and invitations—she had forgotten how it all felt: glorious, that's how, a high you never wanted to end. Her aunt Clara bustled in with a box of Godiva chocolates, stared and gushed adoringly, and fluttered out again to wait in the lobby with two neighbors she had brought with her, to see her niece perform.

Between incursions by the admiring public, Jess scanned congratulatory telegrams and sipped from a bottle of very good wine supplied by the Whitelys. The adrenaline spike smoothed into a more even buzz of happy well-being and satisfaction over a job well done. When the stream of visitors thinned at last, she gathered herself to leave the shelter of the tatty little dressing room and go out with her colleagues and friends—and Nic—to celebrate.

Someone knocked. "Nic?" she called.

It was Johnny Wagner, abandoning his post at the stage door, looking anxious. "Ms. Clausen said not to let him into the theater again, but—"

"Jessamyn?" A tall man in a fur-collared coat leaned hesitantly in past him, hat in hand. "Please?"

Marie drew herself up between him and Jess. "You're not welcome here, Mr. Sinclair."

But Jess motioned her aside. "Thanks, Marie, but I'd like to hear what he has to say. What do you want, Anthony?"

"It's okay, then?" Johnny said, trying to look dangerous.

Jess nodded, but Marie, glaring at Sinclair, barked, "Stick around outside, John. Just in case."

Anthony Sinclair winced visibly, and hot color stained his gaunt cheeks. "Jessamyn, if we could speak privately—?"

"Say what you came to say, Anthony," Jess said tightly, "and I wouldn't drag it out if I were you. Nic will be along any minute to collect me, and I don't think you want him to find you here."

"Or anywhere," Marie muttered. With a final bulldog glare at Sinclair, she turned away and busied herself with the costumes, creating at least the illusion of privacy for Jess and her enemy.

"I never had a chance to explain," Sinclair said earnestly, "and I don't want any unfounded suspicions to cloud your relations with the others, Jessamyn. I—" He swallowed audibly and blinked miserably at the floor.

Then he drew himself up with his eyes squinted half-shut and said quickly, "I wanted Anita MacNeil to take your place so that my wife could step into Anita's role as Magda. Sal was desperately unhappy when she lost her job; she was talking about—about suicide, or retiring and going to live with her mother in Canada and teach school or something equally awful.

"I have an old connection with Walter. I knew I could persuade him to let me import Sal into *The Jewel*. Once you—had left. The thing is, as soon as we're working together again on the stage, Sal and I, it will be all right between us again. You have no idea what it's like, Jessamyn, to love someone like that, to need them so badly—"

Jess watched the sweat bead on his forehead, noted the carefully-combed sweep of his thinning hair, the manicured shapeliness of his large, graceful hands. It was strange, but she felt more sadness than anger. She couldn't guess what he felt, but she mourned and resented the loss of their friendship.

"You did it alone and you did it for love, is that what you're saying?" she said.

He smiled painfully. "Thank you. Yes. Jessamyn, I never meant to hurt you, just to get you to leave the production. I felt then and I feel now only the greatest fondness and admiration—"

She turned away. "Oh, Anthony—please!"

"You don't understand, you're young, you have any number of chances ahead of you. But for Sal and me—" He licked his lips and stood hunched and silent.

"Anita knew nothing about it, then, just as she says," Jess said.

A shamefaced nod.

Jess stared at him. She couldn't think of anything more to say. Her silence said it all.

The hectic spots blazed on Sinclair's cheeks and he reached pleadingly toward her. "They were supposed to frighten you, those idiots, just frighten you, that's all! My God, Jess, I'd been shadowing you myself after Nic left, to scare you, not to hurt you. I never once thought of doing anything to actually harm you—just to scare you, you see."

He smiled hopefully, trying for camaraderie. "You didn't recognize me when I shadowed you, did you? Even you didn't spot me that day I led Johnny off into the bookstore, Marie. God, I had some fun with those disguises!"

"They came at me with a razor, Anthony," Jess said.

"I know, I heard, and I'll never forgive myself." He raised his hands and shook them helplessly in the air. "I made it absolutely clear that there wasn't to be any real threat, no real violence!"

Either he was sincere—or he was acting. It made no difference. Jess said, "Sally Sinclair is used to leading roles. If I'd dropped out, Anita would have played Eva; she's been understudying the part all along. Your wife

would have had to settle for Magda. What would you have
done when she got restless playing a supporting role? How
far would you have gone to make your wife happy, when
she started chafing to take over the part of Eva?''

Sinclair's eyes opened wide with outrage. ''She isn't like
that, Sally would never—''

''But you would; and you did, in my case.'' Jess sighed.
''I'm not pressing charges, Anthony. Nic wanted to, but
there isn't enough evidence, and anyway—I believe in what
Eva says in the play: revenge is an acid that corrodes whatever it touches. You don't have to worry about me going
after you over all this. But don't come here again; there's
no more to say. You'd better leave now, before Nic shows
up.''

Sinclair leaned urgently forward, opening his mouth to
speak again.

Marie said over her shoulder, ''You want to lose the rest
of your hair and have your bridgework dissolve in your
mouth, Mr. Sinclair? I know some tricks, and I know some
people. Mrs. Sinclair wouldn't be so fond of you with your
kneecaps fused. Miss Croft said go away, so go!''

Sinclair went very pale and seemed to shrink into himself, suddenly becoming the skinny old man he would truly
be in a few years' time. Without another word he turned
away down the corridor. His footsteps hastened, although
nothing followed him but glares from Marie and Johnny
Wagner.

Jess turned wide eyes on her dresser. ''Wow. That was
pretty ferocious, Marie.''

''He deserved worse,'' Marie said, banging the dressing-
room door shut. She held an open-topped cardboard carton
in her hands. ''Look at this—aren't these peculiar flowers
to send on an opening night?''

''What?''

Marie took a small pasteboard card from between two
plain pots of bright geraniums which were in the box, tied
together loosely with a scarlet ribbon. She handed the card
to Jess, her expression studiously blank.

The pasteboard shook slightly in Jess's fingers. On its creamy surface someone had inscribed in a firm, flowing hand, *The past can be a prison cell or wings on which to soar. Thank you. v..C.*

Heat bloomed in her body. Her hand flew up involuntarily to touch the two tiny scars on her throat. If he had been there—a man she had held in fierce, sad fondness and hoped never to lay eyes on again—if he had been there, she would have gone to him, gone with him, for another taste.

No. That was a dream, a scene from a delirium that she could manage briefly, or in a play onstage, but not maintain in real life. She was not cut out to be consort to an immortal; she had too much ego of her own, for one thing, because she was an actress, and a good one, by God. But she was not truly Eva, not any of the roles she played, not larger than life; offstage, she was just life-sized.

At that moment Nic burst in looking harried and alarmed. "Was that Sinclair I saw just now, scuttling out of here like a bug?"

Marie nodded. "He just came around to see if he's safe from prosecution," she said darkly. It had hurt her, giving up her crush on the great Anthony Sinclair. On that account alone Jess was not sorry for her hard words to him.

Jessamyn looked up into Nic's angry face, the aggressive set of his jaw. She was sure he meant to go after Sinclair and beat him up as if they were contemporary rivals, not a muscular young man and a rather frail older one.

Vengefulness corrodes everything it touches.

"Nic," she said. "There's cold cream in your right ear." He made a face and dabbed at his ear with his handkerchief, and in that moment he returned to the man she knew: sweet and sober, and maybe someday as good an actor as he was a playwright.

She caught Nic's hand, his warm hand with the slender fingers and big knuckles and the fine golden hairs on the back; a living hand warm with the beat of its own blood under the skin. "Come on, let's go blow off some steam. I could eat six pizzas by myself!"

"Dissolute theater creatures," Marie said with a sniff. "You should be resting up for tomorrow night's performance, not painting the town." She grinned ferociously. "Actually, your best revenge is for you two to become an even more famous theater couple than—than that sorry man and his spoiled wife."

Nic kissed Jess's palm and pressed it to his cheek. "That's the plan," he said. "Oh; you dropped something, Jess."

Jess picked up the card that had come with the geraniums. She fixed it boldly to the makeup mirror by wedging one corner under the scarred wooden frame.

"A note from a friend," she said lightly. "Come on, they're waiting for us. It's going to be a hell of a party!"

"Will this friend be there?" Nic asked in a low voice, his gaze averted as if he were afraid to see something in her face that he could not bear to see.

She grabbed his shoulders and drew him down so she could press her cheek to his and speak privately in his ear. "No, Nicolas. He's sent the flowers from his apartment for me to take care of; that must mean he's gone away, and he wants me to know it. He wants *us* to know it."

"But is that what you want?" He held her by both arms in a tense grip.

"Yes, it's what I want. It's your freedom, and mine too." And his I hope, she thought, but she did not say this. She leaned closer to Nic and kissed him, hungry for the salty taste of his skin, the roughness of the beginning stubble of his beard, and the slightly rank scent of his hair, with the sweat of stagework not yet washed out of it.

"Come on," she said, on a burst of joy too large and rich to contain, "the others will eat everything up. Aren't you starving? We have to start pounding on Walter about that scene change in Act Two, and this is the time to start. Houdini couldn't do his costume changes in that amount of time—could he, Marie?"

"I'm not old enough to know an answer to that," the dresser said haughtily.

In the cab on the way home from the party and late-night buffet at Manrico's All-Night Italian, Nicolas held Jess against his side as she dozed. It was like that, sometimes: the high of performance made it impossible to sleep, until food and company eased you down and left you poleaxed by exhaustion.

He studied her face in the light of passing vehicles—not many, this early in the morning—and of streetlights at the corners of the blocks as they whizzed by. She was no longer the ingenue he had met on the stage that summer and fallen for with a bang.

But this woman with the intriguing asymmetry to her face, filled with sweet gravity in repose, this woman was more than he had ever thought Jess might become. He only hoped that he, too, had grown as much. He hoped that he had grown enough to let the past lie quiet. There were questions he must never ask, because of the strength of his desire to live his life with her. There were secrets he must let her keep.

He didn't need her secrets. He had her. His was the body she leaned into with sleepy trust, his was the life she had chosen to link with her own. Maybe there would be children, who could take the Griffin name without fear. Actors, he thought; between them they could surely produce an actor or two. They would have to talk about that, but not now. Later, after *The Jewel* had closed.

He smiled in the leathery gloom of the cab. He had lost the cursed family treasure and found a future. He had found and won a woman more precious than rubies.

With a small groan of mixed longing and contentment, he gathered her closer against him.

"I ate too much," she murmured drowsily. "Why didn't you stop me? We should have saved some and brought it home for the dogs."

*   *   *

Ivo von Cragga ordered Evian in the first-class lounge. He sat looking out at the airport bustle of moving lights and shapes. Beyond, in the cold night sky, he thought he saw movement, darkness on blackness, and the old dialogue resumed in his head.

What now, Baron? With the Ruby Tear lost, so is your occupation.

Yes, he answered readily, without speaking. I am at your service, Lady.

The task lies uncompleted. What of your vaunted vengeance on the family of Griffin?

I have already had it, generations of it, as you well know, he replied composedly. It is a nasty dish at best. Lately I have fed on such splendor that the taste of ashes no longer appeals.

You mean that if the actress is to be part of that family, then you will no longer harry them for the vengeance that is owed.

He smiled slightly, watching in the reflection in the lounge window mirror the quirking of his lips. You always know my mind better than I do myself, Lady.

So we both thought, came the reply.

But I have not known *your* mind, he said. The balance has been uneven, to say the least.

Silence. He felt the chill of sweat on his face. He could not remember when he had been so afraid. Why did you never tell me that the ruby had been destroyed?

Why did you never ask? A distant answer, not an answer at all.

All this time, all those deaths—

All that blood, she murmured languorously.

But why?

Oh, you are a fool, my young baron! Her voice lashed him, blinded him, paralyzed him where he sat so that he could hardly draw breath. Blood is everything. A family is bound by blood, a tribe traces its members by blood, a nation draws its boundaries in blood. Without the divisions of blood—pagan against Christian, Christian against Muslim, Croat against Serb, region against region, village against village, you against him—it all sinks back into a formless mass; there is no shape, no spirit, no direction. There are only little animals scurrying here and there like mice, forgetting who they are, forgetting each who the other is an instant after meeting. Blood defines; the shedding of blood affirms those definitions, and feeds the spirit of the people that holds them together and tells them who they are.

You, he croaked. Vampire! Drinking the blood of whole peoples—

Because they wish it, Baron, purred the voice, hoarse, like a tiger's cough. Without these divisions and enmities, they are too confused, they flounder and fail. And so I am called into being. And how can I protect my many children, how can I inspire them to protect each other, without the bonds of blood, the taste of blood, the debts of blood?

It will not always be that way, he muttered. Already, it is not that way everywhere. Perhaps you are not immortal, Lady!

Silence again.

He opened his eyes and saw in the seats near him in the lounge a jowly businessman methodically folding a newspaper, a young woman hunched over a laptop keyboard, an older man dozing with big-knuckled hands hanging empty.

He gathered himself and concentrated on the black dialogue inside his mind:

What now? Do you summon me home? If so, you find me about to embark.

Summon you? Not I. What use would I have for you, Baron von Cragga?

He sat up straighter, impelled by a thrill of fear. What?

After all this time and effort, when the ultimate moment came you threw it away. You have forgiven your enemy his debt and shown tenderness to him and his. Your bond with me is sundered by the weakness of your own hand, Baron. Your blood quest is ended. Without blood, you have nothing to offer me.

Wait! he cried, starting up out of his seat in a panic. Where can I go, what shall I do?

Where and what you wish, but never set foot in my domain again.

In a dizzy, nauseous panic he cried, Lady, don't leave me.

There was no reply, only a sudden drawing sensation throughout his body, as if some scorching internal wind blew through his body's cells, sucking up every drop of moisture, all in an endless instant.

Like this, he thought, it's like this, to have all your blood drained by a hungry vampire. It's just like this that the undead body of the thirsty monster dries to powder in a flash before the amazed and flinching eyes of his executioners. It feels like this, from the inside. How horrible, he thought, with distant compassion for his own physical self.

And then what—judgment? Extinction? What was he, in light of what he knew now—murderer, avenger, demon of the house of Griffin? What angel or devil waited, poised to snatch his flying soul from the desiccated body after all those years of error and deception? He hung blind, deaf, and helpless in the grip of this merciless furnace, while high walls of blackness closed in.

Come, Devil, he thought, groping in chaos for some weapon, some defense. Come claim me, come fight!

"Are you all right, sir?"

A young woman in a flight uniform knelt by his chair, peering anxiously at him. She had too much lipstick on, but her face showed real concern.

"Am I?" he croaked, astonished to see her, to hear her, and most of all to speak in reply. His throat felt dry as paper.

"Do you want a doctor?"

Cragga shook his head, then turned to squint out of the window again. There was no denser dark against the sky. There was no observant companion in his mind. He was alone, cut off, abandoned in the place and time he had come to, after all this long hunting.

Oh, I am free, he thought with wonder. And then, *I will regret this, bye and bye. I will live to regret it, when my hair and my teeth drop out with age. If I live that long— this too is a dangerous world, and I exist in it now with only my human will and my human strength. But for the present, it seems, I will live.*

Look at those lights, fairy lights, like in an enchanted wood, into which the young prince pursues the magical white doe (*O beautiful one, I will never forget you!*) and finds himself turned into . . .

Into what? He looked at his spatulate hands, at the broad band of the expensive watch on his wrist, the lustrous fall of fine woolen cloth over his knees, the glowing leather of the carry-on bag on the floor between his feet in their well-made shoes.

Turned into what? What a marvelous question; its answers so brilliantly transparent as to be undetectable. Turned into a dragon, a kobold, an angel?

"What's your flight number, sir?" the concerned young woman was saying. "Let me see your ticket, please."

"No," he said thickly, suddenly having trouble locating the right words in this language that was not his native language. "Thank you. I am all right; I have just a—a reaction, an allergy. It's nothing, it will pass. Just let me sit a moment; I'll be fine."

She finally left him. Other passengers in the lounge looked away and pretended they had not been watching.

Giddy with elation, he peered again at his own face in the window glass: broad-cheeked, strong-looking, the face of an intelligent and resourceful young man of action. (A tear-stained, shock-blank face; how odd.) Surely such a man could get along anywhere, in any age, even without comment and advice from ancient entities of brutal appetite? Surely he could find ways to live as other men lived until his days came to their natural end?

Perhaps he could find good things to do with this life, after having done so much ill. Perhaps not, perhaps what he was could never be "good" in this world of the future.

He was little different at base than the Lady herself—primitive, violent, single-minded, or so he had proven himself through centuries of the hunt.

But he had not killed Nicolas Griffin. His final enemy had offered his throat, his blood, and the last Baron von Cragga had not struck him down. As if waking from some heavy, evil dream, he had found another way. A woman had helped him to do this—one who only played stories of vengeance on the stage, old stories one could learn real lessons from without the spilling of real blood. Yet she was brave all the same. He might learn to be brave in that way.

Who could tell what he might learn or come to be, with the long hunt over at last, the iron claws of the Lady's demand released from his neck? How had he never noticed until now, in his sudden freedom, how tight, how bitter that controlling grip had been?

God, what a thirst he had! What a raging, cracking, driving thirst, unslaked for centuries while that other need was fed in its place. He got up, with an effort, walked unsteadily to the drinking fountain by the wall, and joyfully gulped the cold, cold water until his need was quenched.

Then he folded his camel's-hair coat over his arm, and carrying his one bag in his hand he went to find the monitors where he could read the names of all the destinations to choose from in the great, wide, whirling, pulsing world.

Available by mail from